John Young Sargent

A Latin Prose Primer

John Young Sargent

A Latin Prose Primer

ISBN/EAN: 9783337366773

Printed in Europe, USA, Canada, Australia, Japan

Cover: Foto ©Andreas Hilbeck / pixelio.de

More available books at **www.hansebooks.com**

Clarendon Press Series

A

LATIN PROSE PRIMER

BY

JOHN YOUNG SARGENT, M.A.

Fellow and Tutor of Hertford College, Oxford

Oxford

AT THE CLARENDON PRESS

1888

PREFACE.

THIS Primer is designed for the use of beginners, being introductory to 'Easy Passages for Translation into Latin': a complete Latin version of which has been published for the use of teachers.

The plan adopted is to start from the simplest form of sentence, and proceed gradually to continuous narrative.

The first part contains ten preliminary exercises. These consist of short detached sentences, in which by the use of a limited number of words, a central idea is dwelt upon, turned about, and presented in many different aspects. The object is to make the pupil familiar with the Latin inflections, and to give him practice in the various forms of syntax, direct and indirect statement, interrogation, warning, command, etc., before venturing upon a connected narrative.

To each exercise is attached a list of the Latin equivalents for the words that occur in the English.

The second part consists of aids and explanations for the translation of fifty pieces of English which will be found in the seventh edition of Easy Passages for Translation into Latin.

These aids are—

1. Praeparatio : containing hints and remarks on the method of dealing with the passage under consideration.

2. Constructio : the passage arranged to suit the Latin Syntax.

3. Materia: a list of words applicable for translating the piece into Latin.

For the earlier passages a full vocabulary is supplied: as we proceed the constantly recurring words are omitted.

Later on, these props and helps are gradually withdrawn, only key-words indicating the more important ideas are inserted.

At length the Praeparatio, and finally the Constructio are left out, and a few suggestive words, renderings, or cautions are added as required.

It is presumed throughout that the learner comes prepared with a knowledge of the elementary rules of Grammar, and is fairly familiar with the Latin Accidence and Syntax.

As the Praeparatio and Constructio are not meant to supersede the use of the Grammar, so the lists under Materia are not meant to save the trouble of looking out words in the Dictionary. The method in all cases is intended to be suggestive.

The pupil is expected to use his own faculties in comparing, and examining, and deciding between different words and constructions. To give him an opportunity of thus practising his judgment, a number of synonymous verbs, nouns, and phrases are given, each with a typical example of its usage taken from a Latin author. The quotations have been selected as bearing directly on the point under consideration in each case, and are meant to act as a guide to and authority for the syntax to be used.

I have to thank Mr. J. H. SARGENT, B.A., of Exeter College, Oxford, for valuable help in detecting mistakes and suggesting improvements.

INTRODUCTION.

———◆———

WHY is the writing of Latin Prose such a stumbling-block to Candidates for Matriculation, for Responsions and similar Examinations? Judging from the number of students who, after a long course of instruction at school, are still unable to express themselves grammatically and intelligibly in Latin, one might fancy there was some peculiar and inherent difficulty in Latin, not shared by other languages. But, after due allowance made for idleness and incapacity on the part of the pupils, and for the disproportionate value set upon excellence in bodily exercises, the conclusion cannot be avoided that there must be something faulty in the method of teaching.

Faults and misconceptions as to the teaching of Latin.

It would hardly be correct to say that time enough was not given to the subject, seeing that a schoolboy is haunted by it over a space of several years. But being only one of a vast number of subjects, each demanding time and attention, it has no chance of being thoroughly dealt with, and the boy who by concentrated effort might have learnt to write intelligible and grammatical Latin between the ages of eleven and fifteen, remains a smatterer at eighteen, even if his ignorance has not by that time become invincible.

But besides doling out instruction in Latin composition in such small and weak doses, we make it too much of a mystery. The beginner is so overwhelmed with details that he loses sight of the fact that the object of language is to make known men's thoughts to one another. Latin is presented to him as a kind of puzzle, consisting of words to be put together like bits of mosaic, according to certain rules. It seems never to occur to him that the Romans *talked* Latin, and conversed in homely fashion, on homely topics in happy unconsciousness of the pitfalls of the subjunctive mood.- They are always, as he meets them, making speeches, talking philosophy, describing battles, and dealing generally with subjects remote from the experience of everyday life. And so by common consent they have ceased to be regarded as men and brothers. Rather they are looked upon as fossils, or skeletons at the best, and are treated as if they had never been anything else. Their utterances are supposed to be the result of intricate and mysterious grammatical rules. How Roman schoolboys managed to talk to each other in play-hours, before they had mastered '*as in praesenti,*' '*propria quae maribus,*' and the doctrine of 'stems,' 'roots,' 'tertiary predicates,' and 'past jussives' of a newer jargon, is a problem that is left entirely out of sight. It is long before it dawns on the mind of a boy struggling in a tangle of rules and exceptions, that speech was invented before grammar, and that the Latin language has not been constructed out of rules, but that the whole system of syntax and accidence has been deduced from analysis of an already existing language.

This is said not to depreciate the study of rules, but to suggest in all humility that there may be some misconception as to the best way of learning and teaching a dead language. If Latin is regarded not as a vehicle of thought, but as a subject for dissection and reconstruction merely, and solely as an instrument for investigating the laws of human speech—well and good—it serves a useful purpose, and few subjects could serve the purpose better.

But for the majority of learners surely a more obvious end, and more practical and common-sense methods might be adopted. Cannot Latin be treated more as if it were still a living language? Cannot we use similar means, and employ the same faculties in learning it, as are found useful in learning modern languages? Cannot we, at least when teaching young beginners, dwell more on the language and less on the apparatus? May we not reasonably appeal to the perceptive powers by which a child unconsciously learns his own language, and which are more vivid in youth than the reflective powers? Cannot we enlist the faculties of imitation and association? Cannot we furthermore take advantage of the tongue and ear, instead of trusting almost entirely to the eye, and acquire familiarity by repetition, iteration, transposition and the learning of passages by heart?

Without descending to the inanities of the ordinary guides and conversation manuals, the principle of their method might be adopted with good effect. Let the teacher take a sentence from the lesson that is being construed, say a passage of Caesar, or Nepos, or whatever has been chosen as the easiest for beginners, and working on the materials there supplied, put the sentences into all the different forms in which it is possible to combine them, and so exercise the common sense of the pupils, while increasing their familiarity with the sound and meaning of the Latin words.

Such a method is suggested in the exercises that follow in Part I. It is a method capable of expansion, and may be adapted to circumstances, and the forms can be varied and multiplied by the ingenuity of the teacher. Moreover it will be found useful to commit to memory the lists of words in the Vocabulary in Part I, and in Part II the *examples* quoted under Materia.

It does not belong to the plan of this Primer, which is only an exercise-book, to give the information which may be found in the grammar and dictionary. An elementary knowledge of syntax is pre-supposed, and constant reference to the grammar and dictionary is implied.

For the benefit of those students who endeavour to learn **Trans-lation and retrans-lation.** Latin by themselves, it should be stated that there is a method of acquiring an idiomatic and correct Latin style which is preferable to any other, and that is by translation and re-translation. Let the learner, when somewhat more advanced, take a chapter of Livy and translate it into English. Let him continue to translate a chapter every day. At the end of a week or so let him retranslate his own English version into Latin. Finally let him compare his Latin with that of Livy. If it does not coincide he will see for himself where the fault lies. Then let him learn the chapter of Livy by heart. The merits of this plan are so obvious that they need no further recommendation. Schoolmasters say it takes too much time. To such an argument there is indeed no reply.

Another useful practice is the writing of themes, letters, **Original Compo-sition and Verse Making.** speeches, descriptions, and verses in Latin. Strangely enough this useful method of putting our knowledge into practice, and of learning to think in Latin, has gone out of fashion. The study of Latin has come to be regarded as merely a branch of philology, and an aid to comparative grammar. This is one reason, by the way, for the disrepute into which Latin Verse Composition has fallen. Another is the prevalent misconception of the object of writing Latin Verse, which is embodied in the superfluous disclaimer 'I am no poet,' or the still sillier protest, 'I don't want my son to be a poet.' But it is not with the hope of their producing a Latin Epic, that such disciples are urged 'to strictly meditate the thank-less Muse,' but in order that a most useful mental discipline may not be neglected. In fact, if we allow that the end of learning Latin is to understand the subtlest shades of meaning in the language of the great Latin orators, philosophers, historians and poets, then the comparison of synonyms, the varying of the syntax according to the requirements of the metre, the familiarity with the well-abused 'tags' and quotations, required in the practice of Latin Verse Composition combine to furnish one of the most safe and efficacious means of attaining that end.

There is no reason why original Composition should not be required from the learner at a very early stage : in the shape of short sentences, answers to questions, and paraphrases of some passage taken from a Latin author, according to the plan employed in Part I of the Primer.

It cannot be too steadily borne in mind that the object of writing Latin is to express thought. Rules and critical apparatus are means not ends. It is not a mere knowledge of formulae that is wanted, but the intelligent application of rules to practice. How often in the answers to a paper of critical questions do we find a fluent discussion of the theory of the gerund, an admirable comment on abnormal uses of the indicative and subjunctive mood, a surprising familiarity with the dates, history and comparative value of the readings in Codex A and Codex B, and an ingenuity in deciphering inscriptions, implying marvellous research —if it is not cram—in a candidate still under age. And the most surprising and disappointing part is to find in the Latin Prose Composition of the same candidate a complete ignorance of the commonest idioms, and a neglect of the commonest rules of grammar; and a contradiction in practice of the most ingenious of his own explanations.

Rather, then, as beginners let our aim be *not to talk learnedly about Latin*, but *to talk intelligibly in Latin*.

Let our first desire be to make ourselves understood.

Composition.

The translation of continuous narrative as in Part II, and
Latin Prose as an art. the treatment of Latin prose considered as an art, suggest a different set of considerations, and the following remarks may be found useful to teachers and to students working by themselves. They are meant to obviate those stereotyped blunders which confront the teacher and examiner in the exercises of each fresh batch of pupils or candidates. These errors arise chiefly from want of method, from dwelling unduly on parts to the neglect of the whole, from incapacity to distinguish between words and ideas, between the letter and the spirit, and from an apparent indifference as to what their Latin version must mean if it means anything at all. The attempt to provide against these faults has involved some iteration, but those who have had experience in teaching know well that there are many learners

οἷς οὐδὲ τρὶς λέγοντες ἐξικνούμεθα.

Of understanding the English.

1. It is obvious that before we try to express ourselves in a language not our own, we must know precisely what we want to say *Misunderstanding of the passage* to be translated is a commoner fault than might have been expected. It frequently comes from beginning to translate before the pupil has read the whole passage through, from attending to single words before mastering the general sense, from neglect or inability to distinguish between the several meanings of the same English word, and to determine whether it is used as a conjunction, for example, or an adverb. Take as an instance the word '*Now*,' which may be represented in Latin by four different particles, at least, according to the aspect in which the word is presented to us.

'*Now* this being the case' is '*Quum igitur haec ita sint.*'

'*Now* I know what Love is.' '*Nunc scio quid sit Amor.*'

'And *now* the dawn was at hand.' '*Iam prope lux aderat.*'

'He said Marcus was a wise man. *Now* Marcus is nothing of the kind.' '*Dixit Marcum esse sapientem Marcus autem minime sapiens est.*'

Or take the word '*so*,' which has a different meaning in each of the following sentences.

'And *so* they departed.' '*Itaque discesserunt.*'

'He certainly said *so*.' '*Id certe dixit.*'

'Apollo saved me *so*,' '*Sic me servavit Apollo.*'

'*So* you are to keep the estate.' '*Ergo tua rura manebunt.*'

'Toils *so* many, *so* great, and *so* hard.' '*Tot, tanti, et tam duri labores.*'

Therefore one reading of the English will not be enough, we must understand it in all its bearings, and we ought to be able, before beginning to translate, to put the book down, and repeat the essential statements from memory.

Vocabulary.

2. But not only must we know what we want to say, *we must also be furnished with the words* in which to say it. We are supposed, before beginning to write Latin Prose to be provided with a stock of the commonest words, such as the pronouns, numerals, and a certain number of frequently recurring nouns and verbs. We are also supposed to be thoroughly up in the inflexions and declensions; and to know the concords, and the most general rules of Latin Syntax. Now in regard to modern languages a few common words will go a long way, if judiciously eked out by expressive gestures and grimaces, but for the purpose of composition in a dead language where these arts are not available a good store of words is an absolute necessity.

How are we to get our vocabulary? There are only two ways of providing ourselves with a stock of words in a dead language. One is by committing passages to memory—not strings of single words—but connected passages; the other is by looking out words in an English-Latin dictionary. Neither means can be dispensed with. But a third or supplementary process is still necessary. We must verify each suggested word by looking it out in the Latin-English dictionary. In learning an ancient language we are debarred the great assistance that is derived from constantly hearing and talking. We must supplement this defect by using the dictionary. It is best at first to look out every word you think of using in the Latin-English Dictionary, and to read all the *examples* there given. In this way the student almost unconsciously gets a just idea of the essential signification of each word by comparison of the different aspects in which it is presented to him. And besides this he will be led to associate the word with those other words in the company of which it is generally found, and to connect it with those forms of syntax in which the Latin writers are wont to employ it. All this helps towards forming a correct and idiomatic style. For all correctness in writing Latin Prose depends upon authority. We cannot coin new words, nor are we at liberty to arrange the old ones in other syntax than that of which we have examples. We may not aim at originality. To succeed in that would only make us ridiculous. We could only achieve a solecism at the best.

But not only must the modern writer of Latin Prose employ words sanctioned by the custom of writers of the Augustan and to some extent of the Silver age, but he must arrange and group them according to certain acknowledged models. Whether the limitation is or is not pedantic need not be discussed here. It is enough that certain authors, such as Caesar, Cicero, and Livy, have produced masterpieces of Latin prose, and for the purpose of training in the art of composition we cannot do better than take them for our models.

Variety of Style.

3. *In selecting an author or passage for our model* we must be guided by the nature of the piece to be translated. Is it Narrative? Is it Reflective? Is it Rhetorical? Is it Epistolary? Because a somewhat different style and syntax are appropriate to each. For Rhetorical eulogy or invective, argument or sarcasm, we may seek our pattern in Cicero's Orations, such as the Philippics, the Verrines, the Catilines : or in special speeches found in Livy. If we have to deal with a simple narrative we shall find in Caesar a model unsurpassed for clearness, simplicity and directness. For animated narrative and picturesque description, we must go to Livy, who abounds in moving incidents and memorable scenes, and presents us with a boundless variety of situation, plot and character.

Cicero will be our pattern letter-writer whether the mood be grave· or gay, the subject trifling or important, the sentiments conventional or sincere, for Cicero can be both. And Cicero will show us also how noble thoughts may be expressed in fitting language, when he treats of the duties of life, the phenomena of nature, and the ,problem of a future state.

For colloquial Latin the plays of Terence and the comedies of Plautus may be consulted with advantage, and the Satires of Horace may be pressed into the service.

It is beside the present purpose to say much about the style of Seneca, Pliny or Quintilian. They are all writers of elegant prose. Seneca is highly finished and in places epigrammatic. Quintilian is correct and graceful. And Pliny's letters leave the impression that he was a very highly educated and superior person. I purposely abstain from recommending Tacitus as a model for imitation : any more than I would recommend Carlyle to a foreigner learning English. Tacitus unfortunately has a certain fascination for those who would run before they can walk : and the result is that such ambitious students arrive at imitating his obscurity, with considerable success, and stop short at this interesting stage.

Mental attitude. Sympathy.

4. Since style is the expression of feeling, and varies with the temper of the speaker, a certain *flexibility* of mind, and *sympathy* is necessary in translating from one language into another.   Sympathy both with the subject, and with the author whose style we wish to imitate.   It is not enough to understand the words, we must feel them.   We shall need not only the dry light of intellect, but the warming fire of enthusiasm.   We must take sides in the battle we describe. We must feel indignation at the culprit we denounce.   If the subject is of a lighter kind, such as a familiar letter, where banter and raillery are appropriate, we should assume a certain archness, and even indulge in irony.   If we have a simple story to tell, we must aim at nothing more than to be simple and direct.   In short we must vary our mental attitude to suit the various themes, characters, and events with which we have to deal.   But we must ever keep in mind the dictum of Aristotle, that 'clearness is the highest merit of diction.'

Having fully entered into the spirit of the passage to be translated into Latin, we must try to recollect some passage in a Latin author conceived in the same spirit, and if possible treating of the same theme.   When we have found a suitable passage, we must make it our own.   In order to do this effectually we must identify ourselves with the author.   Suppose it is Livy we wish to imitate, let us try to see with his eyes, to feel as he felt, to reason as he reasoned : let us even adopt for the time being his prejudices.   By such complete devotion only can we hope to catch the trick of his language.

And more generally in order to acquire a classical tone in writing Latin we must surrender ourselves to an illusion : we must go back to the thoughts and feelings of men as they expressed them nineteen hundred years ago, and for the time become Roman citizens.

This will entirely change our horizon and our perspective. We shall survey mankind from the city of the seven hills. The earth becomes flat again with Styx and Tartarus beneath it. America fades away into a mythical Atlantis. The pillars of Hercules form the limit of the western world ; and once more we regard the Britons as ' toto orbe divisos.' We change our habits too, and our way of talking. ' Urbs ' for us means ' Rome,' and ' Roman soldiers ' become ' nostri.' We measure history ' from the foundation of the city.' We date our letters, no longer written on paper, but on waxen tablets with the stylus point, by the ' Kalends,' ' Nones,' and ' Ides.' We mark the hour of day by the sun, disregarding minutes and seconds : the time of night by the relief of sentries. Our husbandmen and mariners look to the winds and stars,

  ' Pleiades, Hyades, claramque Lycaonis Arcton,'

to give them the points of the compass, and the season of the year. Our ships of war are represented by triremes and quinqueremes, and musket and cannon are displaced by pikes and arrows, balistae and missile darts.

At home we lie down to meals. The hunter spends the right ' beneath cold Jove.' We swear, where in English we should not swear at all, ' by Pollux ' and ' Hercules.'

Battles are fought with ' adverse,' ' favouring,' or ' equal Mars ' ; and no intellectual work succeeds ' if Minerva is unwilling.' The distinction of Heathendom and Christendom disappears : the population of the orb of earth is divided into ' Romans ' and ' barbarians,' and ' servant ' becomes synonymous with ' slave.' We talk as if we believed in auspices and divination, and connived at the doctrine of a plurality of gods.

Logical Connexion.

5. Having digested the meaning, and determined the character of the piece, and being equipped with Latin equivalents for the main ideas, it remains to consider the *logical connexion*, so that the several sentences may be united into one framework, of which the parts shall come in natural sequence and be coherent with each other.

If we compare a piece of ordinary English narrative with a passage relating a similar event in Latin, it will be seen that the English passage consists for the most part of independent statements. The Latin will be composed of connected sentences. A page of English bristles with the ever recurring '*and.*' On a page of Latin, one clause glides into another. No gap or roughness, or interruption is visible. And such is the 'callida junctura' of the workmanship, that each sentence seems to grow out of the one preceding, or to lead up to the final climax, by a natural and necessary sequence. The result is a paragraph composed of symmetrical parts ; each clause, sentence, and period uniting to produce a 'sermo totus teres atque rotundus.'

In English the ideas are ranged in a rank, like Milton's shepherds, 'All simply chatting in a rustic row.' In Latin they must be artistically grouped ; and in endeavouring so to group them, we shall have to bring out some into relief, and to thrust others into the background. Some statements will have to be treated as principal, others as subordinate. To find out which ought to be most prominent, we must consider the mutual relation of the several statements, and what proportion they bear to each other. And in order to do this we shall frequently have as it were to read between the lines owing to absence of logical particles in many kinds of English prose. Such an examination will show that some indicate independent facts, while others are of the nature of conditions, causes, consequences, accessories, concessions, or other modifications. These relations must be expressed, first by conjunctions or connecting particles, such as, *quum, quia, si, quamvis, sed, autem, igitur, nam, vero, enim,* and the like; secondly, by the use of moods, the indicative for independent statements, the subjunctive for dependent statements; thirdly, by the use of the participles, the gerunds, the ablative absolute, and various other devices for suspending the crisis, and building up the fabric of a sentence out of many coherent and interdependent parts. Thus instead of making a series of apparently coordinate assertions, as in English, we shall have to gather several into one group in the Latin. We shall have to embrace in one period a variety of clauses expressing different logical relations, but directed to and bearing on the main idea, which they serve to illustrate and embellish. The principal statements will be in the indicative mood, or, when the narrative is oblique, in the infinitive, while the subordinate statements will fall naturally into the subjunctive mood.

When the logical connexion running through the whole passage has been ascertained, it is a good plan to arrange mentally the connecting links, and to form as it were the moulds into which the material is to be run. The first draught may then be made, which will be a kind of *precis.* The leading and essential statements, those without which the piece would be false, or unintelligible, should be put into Latin first. We shall thus have secured a solid foundation on which to build. Our general meaning will be rightly and intelligibly stated, even if we should afterwards go wrong in details.

All this will sound to some very mechanical, but the plan has the merit of being thorough. Some drudgery must be undergone in every discipline. But the labour will soon become lighter from habit. A process which at first requires laborious effort and attention will if persisted in soon become automatic.

We shall find ourselves reasoning and thinking in Latin without conscious effort, and what seems so artificial at the outset will become in time natural and easy.

Order of Words and order of Thought.

6. It remains to speak of the order of words, which at first sight seems to be one of the principal differences between Latin and English. But it will be found, if we look at essentials only, that the order of thought need not differ much in whatever language it is expressed.

The first object of the speaker or writer is to make himself understood, and everything must be subservient to this consideration.

But the attitude of mind and the intention of the speaker will chiefly determine *how* he will make himself understood. Passion will blurt out the uppermost thought first. Reason will take preliminary steps. Reason will first lay down premises, on which to support the main idea, which of necessity must come last. Take for instance the following passages.

It will be seen (1) that the order in each is dictated by the mood of the speaker.

(2) That the order of thought in English need not differ from the order of thought in the Latin.

' *Me Me adsum qui feci in me convertite ferrum.*'

'It is I, it is I'; or better still,—for the language of passion is more apt to be idiomatic than grammatical—

''Twas, 'twas me. Here I am. I did it. Make me the target of your strokes.'

Again,

' *Dissultant ripae refugitque exterritus amnis.*'

'Asunder start the banks, back flies the frightened river.'

And again,

' *Si quid est in me ingenii, judices, quod sentio quam sit exiguum, aut si qua exercitatio dicendi, in qua me non*

*inßtior mediocriter esse versatum, aut si hujusce rei ratio
aliqua ab optimarum artium studiis ac disciplina profecta,
a qua ego nullum confiteor aetatis meae tempus abhorruisse,
earum rerum omnium vel imprimis hic Aulus Licinius
fructum a me repetere prope suo jure debet.'*

'Whatever I have of talent, sirs,—and I am conscious how
little it is; whatever my ability in public speaking,—wherein,
I deny not, I have had considerable practice; whatever my
acquaintance with the subject before us, such as a study of
the liberal arts, and literary training can confer,—which I
confess at no period of my life have I neglected—these
faculties, each and all, ought in an especial degree to be
exerted for the advantage of my client here. Aulus Licinius
has a claim upon my services, amounting almost to a right.'

Here we see that the order of thought can be preserved in
the translation, by accommodating the syntax. And this is
always the best plan to follow if we wish to reproduce the
feeling and tone of the writer, as well as the meaning of the
words. And what is true of translating from Latin into
English is also true of translating English into Latin, if we
regard the sequence of thought rather than the mere succession of the parts of speech. If we alter the logical order
of an author we run the risk of distorting his meaning, by
putting the emphasis in the wrong place.

Articulate thinking, and precise enunciation necessary.

To find out the true sequence of ideas we must distinguish
between words as mere parts of speech, and words as pre-
dication. *The thoughts* must be *articulated* and *divided.*
It will be found that one word, or κατηγόρημα, may consist
of several parts of speech, either disjointed, as 'they would
have heard' or united by means of inflection, as '*audivissent.*'
Such words, or groups, must be kept distinct; and must

follow that order which the writer thinks will best make his meaning and intention clear. The same sense of precision will guide him in the arrangement of the sentences that go to make a paragraph, of the clauses that go to make a sentence, and of the parts of speech that go to make a word.

The habits formed in construing Latin into English react on the process of translating English into Latin. And nothing tends more to dull the faculty of articulate thinking than the practice of reading off the English at sight. This is an elegant accomplishment, and much to be admired when the power has been gained by conscientious and legitimate means, and by carefully following the syntax ; but it ought not to be exacted from boys until they have learnt the accurate measure and precise value of each word. The effect of adopting this practice too early has been extremely mischievous. It has fostered slovenly inaccurate habits of thought, and leads boys, especially those possessed of a superficial quickness, to substitute a hap-hazard paraphrase for an accurate version arrived at through the syntax. Let the learner not think it beneath his dignity to '*take the words.*' Unless he actually utters each word of the Latin, he will not appreciate the exact grammatical and logical value of it. He will omit to define the precise limits of the English equivalent, and so fail to make the two coincide.

The attempt to learn the Latin language 'by sight' is in fact a wilful rejection of the assistance to be derived from using the ear and the tongue, organs especially provided by Nature to help men in learning foreign languages and to retrieve the disaster of Babel. The boy who is forced to enunciate the English only, and to give no voice to the Latin, sees the words in a confused crowd. He gets to know some of them by sight, but the acquaintance hardly ripens into knowledge. He looks at but one side of the objects : he never sees around them or behind them. They are presented in relief only. Hence his version is too frequently a hazy paraphrase with a resemblance more or less grotesque to the original, but wanting in faithfulness and precision. The class of words which the learner who has been condemned to this semi-silent system mostly fails to understand clearly are the abstract words—grammatical and logical particles, conjunctions, adverbs and relatives. Hence the confusion as regards such words as '*talis, qualis,*' '*tamquam, quamquam,*' '*vero, etiam,*' '*sed, enim,*' '*qui, ille,*' and ignorance of the precise meaning of different parts of the verbs, as '*monui, monebam, moneam, monerem, faciat, faceret, fecisset, facere, fecisse, factum iri, facturum fuisse.*'

Single words and Group-words.

To return to the order. It happens in fact that the verb usually comes at the end of a Latin sentence. But this is not because it is a verb, but because the predicate happens - to be naturally expressed in that form in Latin, while the same idea most commonly takes the form of a substantive in English. Take the following sentence for example.

'He-made-up-his-mind (1) to-stay-where-he-was, (2) in-the-possible-event (3) of-the-enemy-having-taken-advantage-of-the-darkness (4) to-make-a-night-escape (5).'

'*Constituit* (1) *ibi-manendum* (2) *si-forte* (3) *hostes-per-tenebras* (4) *nocte-effugissent* (5).'

Here there are *twenty-seven single words* or parts of speech in the English, and *ten* in the Latin. The order of these in Latin differs from their order in English. But the *ideas* follow in the same order in both languages. The group words may be set down at *five*: and they follow in precisely the same succession in both languages; because that is the sequence which the writer consciously or unconsciously considers the best for making his meaning clear.

It is useless to attempt to give rules for the order. The feelings of the speaker in each case will suggest that which is most appropriate. And in translating, in the generality of cases, unless there is some special reason for altering it, the order of the author, whether Latin or English, had better be retained. The *order of thought*, that is: and always with a view to clearness, for σαφήνεια λέξεως ἀρετή.

Prose Rhythm.

7. But there is another influence to be taken into consideration, viz. *Rhythm.*

This applies chiefly to the Rhetorical style. In reading aloud or reciting the most highly wrought periods of Cicero, we become conscious of a certain harmony which a silent perusal does not make apparent. This *prose rhythm*, first consciously elaborated by Isocrates, like a subtle fragrance wafted from the garden of its first cultivator, pervades the style of every acknowledged artist in prose composition since his time, both in classical and in modern literature. This music, εὔμετρον ἀλλ' οὐκ ἔμμετρον is most highly developed in oratorical passages. But in Latin prose it cannot be even felt, much less imitated, unless we use the ear and tongue as well as the eye. Nor can it be taught by rule. We must recite and repeat aloud in order to get the perception of it. We must hear a passage declaimed in order to appreciate it : and we must commit to memory before we can hope to imitate it.

LATIN PROSE PRIMER.

PART I.

1.

EXERCISE.

Water. The heat of the water. Concerning the heat of the water. Let us say a few words concerning the heat of water.

Water is hot when it is seen to boil. This water is hot. I wish it was hot. Hot water hurts those who touch it. This water is so hot that it hurts those who touch it.

I tell you this water is so hot that it hurts those who touch it.

I told you the water was so hot that it would hurt those who touched it. That water in which I washed my hands yesterday morning was so hot that it hurt my hands when I touched it. I wish it had not been so hot. Therefore if you are wise you will not touch this water, for it is very hot. You will confess that it is very hot.

Avoid too hot water.

VOCABULARY.

Water . .	aqua.
Heat . . .	calor.
Concerning	de.
Say . . .	dico.
Few . . .	pauca.
Words . .	verba.
See . . .	video, cerno. *See Dictionary.*

B

Hot . . .	calidus.
Boil . . .	ferveo.
Wish . .	*Say ' O that it were,'* utinam. *See Dict.*
Hurt. . .	noceo.
Those who	ii qui, *with verb, but omit pronouns if participle is used.*
Touch . .	tango.
This, that .	hic ... ille.
So that . .	tam ... ut. *See Dict.*
Wash . .	lavo.
Hand. . .	manus.
Yesterday .	hesternus, *adjective.*
	heri, *adverb.* *See Dict.*
Therefore .	ergo.
If	si.
Am wise .	sapio.
For . . .	nam.
Confess . .	confiteor.
Very . . .	valde, admodum, *sometimes by superlative.*
Avoid . .	fugio.
Too . . .	nimis, nimium. *See Dict.*
Not . . .	non, *direct negative.*

        non, *must come immediately before the word it negatives, as* 'eum colere coepi non admodum grandem natu.' 'Non potest conciliari,' *not* 'Non conciliari potest.'

        non, *when it negatives a sentence must come first in that sentence, as* 'Non sunt in senectute vires.'

        nonne, *interrogative.* 'Nonne fuit satius?' '*was it not better?*'

        haud. *The beginner had better not use* 'haud' *as long as* 'non' *will do.*

        ne, *in wishes, commands, purposes, prohibitions,* 'ne fugite hospitium, neve ignorate Latinos.'

Not even . ne ... quidem : *avoid* 'non etiam.'
And not . neque : *avoid* 'et non.'

2.

EXERCISE.

The force of custom is great. Who says the force of custom is not great? Cicero has said that the force of custom is great. Cicero was accustomed to say that the force of custom was great. Do you believe Cicero when he says that the force of custom is great? You may believe Cicero or not, as you like. Nothing is greater than the force of custom. The force of custom is too great to be overlooked.

Take an example. I offer you an example. Let an example be taken. Hear the following, for the sake of example. The snow is lying on the ground. The fields are covered with snow. It is freezing. All things are rigid with cold.

Marcus is a hunter. Marcus stays out all night in the snow. Many hunters are accustomed to stay out all night in the snow on the mountains. The excessive frost bites them. Frost bites like fire. If frost bites like fire, why do hunters stay out all night? I should be sorry to be frost bitten. They let themselves be frost bitten. They suffer themselves to be frost bitten with an equal mind.

So great is the force of practice and determination. Custom produces habits. Character is determined by habits (*say*, Habits effect that men shall be good or bad).

VOCABULARY.

The . . .	*Omit.*
Force . .	vis.
Custom . .	consuetudo.
Is	sum, es, est.
Great. . .	magnus.
Who . . .	quis.
Says not .	nego.
Cicero . .	Cicero.
Accustomed	soleo.
Believe . .	credo, *interrog.* ' an credis?' ' credisne ?'
	' nonne credis ? ' *'don't you believe ?'*
May . . .	licet.
Or not . .	aut non, *with verb.*
As you like	ut lubet tibi.
Nothing .	nihil.
Than . . .	quam, *or, ablative.*
Too . . .	*Comparative, here.*
To be over-	
looked .	*' Than that it should be overlooked.'*
Overlook .	negligo.
Take Lo ! .	ecce, *or* accipe.
Example .	exemplum.
Offer . . .	do.
Take . . .	capio, sumo.
Hear . . .	audio.
Following .	sequor, *with relative.*
Sake . . .	causa, gratia.
Snow . .	nix.
Lying . .	jaceo.
Ground . .	humus. *See Dict.*
Field . .	ager.
Cover . .	obtego, *not present; the present tense*
	would mean ' are being covered.'
Freeze . .	gelo. *See Dict.*
All . . .	omnis.

Are rigid .	rigeo.
Cold . . .	frigus, *or* gelu.
Hunter . .	venator.
Stay out all	
night . .	pernocto.
In	in, *with ablative*.
Many . .	multi, *or adverb*, 'saepe, plerumque.'
Excessive .	nimius.
Frost. . .	gelu, pruina, frigus. *See Dict.*
Bite . . .	uro.
Mountain .	mons.
Like . . .	sicut, *or*, haud minus quam.
If	si.
Why . . .	cur? quare?
Be sorry .	piget, nolo, aegre fero. *See Dict. Or* 'utinam ne,' 'ne,' *in the form of a wish.*.
Let . . .	patior.
Self . . .	se.
So great .	tam magnus.
Practice .	exercitatio.
Determination	*Here*, meditatio.
Produce .	gigno.
Habit . .	habitus.
Effect . .	*Verb*, efficio ut. *See Dict.*
Good . .	bonus.
Bad . . .	malus.

3.

EXERCISE.

Some men are pugilists. A pugilist is one who fights with his fists. The English fight with their fists. The Romans fought with the caestus. They are both called pugilists. The caestus hurts the limbs. How does the caestus hurt the limbs? The caestus hurts the limbs by bruising. Many have died bruised by the caestus.

Pugilists are a kind of gladiators. Many pugilists have died in the arena the people looking on. It was delightful to the Romans to see men dying, whether bruised by the caestus, or cut by swords, or pierced by spears, or torn by wild beasts. The men and women rejoiced to hear the groans of the dying, to see their blood flow, to watch their faces turn pale.

The Romans were descended from the gods. The gladiators were outcasts or barbarians. Cicero says they were barbarians.

VOCABULARY.

Some	nonnulli, quidam. *See Dict.*
Pugilist . . .	pugil.
One who . . .	qui.
English	Angli.
Fight	pugno.
With	*Ablative of instrument.*
Fist	pugnus.
Caestus	caestus, *use the plural.*
Both	et hi et illi. *See Dict.*
Call	voco, nomino. *See Dict.*
Hurt	laedo, noceo.
Limb	membrum.
How	quomodo.
Bruise	contundo.
Die	morior.
A kind	genus quoddam.
Gladiator . . .	gladiator.
Arena	arena.
People	populus.
Look on . . .	specto.
Was delightful .	juvo, delecto, voluptatem affero.
To see	video.

Man . . . . . . homo, vir. *See Dict.*
Whether, or . . . sive, seu.
Cut . . . . caedo.
Sword . . . . . gladius, ferrum.
Pierce . . . . . . transfigo.
Spear . . . . . . hasta.
Tear . . . . . . dilanio, lacero.
Wild beast . . . . fera.
Woman . . . . . femina, mulier. *See Dict.*
Rejoice . . . . . gaudeo.
Groan . . . . . . gemitus, *verb*, gemo.
Watch . . . . . video.
Blood . . . . . . sanguis.
Flow . . . . . . effundo, *passive.*
Face . . . . . . vultus, os. *See Dict.*
Turn pale . . . . pallesco.
Descended . . . . gigno, orior, oriundus. *See Dict.*
God . . . . . . deus.
Outcasts . . . . perditi homines.
Barbarians . . . barbarus.

4.

EXERCISE.

Great is the force of custom. Pugilists do not groan when bruised by the caestus. They do not begin to utter a groan even.

Gladiators suffer blows. They must suffer blows and inflict them. Good heavens, what blows they suffer. If they did not suffer patiently, they would seem to themselves to be disgraced. They would rather receive a blow than avoid it basely. Some blows may be avoided. Some blows might have been avoided. Some blows are to be avoided, some are not. Some blows can be avoided, some cannot.

The gladiators thought that certain blows ought not to be avoided. They prefer to satisfy the spectators or their master. They wish for nothing better than to satisfy their master. How often is it seen that they wish nothing better than to satisfy their master?

VOCABULARY.

When bruised . . .	quum, *never used with a participle*.
Groan	ingemo.
Not even	ne (*with the word between*) quidem. *See Dict.*
Begin to utter a groan	ingemisco.
Suffer	perfero.
Blows	plaga.
Must	*Gerund, or* necesse est *with subjunctive.*
Inflict	infligo, *or* infero aliis.
Good Heavens . . .	Dii boni !
Patiently	patienter.
Seem	videor.
Disgrace	turpitudo, ignominia, dedecus. *Verb,* dehonestor, afficior ignominia. *See Dict.*
Would rather . . .	malo. *See Dict.*
Receive	accipio.
Avoid	vito.
Basely	turpiter.
May be	licet. *See Dict.*
Are to be	*Gerund of* vito.
Not	*Supply, ' to be avoided.'*
Can	possum.
Ought	debeo, oportet.
Some	nonnulli, quidam, alii. *See Dict.*
Satisfy	satisfacio, *with dative.*
Spectators	populus, *or,* spectator.
Master	dominus.

Better . . . . potius.
How often . . . . . quam saepe.
It is seen . . . . . appareo.

5.

EXERCISE.

A gladiator lies on the arena wounded to the death. Gladiators, when hacked almost to death with wounds, send to ask their masters, what their will is.

'What is your will, O Master? Do you wish that I should die fighting, or be saved? If you are satisfied, I am ready to die. I will lie down and receive the knife. When this morning I entered the arena, I, about to die, saluted the Emperor. I and my comrades said, "Hail, Imperial Caesar, we salute thee, men doomed to die."'

A gladiator never groans. Who, even though he were but a second-rate gladiator, ever groaned? A gladiator does not change colour. What gladiator ever turned pale? Who, when he had at last sunk down, ever winced? ever shrunk from the edge of the steel? Who ever drew back his throat, when ordered to receive the cut?

Such is the influence of practice, custom, resolution. Shall a low fellow, a rascally foreigner, fit only for such a life and such a profession, be able to suffer with such fortitude, and shall a Roman citizen not be able?

VOCABULARY.

Wounded to death . confectus vulneribus.
Hacked . . . . . concido.
When . . . . . . *Omit with participle.*
Almost . . . . . paene.
Send . . . . . . mitto.
To ask . . . . . . quaero, *say 'who may ask.'*

Will . . . . *Say 'what they wish.'*
Do you wish . . . visne ; *for construction see Dict.*
Save . . . . . . servo.
Satisfied . . . . . *Impersonal, 'if it is satisfactory,' 'if enough has been done for you.'*

Ready . . ' . . . . paratus.
Lie down . . . . decumbo.
Receive . . . . . accipio.
Knife . . . . . . culter, mucro. *See Dict.*
This morning . . . hodie mane.
Enter . . . . . . intro.
Salute . . . . . . saluto.
Emperor . . . . . imperator.
Comrade . . . . . socius.
Hail . . . . . . ave.
Imperial . . . . . imperator.
Never . . . . . nunquam.
Who . . . . . . quis.
Even though he were *Omit in the Latin.*
Second-rate . . . mediocris.
Change . . . . . muto.
Colour . . . . . color, *but here* vultus.
At last . . . . . tandem, *or*, ad extremum.
Wince . . . . . horreo, reformido.
Shrunk from . . . declino.
Edge of steel . . . mucro, *or*, ferrum.
Drew back . . . . contraho.
Throat . . . . . collum.
Order . . . . . . jubeo.
Receive . . . . . recipio, accipio. *See Dict.*
Cut . . . . . . ictus, *or*, ferrum.
Such is the influence tantum valet.
Practice . . . . exercitatio.
Resolution . . . meditatio, *properly, 'the result of careful preparation.'*
Low fellow . . . spurcus homo.

Foreigner	peregrinus, barbarus.
Fit only	dignus.
Life	vita.
Profession	locus, *literally*, '*station.*'
With such fortitude	tam fortiter, *or* tanta fortitudine.
Such	'*Such*' *has two meanings*: 1. '*like this,*' '*of such a kind,*' talis *correlative to* qualis, '*as*;' 2. *so great*, tantus *correlative to* quantus, *as.*

6.

EXERCISE.

Gavius was a Roman citizen. Gavius kept crying out that he was a Roman citizen. . It is not lawful to bind a Roman citizen. It is provided by law that no one shall bind a Roman citizen. Who would dare to bind such an one?

Verres ordered Gavius to be bound. 'Let Gavius be bound with chains.'

It is an outrage to bind a Roman citizen. It is a crime to flog him. It is hardly less than murder to put him to death. What would it be to crucify him?

Gavius was crucified by order of Verres. Verres condemned Gavius to be flogged. 'Lictor,'·says he, 'tie his hands; let him be flogged. It pleases me that the prisoner shall be flogged. I am not content with that. Let him be lifted up, and nailed to a cross.'

What an unheard of thing! What a nefarious business! Does it not seem to you a nefarious business? No one will deny it is a nefarious business. There has not been found any man to deny it. All the best citizens, all the most just men, exclaim against the villainy of Verres,

Vocabulary.

Gavius	Gavius.
Cry out	clamo.
Kept	*Sign of imperfect tense.*
Is lawful . . .	licet.
Bind	vincio.
It is provided . .	caveo. *See Dict.*
That no one . .	ne quis.
Dare	audeo.
Such an one . .	civis Romanus, *not* talis.
Order	jubeo.
Chain	vinculum, catena.
Outrage	facinus.
Crime	scelus.
Flog	verbero, virgis caedo.
Hardly less . .	prope.
Murder	parricidium.
Put to death . .	neco.
What would it be	*Translate ' what shall I say' or ' call.'*
Crucify	in crucem tollo.
By order	*Substant.* jussu, *or, participle ablative absolute.*
Condemn	condemno, jubeo. *See Dict.*
Lictor	lictor.
Says he	ait, inquit. *See Dict.*
Bind	colligo.
Pleases	placet, *followed by Dative.*
Content	contentus.
Nail	affigo, *verb;* clavus, *substant.*
Unheard of . . .	inauditus.
Nefarious . . .	nefaria, *or ' nefarious business,' in one word,* nefas.
What a	quae, *also* quam, ' *how.*'
No one	nemo.
Not any man . .	non quisquam.
Find	invenio, reperio.

Best	. . . . .	bonus, *superlative*.
All the	. . . .	*Say, 'each most just.'*
Just	. . . . .	justus.
Exclaim	. . . .	exclamo.
Against	. . . .	in, *with accusative*.
Villainy	. . . .	nequitia.

7.

EXERCISE.

Which is the way to the forum? Does this way lead to the forum? No, you are astray, 'all over the sky,' as we say. I will ask yonder boy which of these two roads leads to the forum. I asked a woman which way led to the forum. I wish I had not asked her. She answered that neither of these two ways led to the forum. He told me to go straight on. Will you be our guide? I will show you the way. Wait here till I come back; the way is short. Go past the temple of Vesta, straight on. We both lost our way again; he went to the left, I to the right. I happened to see a Briton coming towards us. He was on foot. As he was walking, I ran up to him. 'Where, and for how much,' said I, 'can I buy bread, wine, food? Where can I get lodgings?'

He answered, 'I advise you to put up with a tavern-keeper whom I know.'

VOCABULARY.

Which?	. . .	quis? quisnam?
Way	. . . . .	via.
Forum	. . . .	forum.
Lead	. . . .	duco.
Does?	. . . .	anne, an, ne, num, annon.

See Dict.

No	at tu.
Astray	erro, *verb*.
All over the sky .	toto caelo.
Ask	interrogo.
Which of two . .	uter.
Neither	neuter.
Told	jubeo.
Straight	recta.
Will	volo.
Guide	dux.
Show	monstro.
Wait	maneo.
Till	dum. *See Dict.*
Come back . . .	redeo.
Short	brevis.
Past	praeter.
Vesta	Vesta.
Temple	aedes.
Both	uterque. *See Dict.*
Lost	erro.
Left	sinistra.
Right	dextra.
Happened to . .	forte.
Come towards .	accedo.
On foot	pedes, *adjective*.
Walk	ambulo.
Ran up	accurro.
Where	ubi.
How much . .	quantus. *See Dict.*
Buy	emo.
Wine	vinum.
Food . : . . .	cibus.
Get	paro.
Lodgings . . .	hospitium.
Advise	moneo. *See Dict.*
Put up	deversari.

With	apud.
Tavern-keeper .	caupo.
Know	nosco. *See Dict.*

8.

EXERCISE.

From whence do you come?

I came hither by ship from Britain. I arrived the day before yesterday.

Of what country are you?

I am a citizen of the world.

Socrates used to say that he was a citizen of the world. I do not believe you are a Roman citizen.

He said he doubted whether I was a Roman citizen.

Don't you know whether he is a citizen or a barbarian?

I took him for a native of Boeotia.

Britain is a long way from here. Britain is an island. The Britons are said to be rich. The Britons boast they never will be slaves. Are the Britons slaves? Are there any slaves among the Britons? It is not true that all Britons are rich. How few of them are rich! How small a portion of them are rich! How many inhabitants does Britain contain?

Alas! How many are poor! The idler men are, the poorer they become. The more they work, the richer they grow. If they were not idle they would not be so poor. If you are idle you will be poor. If they had been idle they would have been poor.

VOCABULARY.

Whence	unde.
Come	venio.

Ship	navis.
Britain	Britannia.
Come by ship . . .	vehor, appello. *See Dict.*
Arrive	adsum, advenio.
Day before yesterday	nudius tertius, *adjective agreeing with* ego. *See Dict.*
Of what country ? . .	cujas ?
Of the world	mundanus.
Citizen	civis.
Doubt whether . . .	dubito num.
Take for	puto esse.
Native of	natus in.
Boeotia, Boeotian . .	Boeotia, Boeotus.
Briton	Britannus.
Long way	procul.
Island	insula.
Rich	dives.
Boast	jacto, glorior. *See Dict.*
Slave	servus.
Among	apud, '*living among*;' inter ' *in the number of.*'
True	verus.
How few	quotus quisque ! *See Dict.*
How small	quotus ! 'exclamantis et interrogantis.'
How many	quot ? 'interrogantis.'
Inhabitant	incola.
How many	quam multi, 'commiserantis.'
The	quo, eo.
Idle	ignavus.
Poor	pauper.
Become	fio.
The more	quanto magis.
Work	laboro.
Grow	fio.

9.

EXERCISE.

Can you speak Latin? I ask you if you can speak Latin. If you can, speak out. This person is deaf or stupid. Are you deaf or stupid? He is more stupid than deaf. I think he is more stupid than deaf.

I have learnt Latin.

Can you read or write Latin? He said that he had learnt Latin. Did you learn the language at home or at school?

Words fail me.

He is at a loss, he says that words fail him. How old are you?

I am twenty years old.

Are you twenty years old, and cannot say what you wish in Latin?

I am a good football player.

A person of much brains doubtless. Is it the opinion among your countrymen that the soul dwells in the feet, or in the head, or in the breast?

VOCABULARY.

Can	scio. *See Dict.*
Speak	loqui.
Latin, *adv.* . . .	Latine. *See Dict.*
If	an, si. *See Dict.*
Can	possum.
Out	e, *in composition.*
Person	homo.
Deaf	surdus.
Stupid	hebes.
Think	puto.

c

Latin, *subst.* . . .	literae Latinae.
Learn	disco.
Read	lego.
Or	vel, an. *See Dict.*
Write	scribo.
Language . . .	lingua, sermo.
Fail	desum.
I am at a loss . .	haereo.
How old	quot annos natus.
Twenty	viginti.
Year	annus.
Wish	volo.
Good	peritus. *See Dict.*
Football	follis, pila.
Play	ludo, *verb* ; ludus, *subst.*
Of much brains .	egregie cordatus.
Doubtless . . .	nimirum.
Is it	fertne ? *See Dict.*
Opinion	opinio.
Your countrymen	vos.
Soul	animus.
Dwell	habito.
Feet	pes.
Head	caput.
Breast	pectus.

10.

EXERCISE.

I do not understand you.

I wonder that you do not understand my words. Whose fault is it that you do not understand Latin ?

It is hard to understand.

You said you had learnt Latin. How long were you at school ?

Eight years.

You profess to have learnt Latin, yet you cannot ask for bread, I suppose, in Latin. Perhaps you would prefer roast beef. Caesar says that in his days the Britons lived on milk and venison.

It must be somebody's fault. Any one not by nature foolish can learn Latin, if he uses industry.

He says that no one is to blame. He says it must be the master's fault.

Yes, of course it is the master's fault, as the poet says, ' The fault is attributed to the master, that the Arcadian youth has no brains in his head.'

How few Britons can talk Latin. They say it is a dead language. What need to learn a dead language? It suits not every one to learn things not profitable.

Vocabulary.

Understand . .	intelligo.
Wonder . . .	miror. *See Dict.*
Fault	culpa.
That	quod.
Hard	difficilis, *with supine.*
How long . .	quam diu.
Were	utor.
School . . .	ludus literarius.
Go to school .	ausculto magistros.
Eight	octo.
Profess . . .	dictito, aio.
Yet cannot . .	tamen nescis.
Ask for . . .	rogo.
Bread	panis.
Suppose . . .	opinor. *See Dict.*
Perhaps . . .	fortasse.
Roast beef . .	assa bubula.
Live on . . .	vescor. *See Dict.*

Milk	lac.
Venison . . .	ferina.
Must be . . .	fieri non potest quin.
Somebody . .	aliquis, quidam. *See Dict.*
Anyone . . .	quisquam *after negative.*
Anyone who .	quicunque, quivis nisi sit.
Nature . . .	natura.
Foolish . . .	fatuus.
Use	utor.
Industry . . .	industria.
To blame . . .	culpa dignus.
Master	docens.
Of course . . .	scilicet.
Poet	poeta.
Attribute . . .	arguo. *See Dict.*
No	nullus.
Brains	cor.
Head	pectus ; *say, ' that no heart beats in the breast.'*
Arcadian . . .	Arcadicus.
Dead language .	consuetudinem, *or,* usum istius linguae exolevisse.
Suits	convenit.
Every one . .	quivis, quisque. *See Dict.*
Learn	disco, calleo.
Not	nisi.
Profitable . .	quaestuosus.

PART II.

I. As to the method of dealing with a piece of continuous English to be translated into Latin, the following rules will be found useful.

(1) Read over the whole passage more than once, until you are sure that you know the meaning of the English.

(2) Then shut the book, and repeat the substance of the passage in your own words.

(3) Provide the Latin for the key words and leading ideas, either from memory or from the Dictionary.

(4) Try to recollect whether you have read anything like it in a Latin author. Think what Latin that you have read it most resembles; e. g. if the piece describes a battle, you may be sure of finding an account of a battle in Livy or Caesar; then, if there is an opportunity, read a chapter of Livy or Caesar before doing the exercise.

(5) Now trace in outline the connection of thought running through the piece, seizing on the leading ideas, and making a kind of skeleton of the passage, and paying especial attention to the particles that link the clauses together.

(6) Fill in the details.

(7) Construe your version, taking each word separately and pronouncing aloud both the Latin and the English you mean it to represent.

1.

1. *The Dorian army marched to Athens* . . .

PRAEPARATIO.

If we analyse this passage, we shall be struck by the great number of independent statements in the Indicative mood; and by the absence of connecting particles, other than '*and*.' The English says,

'The Dorian army marched .   .   .   .   .

.   .   .   and lay encamped.'

'Aletes had consulted .   .   .   .   .   .

.   .   .   and had been assured.'

'A Delphian disclosed, ...

.   .   .   and Codrus resolved.'

'He went out, ...

.   .   .   and killed, and was killed.'

'The Athenians sent, ...

.   .   .   and the Dorians withdrew.'

If we were to render these *eleven* disjointed statements into Latin, retaining the English syntax, although the result might be grammatical, it could not properly be called Latin Prose. Why not? Because the use of independent statements, and the absence of logical particles are the precise points in which English syntax differs from Latin.

A Latin writer would probably not have more than *five* indicative assertions in this piece. The other *six* would naturally fall into subordinate positions; for it is the tendency of Latin syntax to economise the direct statements. Moreover the relation of one sentence to another would be made clear by appropriate particles. In English these particles are implied, but not expressed.

The passage might be moulded in the following form, to make it read more like native Latin.

CONSTRUCTIO.

The Dorian army having marched to Athens was lying encamped under the walls of the city. Now inasmuch as it had been answered to Aletes, their leader, on consulting the oracle of Delphian Apollo, that the affair would end prosperously for him only in case he should spare (or, *have spared*) *the life of the king of the Athenians, and whereas a certain Delphian, by name Cleomantis, had made known this answer to the Athenians, Codrus their king resolved to devote himself for his country. So having passed out by the gate, clothed in rustic attire, when he had chanced upon two Dorians, and had smitten one-of-the-two with his bill-hook, he was himself killed by the other. Which thing being known, the Athenians sent a herald to demand back the dead king's body. But the leaders of the Dorians, despairing of the outcome of the war, led off their forces from Attica.*

MATERIA.

(The vocabulary is adapted to the original English passage.)

So . . . . itaque, *meaning 'accordingly.'*

The . . . *No equivalent in Latin. Sometimes it may be rendered by* 'is,' *as* 'ea conditione ut arma dederent,' '*on the condition that they gave up their arms.*'

Dorian . . Doricus, -a, -um. Doriensis, *of the people.*

Army . . exercitus : 'comparavit exercitum.'

March . . contendo : 'in fines Sygambrorum contendit.' proficiscor : 'in Illyricum profectus est.'

To . . . ad, *omitted before names of towns.*

Athens . . Athenae, -arum.

†

Lie en-camped.	} in castris esse.

Encamp . consido : 'quo in loco Germani consederant ;' 'castra posuerunt.'

Under . . sub ; *with ablative, of rest*: 'manet sub Jove frigido venator ;' 'sub ipsis Numantiae moenibus constituere.'

With accusative, of motion: 'exercitu sub jugum misso.'

Its. . . . is, ea, id. *Omitted when there is no fear of ambiguity.*

Walls . . murus, moenia : 'dividimus muros, et moenia pandimus urbis.'

Aletes . . Aletes, -is : 'et qua grandaevus Aletes.'

Their . . *Plural of ' his,' expressed by*

(1) *genitive of* is, ea, id, = '*the person or persons aforesaid.*'

(2) *genitive of* hic, haec, hoc, = 'this one,' *of the prominent subject of discourse.*

(3) *genitive of* ipse, *when not referring to the subject.*

(4) Suus, = '*own*:' *referring generally to subject of the sentence*: 'cur de sua virtute aut de ipsius diligentia desperarent ?'

Omitted when not indispensable for making clear the meaning.

Leader . . dux : 'dux femina facti.'

Had . . . *Sign of the pluperfect. In Latin shown by inflection of the verb*: 'consuluerat.'

Previously ante ; *adverb*: 'saepe ante fecerat.'

Consult . consulo : 'Apollinem de re consuluit ;' 'consulit Phoebi oracula.'

Delphic . Delphicus ; *adjective*: Delphis, *at Delphi.*

Oracle . . oraculum ; *singular, of the place*: 'illud oraculum Delphis tam celebre ;' *plural, of the* *response*: 'Codrus petivit oracula, Pythia edidit ; ' 'oracula petivit a Dodona.'

And . . . (1) et ; *of fortuitous or temporary connection* : 'frigus et fames et sitis.'

(2) atque, *spelt* ac *before consonants* ; *of more intimate connection* : 'ex animo ac vere,' *'from the heart, and so truthfully.'*

(3) que ; *enclitic, but rarely added to words ending in* e *short, joins words or ideas closely connected, and forming, it may be, one complete idea* : 'sarmentis virgultisque collectis ad castra pergunt,' *'twigs and brushwood' = 'fuel.'*

In negative sentences '*and—not*' *is expressed by* 'neque—nec : ' 'rem esse in angusto vidit neque ullum esse subsidium quod submitti posset.'

'And he,' ' and she' may be expressed in Latin by qui, quae (*for a relative is equal to a personal or demonstrative pronoun plus a conjunction*) : 'Milites transcendere in hostium naves contendebant. Quod postquam barbari fieri animadverterunt fuga salutem petere contenderunt.' Quod *is equal to* '*and this.'*

Assure . . confirmo : 'illud se polliceri et jurejurando confirmare tutum iter per fines suos daturum ; ' 'quorum omnium testimoniis de hac Dionis pecunia confirmatum est.'

promitto : 'promitto, recipio, spondeo C. Caesarem talem semper fore civem qualis hodie est.'

polliceor : 'pollicitus est ei coenam ; ' 'pollicentur obsides dare,' also 'se daturos esse.'

The same idea expressed by a substantive ;

fiducia : ' prope certam fiduciam salutis praebere.'

fides : ' fac fidem te nihil nisi populi utilitatem
quaerere ;' '*establish a belief* :' 'accipe
daque fidem,' '*assurances.*'

Success . . successus : ' successu rerum ferocior.'

exitus : ' belli secundos reddidit exitus ;' 'for-
tasse haec omnia meliores habebunt exitus.'
As a verb, '*to succeed* :' 'ad exitum spei per-
venire ;' 'bene rem gerere.'

Provided . si, sic—si : 'ea conditione si ;' 'non aliter nisi.'

He . . . ille. *But as the number and person are distinguished by the inflection of the verb in
Latin,* ille *may be omitted unless required
for the sake of clearness or emphasis.*

Spare. . . parco, peperci : 'parcere subjectis et debellare
superbos ;' 'parce pias scelerare manus.'

Life . . . vita : ' adimere vitam alicui.'

salus : 'tua salus agitur ;' 'una salus victis
nullam sperare salutem.'

caput : 'capitis periculum adivi ;' 'de capite
meo agitur.'

Of . . . . *Expressed by inflection of noun in Latin, usually by genitive case, sometimes by dative* :
'nomen huic duci est Philippo ;' '*the
name of this leader is Philip.*'

Athenian . Atheniensis, -is.

A . . . . *Not expressed in Latin when merely used with
noun to express one of a species* : 'Grae-
cus ;' 'tulit dolorem ut vir.' *But when
special attention is directed to an object,
rendered by* quidam.

Friendly . amicus, -a, -um : 'amicum dixit Populi Romani ;'
'amicus non magis tyranno quam tyran-
nidi.'

Delphian . Delphus, -i, '*a Delphian.*'

Name . .   *Verb* : dico, -xi, nomino, voco.

           Noun : nomen, -inis: 'tribunus nomine Manlius.'

Cleomantis   Cleomantis, -is.

Disclose .   recludo, -si ; '*to unlock* :' 'operta recludere;' *poetical.*

           aperio, -ui : 'domino navis quis sit aperit.'

           patefacio, -feci, -facere : 'patefacta est conjuratio.'

           refero, -tuli, -ferre ; '*make known* :' 'referre sermones deorum.'

Answer .   responsum, -i : 'nullo ab nostris dato responso.'

To . . .   ad : 'rem ad senatum rettulerunt.'

           Sign of dative : 'haec nobis nuntiata sunt.'

Codrus . .   Codrus, -i : 'Codrus pro patria non timidus mori.'

Resolve . .   statuo, -ui, -ere : 'Caesar statuerat proelio decertare.'

           constituo : 'bellum gerere constituit.'

           decerno, -crevi, -cretum, -cernere : 'Rhenum transire decreverat.'

Devote . .   voveo, -vi, -vere : 'sua capita pro salute patriae voverunt.'

           devoveo : 'se pro patria devovit.'

For . . .   *Preposition,* '*for the good of* :' so, 'pro bono publico ;' '*instead of* :' 'filiam pro muta agna devovere.'

Country .   patria, -ae, *in regard to birth.*

           ager, -gri, *to the town.*

           rus, ruris, *to town life.*

Go out . .   egredior, -di, egressus est.

At . . . .   *Ablative, meaning,* '*by* :' 'porta egressus est.'

           Sometimes, ad : 'ad aram stabat victima.'

           Sometimes genitive : domi, '*at home* ;' Romae, '*at Rome.*'

Gate . . .   porta, -ae : 'ante portam oppidi.'

Disguise . *By explanatory words* : 'induit pastoralem pro regio habitum ;' 'veste servili in dissimulationem sui compositus, urbe elapsus est ;' 'permutato cum uxore habitu.'

Woodman . agrestis, -is : *adjective and substantive.*

Garb . . cultus : *' dress,' ' fashion of dress.'*
vestitus : *' clothing.'*
habitus : *' garb,' ' fashion of dress.'*

Fall in with obviam, *adverb* ; obvius, *adjective* ; fieri : 'obviam fit ei Clodius.'

incido, -cidi, -cidere, -casum : 'Valerius, cum vinctus catenis traheretur in ipsum Caesarem incidit.'

Two . . . duo, duae, duo ; *accus. masc.* duo *and* duos : 'angues duo maximi ;' *but with substantives that have no singular, as* castra, *with things that go in pairs, as* oculi, *with substantives that have a different signification in the plural from the singular, use* bini, binae, bina.

Kill . . . occido, -cidi, -isum ; *cut down, kill* : 'alter ibi capitur pugnans occiditur alter.'

trucido, -avi, -atum ; *' butcher,' ' kill :'* 'ne pueros coram populo Medea trucidet.'

interficio, -feci, -fectum ; *' slay,' ' kill :'* 'omnes interfecti sunt.'

With . . . *Ablative of the instrument* ; *when company is implied,* 'cum :' 'vixi cum Pansa.'

Bill . . . securis, -is, *fem.*

By . . . a *or* ab *with persons* : ' a rege percussus est ;' *ablative only, of things* : ' securi percussus est a rege.'

Other . . alter, -a, -um, *when two persons or things are spoken of* : alter *is likewise used for the first mentioned, where in English we say ' the one :'* 'alter exercitum perdidit, alter vendidit.'

Now . . . nunc; *adverb of time, at the present time*: *but when 'now' means 'thereupon,' "accordingly,'* say, 'tum vero,' *or* 'igitur,' *or* 'quo facto,' '*which thing having happened,*' or, '*been done.*'

Send . . . mitto, misi, missum, mittere.

Herald . . legatus: 'legatos misit ad indicendum bellum.'
    caduceator, -oris, m.; '*officer with a herald's staff* or *flag of truce*:' 'caduceatori nemo nocet.'

Claim . . postulo, -avi, -atum : 'postulare jus suum.'
    repeto, -ivi, -itum : 'bona sua repetunt.'
    vindico, -avi, -atum : 'sponsam in libertatem vindicat.'
    reposco, -posci, -poscitum : 'Verrem simulacrum Cereris reposco.'

Body . . . corpus, -oris, n. ; '*living*' or '*dead*:' 'arma detracta sunt corporibus hostium.'
    cadaver, -eris, n. : '*corpse unburied.*'

Of . . . . *Sign of genitive*: 'caput equi.' *Often expressed by an adjective in Latin*: 'caput equinum ;' 'regium corpus.'

King . . . rex, regis, m. ; 'rex erat Aeneas nobis.'

Chief . . dux, ducis, m. ; ductor, -oris, m.

Deem . . puto, -avi, -atum : 'turpem putat lituram.'
    habeo, -ui, -itum : 'quem Aegypti nefas habent nominare.'
    existimo, -avi, -atum : 'qui hoc fecit avarum existima.'
    reor, ratus sum, reri : 'et reor a facie Calliopea fuit.'

Deem hopeless desperare de aliqua re : 'non desperavit de salute reipublicae.'

Withdraw . abduco, -duxi, -ductum.

Forces . . copiae, *plural.* Copia *in the singular means* '*plenty.*'

2. *So now in the hour of danger the geese . . .*

First let us find out the precise meaning of the English.

'So.' What does 'so' mean here? It must refer to something gone before, and we shall have to deduce the meaning from the context. It seems to be this. The geese had been kindly treated, being probably sacred geese, and so in the hour of danger the piety of their protectors was rewarded by the geese giving the alarm in time. This passage, like most of the others, must be treated as an extract from a longer history, and we must supply the connection, indicated by the introductory particle (here '*itaque*' will do), either by knowledge or conjecture.

'The geese began to cry and flap, etc.' presumably, '*ut monerent custodes adventare periculum,*' to warn the guards; if so, the 'and' before Marcus would be more logically represented by '*quo sono excitus.*'

'And behold.' A rhetorical mode of calling attention, or expressing surprise, more appropriate to poetry than prose narrative. It may be omitted here.

'And the Capitol was saved.' A closer logical connection than 'and' indicates is implied, and must be expressed in Latin. '*Sic Capitolium servatum est*' would do.

Notice that there are in the English no less than *fifteen* indicative statements tacked on to each other by *fourteen* 'ands.' The Latin idiom would not allow this. By carefully studying the connection of the parts we shall find what is the real value logically of each of these '*ands.*' Some will be found to conceal a purpose, some a reason, some a concomitant circumstance, and they will have to be translated by corresponding conjunctions, adverbs, or forms of speech. When we have separated the essential statements, from the accidental ones, we shall find about *five* remaining important enough to be put into the Indicative mood.

This will be seen in the following arrangement of the sentences.

CONSTRUCTIO.

Accordingly in this dangerous juncture, the noise of enemies approaching having been heard, the geese began to utter a cry through fear, and to clap with (their) wings: by which sound being roused Marcus Manlius, who dwelt hard by in the Capitol, sword and shield having been snatched up, at the same time calling his comrades, ran to the edge of the cliff. There (seeing) a Gaul who had already got a footing on the summit, Manlius having sprung at him with shield dashed into his face, tumbles (him) headlong. And when the fall of him slipping upset (those) next ascending (either *ascendentes*, or *eos qui ascendebant*, for if *eos* is used, *qui* must follow); *the rest* (accusative) *dismayed and, arms having been dropped, embracing the rocks with their hands, the Romans, whom Manlius had summoned to himself, easily butcher. So the Capitol was saved.*

MATERIA.

So . . . . . *Meaning* '*thus*,' sic : ' sic itur ad astra.'
'*accordingly*,' itaque : ' itaque rem suscipit.'
'*therefore*,' igitur : ' sed flagitat tabellarius ; valebis igitur.'

Hour of   hoc tempus periculosum, discrimen : ' in ipso
danger   discrimine periculi amicum destituit.'

Goose . . . anser : 'atque hic auratis volitans argenteus anser Porticibus, Gallos in limine adesse canebat.'

Hear . . . audio : 'audit equos, audit strepitus, et signa sequentum.'

Sound . . . sonitus : 'armorum sonitum toto Germania caelo audiit.'

Enemy . . hostis, '*public* ;' inimicus, '*private.*'
'Pompeius saepius cum hoste conflixit quam quisquam cum inimico concertavit.'

Begin . . . coepi, -isse, *defective* : 'dimidium facti qui bene coepit habet.'
incipio : 'bellum gerere incipiunt.'

Cry . . . . clamo, clamito, *of men* : 'Tiberium in Tiberim clamitabant.'
vagire ; *of children* : 'vox pueri vagientis.'
strepere : 'argutos inter strepit anser olores.'
clangor, *noise* : 'cum magno clangore volitant.'
murmur : 'raucum pro verbis edere murmur.'

Wing . . . ala : 'radit iter liquidum celeres neque commovet alas.'

Clap . . . plaudo : 'alis plaudentem figit columbam.'

Fear . . . timor ; *implying somewhat of timidity* : 'magno timore affectus est.'
metus ; *apprehension of future evil* : 'reddidit ergo metu non moribus.'
pavor ; '*terror*,' '*consternation* :' 'Ulixi cor frixit prae pavore.'

Manlius . . M. Manlius : 'in summo custos Tarpeiae Manlius arcis.'

Capitol . . Capitolium ; *plural* -a : 'fastigium Capitolii et ceterarum aedium ;' 'stabat pro templo et Capitolia celsa tenebat.'

House . . . domus ; '*dwelling*,' '*house* :' 'domi aetatem agere ;' 'venit in M. Laecae domum.'

domicilium, '*abode*:' 'Roma imperii et gloriae domicilium.'

tectum, *literally* '*roof*:' 'ventus de tecto deturbavit tegulam;' '*shelter*:' 'ne tecto recipiatur qui non arma abjecerit;' '*houses*:' 'vos, Quirites, in vestra tecta discedite.'

aedes, '*building*:' 'aedes laxitate conspicuae.'

habito, *verb*: 'habitanda fana apris reliquit et rapacibus lupis;' 'habitans in sicco.'

incolo: 'Germani qui trans Rhenum incolunt.'

Hard by . . juxta, *prep.*: 'juxta murum castra ponunt.'
Adverb: 'forte fuit juxta tumulus.'

Temple . . templum: 'Junonis.'
aedes: 'Minervae dedicavit aedem.'
fanum: 'Dianae Ephesi.'
delubrum: 'fana ac delubra deorum.'

Arouse . . suscito: 'suscitat e somno.'
excito: 'Mauri ignoto et horribili sonitu repente exciti.'

Spring . . exsilio, '*up from* :' 'de sella properans exsiluit.'
desilio, '*down from* :' 'desilit ab alto curru.'
prosilio, '*forth from*:' 'rex ab sede sua prosiluit.'
insilio, '*on to* :' 'in equum insiluit.'

Seize . . . arripio: 'nostri arma quae possunt arripiunt.'

Sword. . . ensis, *poetical*: 'stricto sic ense precatur.'
gladius: 'strictis gladiis.'

Shield. . . scutum: 'scutis ex cortice factis.'

Call . . . vocare: 'Populum Romanum ad arma vocat;' 'auxilium vocat et duros conclamat agrestes.'
advoco: 'viros primarios in concilium advocat.'
evoco: 'nostros ad pugnam evocant.'

D

excieo : 'quid est quod me excivisti ante aedes ?'

inclamo : 'comitem inclamavit ut opem ferret.'

cieo : 'aere ciere viros.'

Comrade. . socius : 'hunc cape consiliis socium.'

Run to . . accurro : 'territa voce sui nutrix accurrit alumni.'

Edge of . . extremus, *adjective* : 'ad extremas fossas castella constituit.'

Cliff . . . rupes : 'ex rupe Tarpeia dejectus.'

Behold . . ecce : 'ecce autem video rure redeuntem senem.'

Gaul . . . Gallus : 'Galli per dumos aderant templumque tenebant.'

Reach . . . attingo : 'enisus arces attigit igneas.'

Summit . . summus, *adjective* : 'feriunt summos fulmina montes ;' 'in summo muro consistendi potestas erat nulli.'

Rush upon . inferre se : 'adeo concitato impetu se intulerunt hostes in nostram aciem.'

incurso : 'incursabo te pugnis.'

Dash . . . illido : 'caput foribus illisit.'

affligo : 'navis est ad scopulos afflicta.'

impingo : 'pugnum in os illi impingo.'

Shield. . . scutum : 'scutum pro clipeo ferre ;' 'scutis magis quam gladiis geritur res, umbonibus incussaque ala sternuntur hostes.'

Face . . . facies : 'feri faciem.'

os, *literally* '*mouth :*' 'alicui laedere os.'

Tumble down detrudo, *active* : 'Stygias detrusit in undas.'

deturbo : 'in mare praecipitem puppi deturbat ab alta.'

Rock . . . scopulus : 'geminique minantur in caelum scopuli.'

saxum : 'tot congesta manu praeruptis oppida saxis.'

Fall . . . cado : 'turris cadens ruinam traxit.'
prolabor : 'equus prolapsus per caput regem effudit.'

Bear down . sterno : 'turbam invadite ac sternite omnia ferro ; ' 'hujus prolapsi casus stravit ceteros.'

Mount . . ascendo : 'proximi ascendentes.'

Rest . . . ceteri : 'cetera turba fugit.'

Dismayed . attonitus : 'talibus attonitus visis, ac voce deorum ; ' 'metu perculsus.'
trepidans : 'tota urbe trepidatur.'

Drop . . . demitto : 'demisit lacrimas ; ' *' let fall,' but generally it implies purpose* : 'per funem demissus.'
omitto, *from inattention or compulsion* : 'armis omissis.'

Cling to . . haereo : 'dextramque amplexus inhaesit.'

Closely . . arcte : 'arctius atque hedera astringitur ilex.'

Roman . . Romanus : 'hunc tu Romane caveto.'

Slaughter . trucido : 'cavete ne capti sicut pecora trucidemini;' 'non jam pugna sed velut trucidatio pecorum.'

Easily. . . facile : 'haud facile emergunt quorum virtutibus obstat res angusta domi.'

Save . . . . servo : 'sic me servavit Apollo.' .

3.

3. *Jupiter himself appeared to a citizen* . . .

PRAEPARATIO.

The English of this piece is not difficult to understand. The motive of the passage is to illustrate the pride and reserve of Pompey, and the frank courtesy of Crassus. The consuls are, of course, Pompey and Crassus.

The syntax need not be very complex here; the more direct we are the better. Clearness is what we have to aim at. What will require the closest attention here is the proper use of the tenses and moods.

First as to the tenses. Common sense will show where the time is present, where past, where pluperfect, where future, and where perfect. The difficulty is to determine where to use the aorist, and where the imperfect. The perplexity arises from two facts.

First, that in English one form can stand for both the aorist and the imperfect, as, 'He behaved haughtily,' may mean, either, '*Arroganter se gessit*,' or, '*arroganter se gerebat.*'

Secondly, that in Latin one and the same form stands for both the aorist and the perfect: as, '*Crassus processit*' may mean, either, 'Crassus has come forward,' or, 'Crassus came forward.'

The aorist and imperfect differ thus:

The aorist *states an occurrence absolutely.*

The imperfect *states an occurrence with relation to some other occurrence.*

The action of the *aorist is momentary.*

The action of the *imperfect is continuous.*

The aorist *resembles a point.*

The imperfect *resembles a line.*

The aorist *narrates.*

The imperfect *describes.*

The aorist is used of a *single action.*

The imperfect of *repeated actions and habits.*

In this exercise, 'appeared' is an aorist, 'bade' is an aorist, 'stood still,' 'said,' 'advanced,' are aorists; 'exclaimed' is aorist, even if '*inquit*,' or, '*exclamat*' be used, because the aorist is not confined to past time. Compare the Greek τύπτε, τύψον, imperative, and ἐὰν τύπτῃς, ἐὰν τύψῃς, subjunctive. 'Deemed worthy,' 'decreed,' are aorists, and 'withdrew' if looked upon as an absolute statement; 'he withdrew once for all' is an aorist.

On the other hand, 'demanded,' 'was haughty,' 'went into the forum,' indicating habit, or repeated action, are more properly treated as imperfects.

The tense or time of the dependent verbs is regulated by that of the principal verbs: e.g. 'Jupiter *tells* him *he is to* warn the consuls;' present follows present : 'Jupiter *has told him he is to* warn the consuls;' present follows perfect: 'Jupiter *told him he was* to warn the consuls;' and similarly in Latin, Greek, and other languages. This sequence depends on a law of thought common to all men. It is a part of the logic that underlies language. It is not peculiar to Latin Syntax.

Next as to the moods.

We must treat of them as they occur in the Latinized version, since in the English they are mostly indicative.

'*Imperavit* (here aorist) *civi ut moneret consules.*' The principal indicatives are so simple they require no explanation : '*Pompeius dixit,*' '*Crassus processit,*' etc.

'*Moneret*' is subjunctive after '*ut,*' expressing a purpose or command.

'*Ne deponerent,*' subjunctive after '*ne*' in a prohibition.

'*Antequam gratiam inter se reconciliassent,*' or '*in gratiam venissent,*' subjunctive, because it was part of Jupiter's command. '*Nihil turpe facio qui Pompeio concedam.*' '*Concedam*' is subjunctive governed by the

conjunction latent in '*qui*.' The relative is always equal
to a pronoun plus a conjunction : here the conjunction
latent is '*si*,' '*if*,' or '*propterea quod*,' 'because :' and
'*qui concedam*' is equal to '*si ego concedam*,' '*if*,' or '*in
that I give way*' '*Quem vos Magni nomine dignati
estis : nec non bis triumphum decrevistis, antequam senator
factus est*,' are all stated as historical facts, and are therefore in the indicative mood.

It is conceivable, however, that 'thought worthy,' and
'decreed,' might be subjunctive, as suggesting a reason
for my yielding to Pompey, '*since* you thought him worthy.'
This depends on the '*animus loquentis*,' i. e. the logical
aspect in which the speaker wishes to present the fact.
Neither the indicative nor the subjunctive would be grammatically wrong here, but the indicative is preferable.

CONSTRUCTIO.

*Jupiter having appeared in a dream to a certain citizen,
ordered him to warn the consuls not to lay down the fasces,
before that they should have been reconciled to each other.
Then Pompey indeed, this admonition having been received,
stood still nor spoke any word* (say *nec*; avoid *et non*).
But Crassus came forward (*ultro*), *and his* (*ejus*, i. e.
Pompeii) *hand having been clasped, 'My citizens,' says he,
'I do nothing mean or dishonourable, in that I* (*qui*, conjunction plus pronoun = relative) *give way to Pompey, whom
as yet beardless you deemed worthy of the cognomen of
Magnus, and moreover* (*nec non*) *twice decreed a triumph
to the same man not yet having reached the senatorial age.'
This so great respectfulness was Cn. Pompeius wont to
exact from his equals ; towards the multitude he bore him-*

*self still more arrogantly. He likewise (the same man)
refused the business of protecting-clients-in-law-courts, on
which formerly the most illustrious citizens had been accustomed to pride themselves : nor did he ever descend into the
forum unless accompanied by a band of nobles.*

Materia.

Jupiter . . Jupiter : 'ab Jove principium, Musae, Jovis
omnia plena.'

Himself . . ipse : 'ipsi te fontes, ipsa haec arbusta voca-
bant.'

Appear . . appareo : 'anguis Sullae apparuit.'

Dream   . . somnium : 'quae somnio visa fuerant.'

somnus, '*sleep*:' 'in somno, in somnis, per
somnum videre aliquid ; ' 'in somnis ecce
ante oculos maestissimus Hector visus
adesse mihi.'

A . . . . . quidam : 'quidam de collegis nostris.'

Citizen . . civis : 'quod civis cum civi agat.'

Bid . . . . jubeo, *accusative, followed by infinitive* : 'eos
abire jussit.'

impero, *dative, followed by* ut *and subjunctive,*
ne, *and subjunctive, or subjunctive only* :
'his uti captivos conquirerent et reducerent
imperavit ; ' 'mihi ne abscedam imperat ; ' 'letoque det, imperat, Argum.'

Tell . . . . dico, ' *to communicate information.*'

jubeo, moneo, ' *to order.*'

moneo ne, '*to tell not to*' . . . 'Macedonas
monebat ne multitudine hostium move-
rentur.'

veto : 'ab opere discedere legatos Caesar
vetuerat ; ' 'edicto vetuit ne quis se
praeter Apellem pingeret.'

Lay down office   depono : 'deponere magistratum, dictaturam, fasces, secures.'

Without . . ante . . . quam : 'neque ante dimisit eum quam certiorem fecit,' *without informing him.*

ut non : 'aiunt nec honeste quemquam vivere, ut non jucunde vivat, nec jucunde, ut non honeste.'

Reconcile . '*To be reconciled* :' 'in gratiam redire cum collega ; ' 'inter se in concordiam redire; ' 'jam vos redistis in concordiam.'

On this . . quo facto : 'itaque,' *first in sentence* ; 'igitur,' *after initial word.*

Pompey . . 'ultima Pompeio dabitur provincia.'

Stand . . . stare, '*not to fall, lie, or sit* :' 'Respublica staret, tu concidisses.'

subsisto, '*halt,*' '*stop* :' 'reliqui in itinere substiterunt.'

consisto, '*to stand still,*' *of things generally in motion* : 'constitit utrumque agmen.'

resisto, '*to stand still,*' *of one refusing to move* : 'ille saepius appellatus respexit ac restitit.'

Say nothing 'nullam vocem emittere ; ' 'tacere neque verbum ullum dicere.'

A . . . . = '*any,*' ullus, -a, -um, *after a negative.*

But . . . . autem, *never first in sentence, answers to* quidem *in preceding clause.*

Advance . procedo : 'in medium lente processit.'

Take . . . prehendere : 'dextra prehensum continuit.'

Hand . . . dextra, *in sign of greeting, or fidelity* : 'avidi conjungere dextras.'

Exclaim . . exclamare, '*to say aloud* :' 'non possum quin exclamem, Euge.'

inquit, ait, *after the first word or words of the quotation.*

Countrymen cives : 'ferte opem, cives mei.'

Quirites, '*civilians* :' 'tradite nostra viris ignavi signa Quirites.'

Do . . . facio : 'quid facitis? quis clamor, ait.'

Ignoble . . inhonestum: 'nihil turpe neque injustum neque inhonestum.'

Mean . . . sordidus : 'pecuniam praeferre amicitiae sordidum putamus.'

First . . . prior, *when two are spoken of*: 'rumpit silentia Pyrrha prior.'

Give way . cedo : 'quacunque movemur aer videtur quasi locum dare et cedere ;' 'cedant arma togae, concedat laurea laudi.'

Deem worthy } dignor : 'non tali me dignor honore.'

Name . . . 'cognomen Sapientis habere ;' 'Aristides cognomine justus est appellatus.'

Beard . . . barba : 'sapientem pascere barbam.'
Adject., '*without a beard*,' imberbis, -be : 'non convenit barbatum esse filium Aesculapium, cum pater Apollo imberbis sit.'

Twice . . . 'bis consul,' '*who has twice been consul.*' 'iterum consul,' '*who is now for the second time consul.*'

Triumph . 'de classe Romana triumphum egit.'

Decree . decerno : 'Senatus Africano triumphum decrevit.'

Senator's rank ordo, gradus, senatorius : 'cujus aetas a senatorio gradu longe abesset.'

Such . . . talis ; tantus, '*so great.*'

Ceremony . observantia : 'observantia qua reges coluntur.'

Demand . . exigo : 'a teste veritatem expectant vel potius exigunt.'

Equals . . par : 'invident homines maxime paribus et inferioribus.'

The multitude vulgus : 'non est consilium in vulgo.' plebs : 'plebem et infimam multitudinem delenire.'

Haughty . .	superbum, arrogantem se praebere, arroganter agere, se gerere.
Withdraw from	detrecto : 'judicandi munus detrectavit.'
Advocate . .	'qui modo patronus nunc cupit esse cliens.'
Business of an advocate	patrocinium : 'patrocinium feneratorum suscepit ;' 'causa patrocinio non bona pejor erit.'
Illustrious .	illustris : 'illustrissimi et clarissimi viri.'
Pride oneself on	gloriari : 'nulla re magis gloriabantur quam decepto per indutias rege.'•
Forum . . .	forum : 'in foro ambulare ;' 'in forum descendere.'
Never . . .	'nunquam, si credis, amavi hunc hominem.'
Unless . . .	'nisi victor in castra non revertam.'
Surround .	stipo : 'magna stipante caterva ;' 'Catilina stipatus choro juventutis.'
Company .	globus : 'ex illo globo nobilitatis.'
Nobles . .	optimates : 'plebis et optimatium certamina.'

4.

4. *Julius Atticus, the father* . . .

PRAEPARATIO.

The point of the anecdote is to illustrate the caution, or cunning, of Julius Atticus ; and the unselfishness of Nerva, which is emphasised by the phrase 'good-natured peevishness.'

'Father:' put in this way because Herodes Atticus happens to be better known than Julius.

'Must have ended his life in poverty,' is to be taken as one idea, otherwise '*end*' will be translated by '*die*,' or '*finish*.' It means nothing of the kind. It means '*would have had to remain a poor man to the end of his days*.'

' Might have asserted : ' what does ' might ' mean here ? *'Had the power,'* or, ' *had the right* to assert.' ' Might ' is not an auxiliary verb here. There is nothing subjunctive about it. It is a simple indicative statement. *'Ei licuit,'* or ' *licebat.'*   •   •

' Equitable,' implies a reason accounting for Nerva's refusal to accept the money. This must be taken notice of in the Latin. ' Cautious,' in the same way suggests the motive of Julius.

' Subject,' *not* ' *subjectus,'* all notion of conquest and oppression has disappeared from the word as used here.

' Then ' *not* temporal.

CONSTRUCTIO.

For Julius Atticus, Herodes' father, life would have had to be completed in the lowest poverty, unless he had found a treasure, buried under the ancient house, which only relic of his patrimony he had inherited. And, indeed, it was lawful to Caesar, if he liked to act by law, in the name of the fiscus (not in the English text, but in the spirit of it, and admissible for the sake of greater clearness) *to claim that treasure for his own. When, however, Atticus, having got so much lucre unexpectedly, carried the matter of his own accord to the treasury, Nerva, a man of the greatest equity, who then held the imperial power, was unwilling* (aorist, not *nolebat* but *noluit,* because he gave effect to his unwillingness by once for all declaring it) *to accept even the least part of that money : nay more, he exhorted Atticus not to hesitate to use so manifest a gift of Fortune himself. But the Athenian, sly man, even then persisted in refusing, saying that they were too great riches for a private man ; that he knew not* (*how*) *to use so great wealth. To whom Nerva, with a certain asperity not unkind, 'Abuse it then,' says, ' since it is your own.'*

MATERIA.

Father . . pater: 'natum ante ora patris, patrem qui obtruncat ad aras.'

Herodes . . Herodes, -is.

Must . . . (1) *Absolute necessity is expressed by* necesse est: 'homini necesse est mori.' *Greek,* ἀνάγκη.

(2) *Compulsion of duty or circumstances by the gerundial forms*: 'nunc est bibendum;' 'in primis evitandus est magister aridus.' *Note, neither the gerund nor the gerundive implies mere possibility, or capability.*

(3) *Need, propriety, duty, by,* opus est, oportet, debeo.

End . . . finire: 'vitam finivit voluntaria morte.' *But ' to end,' here does not mean ' to put an end to,' but ' to live out,' ' to continue to the end':* 'qui omnem vitae suae cursum in labore corporis conficeret.'

Poverty . . paupertas, *prose*; pauperies, *poetical*: 'paupertas vel potius egestas ac mendicitas.' inopia: 'res angustae inopiam pariunt.'

Discover . . invenire, *first, of accidental discovery*: 'Scipio mortuus in cubiculo inventus est.' *Also of finding by search*: 'inveniam rimam.' reperio, *generally implying recovery or search*: 'perscrutabor fanum si inveniam aurum: sed si repperero non statim auferam;' 'facile invenies pejorem, meliorem neque tu reperies.'

Treasure . . thesaurus: 'thesaurum invenit; effodit aulam auri plenam.'

opes : 'effodiuntur opes irritamenta malorum.'

Bury . . . obruere ; condere, ' *to hide by burying.*'

Old . . . . *Of persons 'no longer young,*' senex.

To mark the exact age, natus : 'viginti annos natus.'

Of things, 'full of years,' annosus : 'annosa cornix.'

vetula ; *of a woman, in disparagement* : 'vetula et multarum nuptiarum.'

vetus ; '*not new* :' 'veteres naves.'

vetustus ; '*showing marks of age* :' 'templa vetusta.'

antiquus ; '*belonging to former days* :' 'homo antiqua virtute.'

priscus ; '*belonging to the early ages* :' 'prisca gens mortalium.'

Remains . . reliquiae : 'reliquiae copiarum.'

As verb, resto : 'dona pelago et flammis restantia.'

supersum : 'omnes qui supersint de Hirtii exercitu.'

Patrimony . patrimonium : 'patrimonio ornatissimo spoliari ;' 'paterna bona et avita.'

res : 'rem familiarem perdidit.'

According to *Ablative* : 'lege agere.'

ex : 'ex sententia evenit.'

pro : 'pro re ac tempore.'

Might . . . '*Might have asserted,*' 'licuit' *or* 'licebat exigere,' *implying a right.*

'*May have asserted,*' *implying uncertainty* : 'nescio an exegerit.'

'*May assert* :' 'licet exigere.'

The time in Latin is given by the governing verb : in English by the governed verb.

Assert a claim vindico : 'haec jure Quiritium pro suis vindicant.'

postulare : 'aequum postulat ; da veniam.'

assero : 'nec laudes assere nostras.'

Trove . . . 'thesaurus forte, casu, inventus ; ' 'lucrum insperatum.'

Voluntary . sponte sua, ultro.

Inform . . *Legal,* deferre ad ; indicare, *especially of turning king's evidence.*

palam dicere : 'palam agere coepit et aperte dicere.'

Luck . . . fortuna : 'dum fortuna juvat.'

Equitable . justus, aequus : 'et servantissimus aequi.'

Fill the imperium : 'qui tum erat summo in imperio.'

throne potestas : 'summam potestatem obtinebat.'

praesum : 'imperio, reipublicae, rei Romanae praeerat eo tempore.'

Refuse . . recuso : 'recusavit amicitiam Populi Romani ; ' 'nec tibi comes ire recuso ; ' 'sententiam ne diceret recusavit.'

nego : 'negat se ad hostem iturum (esse).'

nolo : 'noluit accipere pecuniam.'

Part . . . pars : 'vix quarta parte diei praeterita.'

Use . . . . utor : 'utere tuis oculis.'

Scruple . . dubitatio : 'sine ulla dubitatione.'

dubito, *verb* : 'quid dubitamus pultare fores.'

religio : 'religio mihi non est quominus utar ea pecunia.'

Present . . donum : 'timeo Danaos et dona ferentes.'

Cautious . . cautus : 'cauto animo.'

vafer : 'hominis vafri facinus.'

Insist . . . dictito : 'nonne es quem semper te esse dictitasti ? '

Negatively, gravor : 'sed primo gravari coepit.'

Too . . . . *Adverb,* nimis : 'nimis longo satiate ludo.'

nimium : 'nimium diu ; ' 'nimium ne crede colori.'

Substantive : 'auri nimium fuit.'

Adject. nimius : 'nimiâ arrogantiâ,' 'nimius mero,' 'nimius sermonis,' '*too much given to.*'

For . . . . nimio plus quam decet, quam satis est ; plus aequo.

Subject . . privatus homo : subjectus *would imply conquest* : 'parcere subjectis et debellare superbos.'

Know not   nescio, *with infinitive* : 'nescire, dixit, Tar
  how   quinios privatos vivere.'

Abuse . . abutor : 'quousque tandem, Catilina, abutere patientia nostra ?'

Then . . . ergo, *or* vero *after pronoun* : 'tu vero.'

Reply . . . ait, inquit, *if the reply is stated in oratio recta.*

- Monarch . . *Not* rex, *speaking of Nerva.*

Good-
  natured } benevolus : *substantive,* bonitas.

Peevishness morositas, asperitas ; *but* 'asperitas non insuavis' *might express the oxymoron.*

For . . . . *Conjunction.*

nam *introduces a direct reason* : 'percontatorem fugito, nam garrulus idem est.' *Always first in clause.*

enim, *less emphatic, never first in clause.*

quoniam, '*since,*' '*seeing that,*' *relative conjunction* : 'quoniam ita vis, ibo tecum.'

5.

5. Day at last dawned . . .

Praeparatio.

In this and the following passage is described the successful issue of the stratagem by which Hannibal got possession of Tarentum.

The style to imitate is that of Livy, who narrates the

same events, but does not dwell on precisely the same details.

We must try to give such an account as cannot be misunderstood by a reader fairly acquainted with the Latin language ; and in every exercise our Latin ought to be self-interpreting. We ought not to be driven to refer to the English in order to interpret our own meaning. It is a good plan for a worker, before showing up his own version, to construe it carefully over, taking each word and uttering the English equivalent ; or, better still, to ask a candid friend to construe it. The weak, ungrammatical, or inadequate renderings will thus be exposed.

' They were safe . . . their bodies.' Consider whether this sentence conveys the reflections of the Tarentines, what they said to themselves, or whether it is a part of the direct narrative, and is what the historian says.

CONSTRUCTIO.

Day at length dawned, but not thereby was the reason of last night's tumult made quite manifest to the majority of the Tarentines : who, although they perceived themselves safe, with houses and goods unhurt, and knew that it was a Roman trumpet, which alone had sounded[1] *a war note, yet saw Romans everywhere slain, Gauls spoiling. It took away doubt (when) heard, (did) the voice of the crier, who, in Hannibal's name, was bidding the Tarentines to be present into the forum without arms ; at the same time, some of their own men, running in various directions through the town kept shouting, ' that they were now free,' and kept pro-*

[1] *Quae cecinisset :* subjunctive, because it was a part of what the Tarentines knew, said, or thought ; not a statement made by the historian on his own authority.

claiming the Carthaginians authors of the new liberty. Then those who most favoured the Roman cause swiftly fled to the citadel; the remaining multitude hastened to the forum.

Materia.

Day dawned dilucesco; *impersonal* : 'jam dilucescebat cum signum consul dedit ;' 'diluxit, patet, videmus omnia.'

illucesco; *personal* : 'qui dies ut illuxit, mortui sunt reperti.'

At last . . tandem; '*after long delay :*' 'tandem vulneribus defessi pedem referre coeperunt.'

demum, *often preceded by* nunc, tum, '*not till then,' also absolutely* : 'noctu demum rex recessit.'

denique, '*finally,' ' lastly,' but also like* tandem : 'nil nostri miserere, mori me denique coges ?'

But . . . sed, *always first in a sentence*; autem, *never first.*

Clear up . expedio : 'hoc mihi expedi primum.'

patefacio : 'omnia illustrata, patefacta, comperta sunt a me.'

Quite . . satis : 'non satis honeste.'

Mystery . res obscura ; ratio rei ; causa timoris.

Alarm . . tumultus : 'tumultum magis quam certum nuntium castris intulerunt.'

Night . . nox : 'quid proxima, quid superiore nocte egeris.' Proximus, *may mean either,* '*next preceding,'* or ' *next following :*' ' se proxima nocte castra moturum.'

Adjective, nocturnus : 'labores diurnos nocturnosque suscipere.'

The mass of plerique : 'plerique Belgae;' 'plerique eorum;' ' plerisque ex factione corruptis.'

major pars ; maxima pars.

E

Tarentum .	Tarentum.
Tarentine .	plebs Tarentina, Tarentini.
They . . .	se; *that is, they found 'themselves' safe.*
Safe . . .	tutus: 'tutus a periculo,' *suggesting contemporaneous danger.*
	salvus; *'saved,' 'safe and sound after danger*:' 'exercitum salvum transduxit;' 'salvus rediisti.'
	incolumis; *'unhurt*:' 'integer et incolumis;' 'salvus et incolumis;' 'sospes et incolumis.'
Unplun-dered }	'bonis intactis.'
Unmas-sacred	integer: 'omnibus rebus integros incolumesque esse.'
Blast of war	'bellicum canit tubicen;' 'Philippum, ubi primum bellicum cani audisset, arma capturum.'
Trumpet .	tuba: 'signum tuba dare;' 'at tuba terribili sonitu taratantara dixit.'
Yet . . .	tamen, *'for all that,' sometimes strengthened by preceding* tametsi: 'quae tametsi Caesar intelligebat, tamen ab incepto non desistebat.'
Soldier . .	miles: 'milites conduxit quingentos.'
Lie . . .	jacere: 'strata jacent sub arbore poma;' 'corpora per campos ferro quae fusa jacebant.'
Spoil. . .	*Substantive,* spolia: 'cruenta spolia detrahere.'
	Verb: 'corpus jacentis uno torque spoliavit.'
Suspense .	dubitatio: 'aestuabat dubitatione.'
End . . .	tollere: 'tollit metum mortis.'
Crier. . .	praeco: 'audita voce praeconis magnum gaudium fuit.'

Summon . cito ; '*to summon by name :*' 'citari patres per
praeconem jussit.'
voco, advoco, convoco : 'ad concionem vocat
populum.'
jubeo : ' cives adesse jubebat.'

In the name verba : ' denuntiatum est Fabio senatus verbis,
of ne discederet,' etc.

Appear . . ' Verres statuerat ad judicium non adesse.'

Market place forum : ' et mane in medio plaustra fuere foro.'

Without . sine : ' sine re, sine fide, sine spe, sine sede.'

Repeat . . repeto : 'haec decies repetita placebit.'
itero : ' clamor segnius saepe iteratus.'

Shout . . clamito : '" ad arma," et " proh vestram fidem,
cives," clamitans.'
vox : 'constitue nihil opis esse in hac voce,
" civis Romanus sum."'

Liberty . . libertas : 'quid est enim libertas ? potestas
vivendi ut velis.'
Adjective : 'libera jam respublica ;' 'io, io,
liber ad te venio ;' 'miles, io, magna
voce triumphe canet.'

Countryman popularis : ' lex Solonis popularis mei.'
suus : 'cupio abducere puellam ut reddam
suis.'

Run round discurro : 'discurrunt circa deûm delubra ;'
' ilicet ad portas tota discurritur urbe.'

Deliverer . liberator : ' nostri liberatores.'
auctor libertatis.
vindex : 'audita vox una, " provoco," vindex
libertatis.'

Cartha- Carthaginiensis : urbs Carthago.
ginian Poenus : ' Poenorum crudelitas.'
Punicus : ' Punica fides.'

Partisan . . fautor : ' clamor ab utriusque fautoribus oritur.'
studiosus : ' studiosi nobilitatis.'

E 2

Verb : 'qui rebus Atheniensium studebant ; '
'qui rei Romanae maxime favebant.'

Make haste propero : 'properes anni spem credere terrae.'

Escape to confugere ; '*fly for shelter* :' 'in arcem con-
fugerunt.'

Crowd to . concurro : 'concurrunt ad curiam.'

confluo : 'multi confluxerant et Athenas et in
hanc urbem.'

'con' *denotes a point of meeting,* 'dis' *in*
discurro *separation in various directions.*

But confluo *rather suggests that the speaker
comtemplates the scene from the point of
meeting. A narrator at a distance would
rather say* contendit, *the* 'con' *here
signifying a purpose, or intention, in the
minds of the crowd.*

6.

6. *They found the market place* . . .

PRAEPARATIO.

'*Carthaginian* :' instead of Roman troops, whom they
supposed to be still in possession of the town of Tarentum.

'*Great general.*' If there is the slightest room for doubt
or obscurity, say '*Hannibal.*'

The most important point for the translator is to distinguish the force of the several clauses ushered in by
'*that*' in the English. The following analysis will explain this.

'They find the forum, etc., and the general of whom
they had heard, etc., about to make a speech. He, in

Greek, etc., called them to witness *that* he was there in order *that*, etc.'

'*that* the Tarentines, etc.' (*information* is here given, therefore the *infinitive* is the proper mood).

'*that* they were to go home,' and

'*that* each was to write, etc.,' (*that* implies a *command* here, therefore the *imperative of oblique narration* is to be used):

'*that* this would be a sufficient, etc.' and

'*that* no house so marked would be, etc.' (*information* therefore *infinitive*).

'At the same time they were to take care not to, etc.' (*warning*),

'*that*, if any, etc., he would punish him as an enemy' (*information*):

'*that* whatever goods, etc., became rightly a prize' (*information*).

'And so' (*narrative* resumed).

CONSTRUCTIO.

The forum they find occupied by a Punic praesidium, and the great general himself, whose so great fame had spread among all, about to harangue. He, using as it is said, Greek speech, protested, as at other times also he was wont, that he had come for this reason, viz. that he might free all the dwellers in Italy from Roman domination : that there was nothing therefore to the Tarentines which was-to-be-feared : let them go home ; over his door let each for himself write, 'this is the house of a Tarentine ;' that this would be enough of protection : that doors so distinguished would not be violated. At the same time, let them beware of writing this title falsely. If any Tarentine should have used this fraud, against that (Tarentine) he would proceed as against an enemy. Whatever anywhere of Roman goods there might be, rightly became booty for the soldiers. Accordingly all the houses in which Romans had lodged were given to the soldiers to be ransacked, and not less than hope was the amount of spoils, which was gotten from thence, as Polybius affirms.

Materia.

Find . . .	invenio : 'naves ad navigandum paratas invenit.'
Market place	forum, 'boarium,' 'piscatorium:' 'hostes in foro ac locis patentioribus cuneatim constiterunt.'
Regular .	justus : 'justum iter conficere.'
	rite : 'creatus rite tribunus;' 'religatos rite videbat carpere gramen equos.'
Troops . .	copiae ; *'forces:'* 'cogere copias Brundusium.'
	miles : *in Caesar and Cicero used in the plural; by post-Augustan writers collectively in singular* : 'armato milite complet.'
	praesidium; *'garrison:'* 'occupato oppido praesidium collocat.'
Occupy . .	occupare : 'totam Italiam suis praesidiis obsidere atque occupare cogitat.'
Great . .	magnus : 'tu bis denis grandia libris qui scribis Priami proelia magnus homo es;' 'nemo igitur vir magnus sine aliquo afflatu divino unquam fuit.'
General .	imperator : 'cum pro se quisque in conspectu imperatoris operam navare cuperet.'
	dux : 'ducis in consilio posita est virtus militum.'
Hear . . .	accipere : *verb* : 'reliquos deos ne famâ quidem acceperant.'

aures : *subst.* 'si vestras forte per aures Trojae nomen iit.'

fama : 'hac tanta celebritate famae cum esset jam absentibus notus;' 'cum fama per orbem terrarum percrebuisset illum esse Romam iturum.'

Address . oratio : 'advocat contionem, habet orationem.'

contio : 'legi contionem tuam.'

contionor : 'haec velut contionanti, Minucio circum fundebatur tribunorum multitudo.'

sermo : 'sermo est oratio remissa et finitima quotidianae locutionis;' 'Caesar sermonem habuit.'

verba : 'ita verba fecit.' *But* 'dare verba alicui,' '*to cheat.*'

Speak to . alloquor : 'senatum composita in magnificentiam oratione allocutus est.'

Greek . . Graece : *adverb* : 'cum ea quae legeram Graece, Latine redderem.'

sermo : *subst.* : 'ut quae philosophi Graeco sermone tractavissent, ea Latinis literis mandaremus;' 'Graecae linguae scientiam habere.'

Apparently videri : 'ut videtur;' 'si ornate locutus est, sicut fertur et mihi videtur.'

Usual . . soleo : *verb* : 'qui mentiri solet, pejerare consuevit;' 'cum audissem Antiochum ut solebam.'

consuetudo : *subst.* : 'consuetudine sua Caesar sex legiones expeditas ducebat;' 'non est meae consuetudinis rationem reddere.'

mos : 'apis Matinae more modoque.'

Free . . . liberare : 'populum metu liberabit.'

Dominion . dominatio : '*despotism*,' '*mastership*,' *connoting servitude.*

regnum, '*monarchy.*'

imperium ; '*sway* :' 'sub populi Romani di-
cionem imperiumque cadere.'

dicio, '*sovereignty.*'

Have to fear } 'nihil vobis metuendum est.'

Home . . domum : 'Suebi domum reverti coeperunt.'

Write upon inscribo : 'in statua inscripsit, "Parenti optime merito."'

Over . . . supra : 'supra tribunal et supra praetoris caput.'

Security . praesidium : 'hanc sibi rem praesidio sperant futuram.'

tutela : 'tutelam januae gerebat;' 'intelligi volumus salutem hominum in Jovis esse tutela.'

Each . . . quisque : 'quod cuique obtigit id quisque teneat;' 'sibi quoque tendente ut periculo prius evaderet.'

Mark . . noto : 'creta an carbone notati?'

Violate . . violo : 'fines eorum se violaturum negavit.'

Mark . . titulus : 'domus proscribebatur si quis emere vellet : venit Athenodorus, legit titulum.'

Must not . ne : 'hominem mortuum in urbe ne sepelito.'

nolo : 'noli putare.'

cave : 'cave dixeris.'

Quarters . hospitium : 'ibi milites benigne excepti divisi-que in hospitia.'

Treason . fraus : 'occasionem fraudis ac doli quaerunt.'

Death . . nex : 'neci datus est;' 'nece vel morte afficere sontes.'

As an enemy tamquam : 'in illum tamquam in hostem animadvertere placuit.'

All . . . quidquid : 'quidquid ubique bonorum esset.'

Lawful . . jure : 'non quaero jure an injuria sint inimici.'

Prize . . praeda : 'argentum omne cessit in praedam militibus ;' 'praedam militibus donare.'

Quarter.	.	deversor: 'cum Athenis apud eum dever-sarer.'
Plunder.	.	diripere: 'tecta milites diripiunt.'
Gain .	. .	potior; *of something definite to be obtained*: 'spes urbis potiundae.'
		percipio: 'serere, percipere, condere fructus;' 'praemia perceperunt.'
		adipiscor; '*get by overcoming difficulties*:' 'adeptus est summos honores.'
		comparo; '*procure*:' 'gemmas, signa, tabulas aliamque supellectilem comparaverat.'
Harvest	.	lucrum: 'qui ex publicis vectigalibus tanta lucra fecit.'
		copia: 'exercitus omnium rerum abundabat copia.'
Hope	. .	spes: 'scio multa praeter spem multis bona evenisse.'

7.

7. *Upon receiving this answer . . .*

PRAEPARATIO.

A connecting particle must be inserted between the first and second sentences : '*deinde*' would be suitable.

Instead of the co-ordinate statements '*Geryones convoked—and they contended—and cursed—the noble chief said*,' in Latin the whole might be welded together, so that each statement would fall into its proper position, subordinate, supplementary, or concomitant, and assume its proper logical value in regard to the whole: and in like manner the parts of the speech of Maiobanes in oblique oration will fall into grooves suitable to each : the guiding principle being to economise the main verbs—

the indicatives in oratio recta, the infinitives in oratio obliqua—and to defer the main statement to as late a stage as is consistent with clearness. The change from oratio obliqua to oratio recta must depend upon the taste and discretion of the translator. The object in view must always be clearness: sometimes this object is attained by a vivid, dramatic method; sometimes by reasoned argument; sometimes by simple statements; sometimes by connected periods.

CONSTRUCTIO.

This answer having been received, the consul, very many villages having been burnt, moved his army nearer to the camp of Maiobanes. Thereupon it was begun anew to treat concerning terms. An assembly having been convoked, when it pleased the rest that Geryones should be given up, who had come to them as a fugitive with such unlucky omens, Maiobanes, with innate magnanimity, said, that Geryones was a good man, and deserved well of him, who, when coming thither he had brought many gifts worthy of a king, had also taught himself and the queen to perform choruses and to dance, which thing he esteemed at not a little. 'Wherefore,' says he, 'I will not desert Geryones, since he has fled to me; and I pledge myself that I will defend him: and I would rather suffer all extremes than give a handle to detractors, so that they should say that I betrayed a guest.'

MATERIA.

Adelantado   praefectus; *generally followed by the name of his office*: aerarii, classis, castris, legionis, praetorio.
                 consul.

Burnt . .   incendo; '*set fire to*:' 'aedificia vicosque incendunt.'

uro ; '*consume with fire*:' 'cum frondibus uritur arbos.'

cremo ; '*burn to ashes*:' 'mortali corpore cremato.'

ardeo ; '*to be on fire*:' 'tua res agitur, paries quum proximus ardet.'

Approach . admoveo; '*bring towards*:' 'dum ne exercitum propius urbem Romam cc millia admoveret.'

Negotia- ago ; '*negotiate*:' 'agere de contionibus;'
tions 'quum de Catilinae conjuratione ageretur.'

Assembly . contio; '*meeting*:' 'advocat contionem, habuit orationem consul.'

Contended flagito ; '*demand peremptorily*:' 'semper flagitavi ut convocaremur.'

posco ; '*require*:' 'poscimus ut coenes civiliter.'

placeo, *inpersonal*; '*it is my will*:' 'senatui placuit ut C. Pansa mitteretur;' 'deliberatur de Avarico, incendi placeret an defendi.'

Ought . . debeo ; '*owe*,' *personal* : 'debemus mori.'

oportet, '*it behoves*:' oportuit, '*it behoved*,' *impersonal*.   *But if* flagito, posco, *or* placet *be used, the obligation will have been sufficiently expressed without* debeo *or* oportet.

Given up : trado ; '*give up*:' 'trade mihi istuc argentum.' '*betray*:' 'tibi trado patriosque meosque Penates.'

Cursed . . exsecror ; '*execrate*:' 'superbiam regis exsecrantur.' *But rather use a paraphrase*: 'qui mala avi, infaustis ominibus ad se venisset.'

Good. . . probus, '*honest*;' *opposed to* improbus.

frugi ; '*worthy*,' '*honest*:' ' Piso frugi,' '*Honest Piso*.'

bonus; '*good,*' *generic term* : 'vir bonus est quis? qui consulta Patrum, qui leges juraque servat.'

Deserved well   bene mereor : 'eum de se optime meritum judicabat;' 'dixit eum de republica meruisse optime.'

Royal . .   rege dignus; '*worthy, either to be given to, or received by, a king* :' 'tribuere id cuique quod sit quoque dignum.'

Give, gifts   dona : 'te potius quam tua dona sequar.'

Teach . .   doceo : 'pueros elementa docebo;' 'docemur disputare, non vivere honeste.'

Wife . . .   conjux; '*wife,*' *or,* '*husband* :' 'Jovis et soror et conjux;' 'exemplumque mihi conjugis esto bonae;' 'conjugis audisset factum quum Porcia Bruti.'

     uxor : 'uxor amans flentem, flens acrius ipsa, tenebat.'

Choral songs   chorus et cantus. *Verb,* cantare : 'si vox est, canta : si mollia brachia, salta.'

Dance . .   ad numerum movere pedes : 'in numerum Faunosque ferasque videres ludere.'

     choros vel choreas agitare.

     saltare : 'nemo saltat sobrius.'

     moveri : 'festis matrona moveri jussa diebus ;' 'motus doceri gaudet Ionicos.'

Account .   magni, parvi, maximi facere; *genitive of price* : 'senatus auctoritatem sibi maximi videri;' 'magni aestimabat.'

Desert . .   desero : 'jurant omnes se exercitum ducesque non deserturos neque prodituros.'

Flee to . .   confugio : con- *in composition with verbs implies an aim or purpose. Here the purpose is protection* : 'jacere,' '*to throw* :' 'conjicere,' '*to throw at.*'

Pledge . .   fidem obligo; '*to give one's word of honour* :'

'obligare fidem suam se ita facturum esse ;' 'spondeo, recipio in me, promitto, me nunquam amicum esse proditurum.'

Would rather   'mallem errare cum Platone quam cum istis vera sentire ;' 'Cato jam servire quam pugnare mavult.'

Extremity.   'ad extrema ventum foret ;' 'potius omnia pessuma pati quam flagitium in se admittere.'

Detract . .   obtrectare: 'obtrectantium clamores negligit.'

Substantive: 'obtrectatores et invidi Scipionis.'

Cause . .   causa: 'ea est causa cur objurgent.'

ansa; '*handle*:' 'mihi ad reprehendendum ansas dederunt.'

Speak ill .   'aliud est male dicere, aliud accusare.'

Deliver up   prodo; '*betray*:' 'classem prodidit praedonibus.'

trado; '*surrender*,' *whether perfidiously or by necessity, or voluntarily*: 'obsides, arma, perfugae traditi sunt.'

Guest . .   hospes; '*guest*:' 'hospite venturo, cessabit nemo tuorum.'

hospes; '*host*:' 'alter ad cauponem devertit, alter ad hospitem ;' 'non hospes ab hospite tutus.'

8.

8. *Now when the Delphians heard . . .*

Praeparatio.

'*Were seized*,' say, '*the greatest terror invaded*;' active voice, aorist tense.

'*Delphos,*' place first in the sentence, for the sake of perspicuity.

'*Oraculum,*' in the singular number, commonly stands for the place ; and inquirers are said to consult the God. Use the historic present, to show that you sympathise with the Delphians, and accompany them step by step.

'*Answered.*' '*Respondit,*' with '*ita,*' is followed by the *oratio recta* ; without '*ita,*' by the *oratio obliqua.*

'*Bade* : ' the idea of bidding is incorporated in the past jussive after '*respondit.*'

'*That he was able* : ' the direct statement will be in the infinitive imperfect after '*respondit.*'

'*Began to think about* : ' express by the imperfect tense.

'*After which* : ' use '*deinde*' after '*primum*' in the sequence.

'*For safety.*' Latin, '*that they may be safe,*' '*ut sint tuta* : ' or, '*that they might be,*' '*ut essent.*' Which is best after the historic present ? See Grammar.

'*Quitted.*' Distinctly an *aorist.* The historic present would be out of place here.

CONSTRUCTIO.

The Delphians then, when they perceived in how great peril they were involved, were seized with the utmost terror. And so they go to the oracle, to inquire respecting the sacred treasure, whether to bury it in the earth, or to carry it away to another land would be better. To them consulting the god answered, that they were to (or *let them*) *leave the treasure untouched, that he could guard his own things without aid from others. They therefore, this answer having been received, proceeded to provide for their own safety. And first indeed they send the women and children over sea into Achaia. Next the majority of those left, having climbed up to the highest ridges of mount Parnassus, hide their goods, in order that they might be the safer, into the Corycian cavern. The rest escape to Amphissa to the Locrians. Thus all the multitude of Delphians, except sixty citizens and the prophet himself, departed out of the city.*

MATERIA.

Danger . . discrimen ; '*a crisis* :' 'sensi in summo rem esse discrimine ;' 'aliquem in discrimen capitis adducere.'

periculum; *literally* '*trial* :' 'salus sociorum in summum periculum ac discrimen vocatur;' *also,* 'in lubrico versari;' 'in praecipiti esse.'

Bury . . . sepelio ; '*a corpse* :' 'nec tumulum curo, sepelit natura relictos.'

humare ; '*to inter* :' *rare.*

condo ; '*to store away* :' 'animam sepulcro condimus.'

defodio ; '*to dig a hole and hide* :' 'necatum hospitem defodit.'

obruo ; obruere thesaurum, '*for the sake of hiding it* :' condere, '*with a view to saving it.*'

Carry away auferre : 'multa domum suam Verres auferebat.' *Here the prominent idea is that of depriving another* : 'abstulit clarum cita mors Achillem.'

aveho: 'frumentum navibus avexerunt,' *of cargo and passengers. Prominent idea, locomotion.*

asporto ; *prominent idea, weight of material* : 'sua omnia Salamina asportant.'

'ab' *regards the place from which*: 'cum,' *the object for which*: *as*, 'frumentum ex finitimis regionibus in urbem convehunt;' 'sarcinas in unum locum conferunt,' i. e. utilitatis causa : 'ad' *regards the place to which*, *as*, 'equo advectus ad fluminis ripam.'

Leave . . relinquo, *never* linquo : '*suffer to remain*,' 'thesaurum intactum reliquit.'

abstinere ab : '*let be*,' 'potin' a me ut abstineas manus?' '*can't you leave me alone?*'

sino : 'Medos equitare inultos;' *or, by negativing the opposite* : 'quieta non movere.'

'*to depart from*:' 'excessit ex hac urbe;' 'uxor a Dolabella discessit.'

'*to leave behind one*:' 'filiam moriens reliquit adolescentulam.'

Help . . . auxilium : 'unde auxilium petam?' 'non tali auxilio nec defensoribus istis tempus eget.'

opis, *fem.*, *no nominative; properly,* '*power*:' 'omni ope atque opera enitar.' *Plural*, '*riches*:' 'magnas inter opes inops.'

then '*help*:' 'ferte opem, cives!' 'non possum id efficere sine ope tua.'

Protect . . tueor ; '*look after and guard*:' 'canis a furibus tuetur domum.'

protego ; '*shelter*:' 'scuto illum protegebat;' defendere, '*to guard by warding off*:' 'defendo a frigore myrtos:' *and conversely*, '*to ward off in order to guard*:' 'defendit aestatem capellis;' 'serva cives : defende hostes quum potes defendere.'

Think about agito : ' bellum agitat in animo.'

concipio : 'fierine potest quod ego mente concipio ? '

specto : 'ad suum magis ille commodum quam ad salutem reipublicae specta-bat.'

cogito : ' is qui nocere alteri cogitat.'

Send across transmitto : 'cohors Usipiorum in Britanniam transmissa est.'

ablego, *'send away:' suggesting a desire ' to get rid of:'* 'ablegavimus eum foras ; ' 'cives procul ab domo relegati.'

dimitto, *'to let go:'* 'obsidem incolumem dimisit.'

Climb . . scando, *generic:* 'timor et minae scandunt eodem quo dominus.'

inscendo, *with a view to ' ensconcing oneself:'* 'navem inscendi ; ' 'in currum inscen-dere.'

escendo, *commonest form; locomotion upwards the prominent idea.*

ascendo, *motion upwards towards a point.*

enitor, *' to clamber up,' implying an effort :* 'in summum verticem enisus ; ' 'hac arte Pollux, hac vagus Hercules enisus arces attigit igneas.'

Place for pono, *generic* ; *'put,' 'place.'*

safety loco, *prominent idea, relative position in which the object appears in consequence of so placing it.*

colloco, *with a certain object.*

statuo, *' set up.'*

repono, *'place back again,' ' to store up.'*

condo : 'minas viginti in crumenam condidi.'

conferre servandi causa.

abdo : ' se in proximas silvas abdiderunt.'

F

To effect es- **cape**	incolumis pervenio ; fugio, '*I flee*;' fugi, '*I escaped*: ' 'insequeris, fugio ; fugis, inse-quor : haec mea mens est;' 'ensesque nefandi quos fugi,' *the completion of a purpose may sometimes be expressed by the aorist tense.* effugere, '*to flee out of danger,' looking behind.* confugere, '*to flee for refuge,' looking forward.* evadere, '*to escape.*'
Quit . . .	discedo : 'procul hinc discedite.' relinquo : 'Aeoliam Pitanen a laeva parte relinquunt.'
Except . .	praeter, *preposition* : 'omnes praeter unum.' nisi, *conjunction* : 'nil nisi pontus et aer.'

9.

9. *The son of Croesus, although . . .*

Praeparatio.

The syntax here will not require much alteration, and the meaning can hardly be misunderstood. The synonyms require most attention. What are the corresponding Latin terms for '*talk*,' '*speak*,' '*utter*,' '*speak out*,' '*cry*,' '*say*?' See the Dictionaries.

Again, discriminate between '*mute*,' '*dumb*,' '*speechless*,' '*tongue-tied*,' '*voiceless*,' '*silent*;' and having determined the meaning in English *first, then* search for equivalent Latin words.

Attention must also be paid to the tenses, so as to distinguish between the *aorist* and the *imperfect,* or *continuous,* tense.

The *aorist* recounts an '*act.*'   The *imperfect* describes a '*state.*'   'Was old enough,' *imperfect tense*; 'was unable,' *imperfect*; 'could not,' *imperfect*; 'was thought,' *aorist*; 'was going,' *imperfect*; 'opened,' *aorist*; 'broke,' *aorist*; 'spoke out,' *aorist*; 'not to kill,' *past jussive*: 'let him not kill;' 'lowered,' *aorist*; 'was spared,' *aorist*; 'had,' *aorist.*

See page 36 supra, on these two tenses.

CONSTRUCTIO.

The son of king Croesus, when already he could speak, as far as age went, was unable-to-talk, and when now he had grown ever so much, could not articulate a word; but was long accounted dumb.   But when, against his father, vanquished in battle, the city in which he dwelt being already taken, an enemy with drawn sword, ignorant that he was the king, was making a rush—the lad opened his mouth striving to cry out, and by that effort broke the impediment of his breath and the knot of his tongue, and spoke out plainly and articulately, calling to the enemy, ' that he must not kill king Croesus.'   Then the soldier lowered his sword, and his life was remitted to the king, and the boy began to speak from that time forth.

MATERIA.

As far as   . per: 'per me equidem sint omnia protinus alba.'

Speak. . .   fari, '*to make use of the faculty of uttering articulate sounds*;' *hence* infans, ' puer nescius fari.'

loqui, ' *to speak as an intelligent being,*' ' *to talk* :' 'pecudesque locutae, infandum !'

dicere, ' *to say,*' ' *to express one's ideas in order.*'

Dumb . . . infans, '*not able, or daring, to speak* :' 'omnium
infantissimus viderer.'

mutus, '*dumb* :' 'mutum esse satius est quam
quod nemo intelligat dicere.'

elinguis, *literally and figuratively* '*tongue-
less* :' 'convicit et elinguem reddidit.'

infacundus, '*not ready of speech* :' 'infacun-
dior et lingua impromptus.'

Dwell . . . habito, *generic,* '*to live in a place* :' 'nulli
certa domus : lucis habitamus opacis.'

incolo, '*inhabit,*' *especially of tribes or nations* :
'trans Rhenum incolunt ;' 'sic veteres
sedes incoluistis, avi.'

Open . . . aperio, *generic* : 'aperire oculos.'

patefacere, '*set open* :' 'patefecit hostibus
portas.'

recludo, '*unlock.*'

resero, '*unbar* :' 'urbem illi reserare jubent,
et pandere portas.'

pando, '*spread wide.*'

diduco : 'diduxit rictum,' '*he grinned.*'

hiscere, '*to gape,*' '*to open the mouth to speak* :'
'raris turbatus vocibus hisco.'

Try . . . . experior, '*make trial of* :' 'veneni vim.'

. periclitor, '*to put to the test of use* :' 'quid
nostri auderent, periclitabatur.'

tento : 'tentavi quid in eo genere facere
possem ;' '*I tried what I could do.*'

probare : 'mucronem cultri,' '*to prove,*' '*try.*'

conari, '*to attempt* :' 'equites in castra
irrumpere conati sunt.'

nitor : 'summa ope nituntur ne . . .'

Burst . . . rumpo, *implies violence, looks to freedom* :
'rupit vincula.'

solvo, '*unloose,*' *looks to freedom* : 'tauris
juga solvit arator.'

frango, '*break*,' *looks to the destruction of a thing*: 'perfidus ensis frangitur.'

Impediment nodus, '*knot*:' 'primus Abantem oppositum sternit belli nodumque moramque.'

vinculum, '*a bond*:' 'nodos et linea vincula rupi.'

haesitantia linguae laborare, '*to have an impediment in one's speech.*'

Tongue . . lingua : 'linguae scalpello resectae liberantur.'

Articulately articulatim : 'verbum a verbo articulatim discernere.'

articulate, plane, distincte eloqui : *but* distincte *refers rather to the matter.*

Verb: 'mobilis articulat verborum daedala lingua.'

Spare . . . parco, '*to use stingily*,' *with dative*: 'nec impensae, nec labori, nec periculo peperci.'

'*show mercy to*;' 'mulieribus et infantibus parcere solent.'

vitam concedere alicui.

Use. . . . usus : 'partium corporis necessarii usus.'

facultas : 'fandi facultatem recepit.'

Voice . . . vox, '*faculty*,' *or* '*mode of utterance*:' 'nec vox hominem sonat ;' 'magna voce exclamavit ;' 'vox faucibus haesit.'

10.

10. *A party had been sent* . . .

PRAEPARATIO.

For the sake of clearness say 'a party of *Spaniards.*'

'Had always been friendly,' '*and* were,' etc.

A Latin writer would probably recognise the supplying of provisions as a consequence of the friendship, and not merely a co-ordinate fact.

In Latin the logical connecting links should be expressed. In English they are often suppressed : say therefore, ' *and so,*' or ' *then*, by chance the Cazique.'

' The Spaniards were looking,' being merely a concomitant fact, would be better expressed in Latin by the *ablative absolute.* ' *And the* animal,' use the relative in Latin. 'The Spaniard,' etc.; express the logical connexion, and say ' was *so* wild *that* it could hardly be restrained : ' use the passive here for the sake of greater clearness.

' *And* unfortunately,' etc. In continuation of the syntax that precedes, ' *then,*' '*accordingly,*' will suit better than ' *and.*' Or, from another point of view, ' *but*' adversative might be a suitable particle here.

' If *he* were to set the dog *at him.*' For the sake of greater clearness, instead of ' *he,*' ' *him,*' say, ' if *the dog* were set at *the man.*'

Use a connecting particle between the two sentences.

' His *friend.*' The friendship is not the important point here : say, ' *the other.*' As to the order, reserve the important statement, ' at him,' till the last. ' *But with this.*' The relative is here the best connecting link, as it contains in itself the conjunction and the pronoun. ' *Qui*' never means ' *he,*' ' *this,*' ' *it, merely,* but is equivalent to ' *he,*' ' *this,*' ' *it, plus the conjunction*: e. g. ' *qui*' may mean ' *but he,*' ' *he however,*' ' *because he,*' ' *although he,*' ' *in order that he,*' but is never equal to ' *he* ' alone.

' *Master.*' The fact of ownership is not the important point here, but by way of compensation may be inserted in some other place, where it would not be so intrusive, e. g. ' *dominus*' may stand for ' *the Spaniard* ' above. The most prominent quality of the master here is the holding back of the dog : therefore say, ' *e manu retinentis.*'

CONSTRUCTIO.

A chosen band of Spaniards had been sent to Saxona, for the sake of procuring bread; for the inhabitants of that land, in consideration of ancient friendship, had been accustomed to supply food to the Spaniards. And by chance then the Saxonian king, holding a staff in his right hand, was urging on his men to hurry the work, the Spaniards looking on ; of whom one had with him a Molossian dog, of great ferocity, which all the' time kept raging excitedly at the king, so that (it) could scarcely be held in. He therefore, whose the dog was, having spoken with angry gods surely, said to one next (him), ' how great a thing it would be if the dog were let fly at the man !' Then the other, in jest, nor doubting but that the dog could be restrained at the master's pleasure, using a hunting expression, ' Hie ! seize him !' says he. By which voice instigated the dog burst from the hand of him holding it back, made at the king with his teeth, and killed him foully mangled.

MATERIA.

Party . . manus, '*a band*,' *seldom without an accompanying epithet : as*, parva, lecta.

agmen, *or* caterva, *would lay too much emphasis on the idea of crowding, and marching. The noun might even be omitted here altogether*: *we might say*, 'missi sunt Saxonam ab Hispanis qui panem compararent.'

To . . . . *A purpose may be expressed in several ways :*

(1) Nonnulli homines missi sunt ad panem comparandum.

(2) Panis comparandi causâ.

(3) Ut, *or* qui (=ut illi) panem compararent.

(4) *Less frequently, the supine active after*

> *verbs of motion* : 'spectatum veniunt, veniunt spectentur ut ipsi.'

(5) 'Adsunt visuri eam epistolam.'

Supply . .	praebere, '*to furnish,*' '*to lend,*' *out of one's means.*
	ministrare, *as an inferior* ; *and figuratively* : 'furor arma ministrat.'
	suppeditare, *in abundance* : 'frumentum ex provinciis suppeditare;' 'aqua suppeditabatur templis.'
	suppeto, *neuter, with dative of person, like Greek* ὑπάρχει, '*there is store of* :' 'pauper enim non est, cui rerum suppetit usus.'
Provisions	cibus, '*food* :' 'non hic cibus utilis aegro.'
	frumentum, res frumentaria, '*victualling for an army,*' '*stores.*'
	commeatus, '*supplies,*' '*commissariat.*'
	victus, '*sustenance* :' 'major pars victus eorum in carne consistit.'
	cibaria, '*victuals,*' *with reference to immediate consumption.*
Cacique .	rex, *in regard to their subjects.*
	regulus, '*petty ruler,*' *in regard to the king of Spain.*
	dux, *a generic title, in regard to their position and duties.*
	proceres, *in plural,* '*governing class.*'
Of the place	ejus terrae, *or* is qui ibi imperium obtinebat.
Stick . . .	baculum, '*a staff* :' 'baculumque tenens agreste sinistra ;' 'pera, polenta, tribon, baculus, scyphus, arcta supellex.'
	scipio, '*a staff of office,*' '*baton.*'
Hasten . .	celerare, '*to act with speed,*' '*to get forward,*' *active and neuter.*
	festinare, '*to make haste* :' 'quae causa cur Romam festinaret ?' 'festina lente.'

maturare, ' *to get a thing done in good time.*'

properare, '*to do a thing in a hurry* : ' ' multa,
forent caelo quae mox properanda sereno,
maturare datur.'

Dog . . . canis, *common* (*but mostly feminine when used
generically*) : 'cave canem ;' ' canibus
venari leporem.'

canes venatici, '*hunting dogs,*' '*hounds,*' '*point-
ers.*'

Molossus, '*a mastiff* : ' 'acer Molossus.'

Wild . . . avidus, cupidus : 'tam incitate in regem
furebat, ut vix cohiberi posset.'

Unfortu- quod male, infauste, accidit : ' omine sinistro
nately incepit opus.'

diis iratis : ' egit certe dis iratis.'

Set at . . immittere, '*to let loose at* : ' ' si efferatos in eum
equos immittitis.'

incito, ' *to urge on* : ' ' incitare currentem.'

Rush at . petere, ' *to make for* : ' ' mordicus et calcibus
appetens.'

se immittere in aliquem : ' immisit se in arma-
tas hostium copias.'

se incitare ad : ' quum ex alto se aestus inci-
tavisset.'

se injicere in : 'sese flammis injecerunt;' '*threw
themselves into.*'

Mangle . . lanio, dilanio : 'corpora a feris laniata ;' 'Clodii
cadaver canibus dilaniandum reliquisti.'

lacero : ' corpus uti lacerent volucres in morte
feraeque.'

discerpo : ' discerptum late juvenem sparsere
per agros.'

11.

11. *Alcibiades the Athenian . . .*

Praeparatio.

Following out the principle of suspending the main
statement as long as possible, and so economising the
indicative assertions, we shall be able to reduce the
number of verbs in the indicative mood very considerably,
in putting this English passage into Latin. The statements to be retained are, 'Alcibiades *threw away* and
broke. The fashion *ceased.*'

Constructio.

Alcibiades the Athenian [*when as a boy he was being
educated at the house of his uncle Pericles in liberal arts and
studies, and Pericles had ordered Antigenides the flute player
to be sent for,—in order that he might teach him to play the
flute* (*which was then considered very genteel*),*—when he had
applied the flute handed to him to his mouth*], *shame-struck
by the distortion of his face threw away and broke it. When
this had become known, the fashion of flute playing ceased by
general consent.*

Materia.

At the house of	apud : 'intro nos vocat ad sese ; tenet intus apud se.'
Uncle . .	*on the father's side,* patruus : magnus, '*great uncle.*'
	on the mother's, avunculus.
Bring up .	educo : 'in gremio matris educatus.'
	instituo, '*to train in some branch of know-ledge :*' 'oratorem.'

Instruct .	erudire, '*teach*: ' 'aliquem in jure civili.'
	'*train*:' 'Marcum adhuc omnino rudem ad dicendum instituit.'
	doceo, '*teach.*'
	in morals, praecipere, *with dative of person.*
	'*give directions*,' monere, mandare.
Accomplish-	artes, studia, disciplinae : *summed up in one*
ments	*word,* humanitas.
Flute . .	'tibīcen,' '*player* : ' 'tibiis canere,' '*to play.*'
Genteel . .	honestum: 'Cretes latrocinari honestum putant.'
Put to . .	adhibere, '*apply* :' 'medicas adhibere manus ad vulnera.'
	'*move to* : ' 'vincto ardentes laminae admovebantur.'
	'*put to* :' 'manum ad os apposuit more eorum qui secreto aliquid narrant.'
Distortion	deformitas : 'quae si in deformitate corporis habet aliquid offensionis, quanta illa depravatio et foeditas animi debet videri?'
Become	percrebresco : 'percrebruit ea res, et in ore et
known	sermone omnium coepit esse.'
	'*get abroad* : ' 'exire et in vulgus emanare.'
	palam fieri : 'ne res ea palam fieret.'
Cease . .	desino, '*leave off doing* :' 'veteres orationes a plerisque legi sunt desitae.'
Fashion . .	obsolesco, '*go out of* : ' 'obsolevit jam oratio.'
	cado : 'pellis cecidit vestis contempta ferina.'

12.

12. *While the king lay . . .*

PRAEPARATIO.

First find out who Tanaquil, and Servius were, and all about them.

'To keep out the people,' '*ut plebs arceretur,*' though stated as a purpose in the English, may be put as co-ordinate with the other part of Tanaquil's command, 'and the people to be excluded.'

The logical connexion, which is the guiding principle in Latin syntax, will require that the clauses shall be somewhat differently divided. The simple expedient of tacking one sentence to another by '*and*' would not suit the Latin idiom. We must digest the various statements, select the leading thoughts, and find the key words, so that gradually the subordinate ideas may fall into their proper places, and be moulded in suitable forms : always keeping in view the main object,—perspicuity.

CONSTRUCTIO.

While the king soaked in blood lies dying, a clamour is made and tumult of citizens in the city. Tanaquil, when she had ordered the palace to be closed—all men to be prohibited from entrance—addresses the people from the upper part of the house, through the window ; (saying) that the king wounded. by the blow was not dead ; that he had given orders that Servius should discharge the royal duty until himself should have got well. Accordingly Servius sitting on the royal seat continued to administer justice (imperfect tense), *and performed the customary functions of the king. Nor however, when presently it became known, that Tarquin had expired, did Servius abdicate the kingship, but for a time reigned not at the bidding of the people, without the will of the fathers. Afterwards, when by promising all things—by giving lands—he had conciliated to himself the majority of the citizens, comitia being held, he effected that he himself should be created king.*

Materia.

In . . . . *The Latin must be more explicit*: 'sanguine perfusus.'

Noise . .   sonitus, '*sound*.'

strepitus, '*confused din* :' 'rotarum.'

stridor, '*creaking* ;' 'januae.'

crepitus, '*clatter* :' 'armorum.'

fremitus, '*roaring* :' 'leonis ;' 'maris.'

Tumult. .   clamor, '*of voices* :' 'agminis clamor fremitus-que,' *of an army on the march.*

tumultus : 'caecos instare tumultus.'

Arose . .   fio : 'fit rixa.'

orior : 'bella repente orta sunt,' *or* 'exorta.'

coorior, *when the operation of a number is spoken of*: 'risus omnium coortus est.'

'*spring up*;' 'exoriare aliquis nostris ex ossibus ultor.'

exsisto : 'magna inter eos exstitit controversia.'

nascor : 'profectio eorum nata est a timore de-fectionis.'

Keep out .   arceo : 'lupum a praesepibus arcent.'

excludo : 'eos manibus excluserunt.'

prohibeo : 'omnes ab aditu prohibebantur.'

Window .   fenestra : 'plena per insertas fundebat luna fenestras ;' *glass*, vitreae, (*not mentioned before the fourth century after Christ*).

Wounded .   saucius, sauciare, *of any wound, contusion, or sore* : 'sauciat ungue genas.'

vulnus, vulnerare, *more severe, implying a cut or lesion of the body by a violent act* : 'servi nonnulli vulnerantur : Rubrius in turba sauciatur,' '*bruised in the crowd*.'

Instead . . pro, '*on behalf of*,' 'pro aliquo necari.'

loco : 'in loco parentis.'

vice : 'fungar vice cotis.'

Until . .	dum : 'ea redemptio mansit dum judices rejecti sunt.' *With Subjunctive when purpose is implied* : 'differant in aliud tempus dum ira defervescat.'
	More definite, tantisper : 'ut ibi essent tantisper dum culeus compararetur.'
Recover .	convalesco : 'aegri non omnes convalescunt.'
	sanus : 'sanus fiet ex eo morbo.'
	emergo : 'incommoda valetudo qua jam emerseram.'
	vires revocare, reficere.
	recolligo : 'recolligenti se a longa valetudine.'
Fill the	obire : 'consularia munera obire.'
place .	fungi, 'aedilitate,' 'reipublicae muneribus.'
	explere : 'amicitiae munus explebo.'
Conduct .	administrare : 'provinciam,' 'rempublicam.'
	gerere : 'suam rem bene et publicam.'
	gubernare, '*steer* :' 'navem.'
	moderari, '*guide and check* :' 'equum.'
Resign . .	abdicare se regno, magistratu.
	abscedere civilibus muneribus.
Rule . . .	regere, *active transitive* : 'tu regere imperio populos, Romane, memento.'
	regnare, *neuter intransitive* : '*to reign.*'
	impero : 'imperante Tiberio ;' 'regnante Tarquinio.'
All kinds of	nihil non promisit.
	omnia pollicendo.
Choose . .	lego, *generic* : 'legere judices,' '*jurymen.*'
	deligo, *by preference* : 'socium sibi imperii delexit.'
	eligere, *out of many* : 'ex malis minimum.'
	opto, *by preference* : 'optet utrum malit ;' 'cooptare collegas.'
	creo, '*to elect to an office* :' 'rex creatus est.'

13.

13. *The prefect set out . . .*

PRAEPARATIO.

The style of Livy will be found most suitable for this and the two following passages. Let us then try to assume the character of the Latin historian for the time, and to see things as he might have seen them, and to describe them in such language as he might have used. It is sometimes worth while to strengthen this illusion by substituting proper names that occur in Roman history, such as Caesar, Cleopatra, for the modern ones; and to replace the original names after the piece is done, when their contact can no longer barbarize the context. The treatment of proper names is somewhat perplexing, and no universal rule can be laid down. The simplest way is to give the word a Latin termination, and make it declinable. As Caradoc becomes *Caractacus*, Dejotar, *Deiotarus*, so here Ovando may be Latinized into *Ovandius*. In English the same personage is described by many synonyms for the sake of variety. For instance Ovando, 'the Prefect,' 'the Governour,' 'the Adelantado,' all refer to the same personage. Sometimes the synonym is one that describes him by some temporary · or accidental condition, as ' the invader,' ' the guest,' or it might be, 'the murderer,' 'the speaker,' 'the dissembler.' But in Latin we must be guided by the requirements of clearness, rather than the desire of variety, and go straight to the point. Therefore at starting we had better introduce him by his proper name.

In arranging the words, put ' *regina* ' and ' *praefectum* ' together: thus, ' *ut praefectum regina honestaret.*'

'They said' is not to be translated: you imply it by putting 'would be,' in the Infinitive Mood.

CONSTRUCTIO.

When the queen heard that Ovandius having set out with seventy horsemen, and two hundred footmen, was on his way, being desirous of honouring him, perhaps also suspecting what he was plotting in his mind, she called together to herself all her allies and tributary chieftains, then with a great company went forth to meet him for the sake of saluting. Various shows were prepared for the purpose of delighting the minds of the guests: and at last Anacona seemed to herself, just as she had conciliated the favour of the former prefect, so now to have softened the mind of the grim Ovandius (or the stern temper of Ovandius). But certain of the old followers of Roldanius, who were about Ovandius, kept saying that new things were being agitated, let him provide then, and crush the nascent evil, for that would be (they said) much harder to do, if sedition should have blazed out into war.

MATERIA.

Set out . . proficiscor: 'ab urbe in Volscos ad bellum gerendum profectus est consul.'

Suspicion . *Subst.*, suspicio: 'in suspicionem cecidit;' 'inter eas gentes nulla suspicio deorum est,' '*no idea of.*'

Verb, suspicor: 'Suspicatus est aliquid de M. Popilii ingenio;' 'me suspicatur habere aurum domi;' 'quid animo intendat ex his suspicari possumus.'

Intention . *Subst.*, consilium: 'consilium est aliquid faciendi aut non faciendi excogitata ratio.'

propositum : 'quidnam propositi aut volun-
tatis Pompeius habebat ? '

Verb : 'sibi erat in animo per provinciam iter
facere.'

cogito : 'huncne tu in aedes cogitas recipere ?'

destino : ' infectis iis quae agere destinaverat.'

struo : 'struere et moliri insidias eum puto.'

intendo : 'vereor ne quid mali intendat animo.'

Summon . voco : 'aliquem in contionem vocare.'

advoco : ' viros primarios in consilium ad-
vocavit ; ' ' advocata contione.'

convoco : 'principes Trevirorum ad se con-
vocavit.'

arcesso : ' quum ab aratro arcessebantur qui
consules fierent ; ' ' *were sent for.*'

Feudatories vectigales reges.

Do honour *Verb*, honestare : ' vos me, Patres, decretis
vestris honestavistis.'

honoro : ' nemo tum virtutem non honorabat.'

Subst., honos : ' honore affecit ; ' ' honoris
causa ; ' ' huc honoris vestri venio gratia.'

colo : ' colere deos decet.'

observo : ' tu me observasti ; ' '*paid me respect.*'

saluto : 'prima luce egressus est patroni
salutandi causâ.'

Coming . . *Subst.*, adventus : 'adventum ejus expecta.'

Concourse . caterva : ' regina incessit magna comitante, vel
stipante caterva.'

Amusements *Objective*, ludi, oblectamenta, delectamenta,
ludicra.

Subjective, animus : 'Romanos animine causâ
quotidie exerceri putatis ? ' ' *Do you think
the Romans are drilled every day for the
sake of amusement ?*'

Provide . . paro : 'quod parato opus est, para.'

provideo, (1) *dative of object* : 'rei frumentariae providendum est.' *Or* (2) *accusative, of neuter pronouns* : 'providet ea quae ad usum navium pertinent.'

Propitiate .   placare, '*to allay anger.*'

propitiare, '*to render gracious,*' *generally of the gods.*

mollire animum.

gratiam sibi conciliare.

Severe . . .   durus : 'durum ingenium.'

tristis : 'oderunt hilares tristem, tristesque jocosi.'

austerus, '*sour :*' 'austerior graviorque esse potuisset.'

atrox : 'atrocem animum Catonis.'

severus : 'vultu tristi ac severo.'

torvus : 'optima torvae forma bovis.'

trux : 'trux aspectu.'

Last . . .   superior : 'superiore anno;' ' proximâ nocte ; ' '*immediately preceding.*'

Follower .   *Subst.,* assectator : 'quidam vetus assectator.'

Verb, sequor : 'qui sequebantur.'

Adject., Socratici, '*followers of Socrates.*'

About . .   circa : 'unus eorum qui circa regem erant.'

Tell . . .   dictito, '*keep saying.*'

Insurrec-   seditio : 'seditionem atque discordiam con-
tion   citare.'

At hand .   instare : 'instare tumultus et operta tumescere bella admonebat.'

Look to. .   provideo : 'cura ut provideas quae opus sint.'

praecaveo : 'nisi praecaveas vix effugies.'

consulo : 'consulto opus est ;' 'consulite in medium, et rebus succurrite fessis.'

Suppress .   comprimo : 'comprimere seditiones.'

reprimere, *for a time* : 'lacrimas repressit ; ' ' res non extincta sed repressa.'

opprimo, '*to overwhelm.*'

supprimo : ' supprimere rumores.'

restinguo : ' nutritur vento, vento restinguitur ignis.'

cohibeo, ' *keep within bounds.*'

coercere, ' *keep within bounds,*' ' *restrain.*'

Difficult . difficile factu : ' res arduae ac difficiles.'

Break out . exardesco : ' milites in perniciosam seditionem exarsuri ; ' ' iracundia exercitus in eum exarsit : ' *if* ' exardesco ' *is used for* ' *break out,*' restinguo, *or* extinguo *should be used for* ' *quell.*'

14.

14. *Ovando listened to these men* . . .

PRAEPARATIO.

' Must ; ' what is the kind of obligation intended by ' *must*' in this place ? Does it mean that Ovando was forced in any way ? Or, is the necessity a logical one, affecting the opinion of the narrator ? Does it mean ' *I cannot help thinking that Ovando wished to believe ?* '

' Tournament ; ' when there is no special equivalent in Latin, we must use some general term that will cover the English word : ' *ludicrum certamen,*' like the Trojan games described in the Aeneid, v. 545, would be near enough.

' A Tiberius,' taken as a ' *type of dissemblers* ; ' so, ' *alter Oedipus,*' for ' *a shrewd guesser.*'

' Poor.' A direct appeal like this to the pity of the reader made by the writer is not usual in Latin Prose ; a Latin author does his best to narrate facts in the most truthful manner, and then leaves them to produce their own effect on the reader. ' *Poor* ' may either be left

out, or the idea may be brought in by way of compensation somewhere else: as, '*tam durae sortis indigna,*'
'*expers fraudis,*' or '*fato immerito.*' But probably '*muli-
ebri simplicitate*' will sufficiently express the sentiment
of compassion for the unfortunate lady, and compensate
for the omission of the epithet '*poor*' applied to '*queen.*'

CONSTRUCTIO.

*To whom advising these things, Ovandius, since he himself
was of a mind predisposed to believe, having professed to give
credence, as if he were convinced that a tumult was impending,
gives order to his cavalry, that, on a certain day after the
hour of dinner, they must mount their horses as if for (under
show of) a mock contest; at the same time the infantry must
be present at (to) the same place prepared for acting. He
himself, an artist of dissimulation skilful as no other, goes
to play with the discus: presently certain (people) begging
him to come to see the games, he gets into a passion with
them as if inopportunely calling him away. Anacona with
womanish simplicity, as if about to walk into nets voluntarily, tells the prefect, that her allies too are very desirous to
see that spectacle.*

MATERIA.

Listen . . aurem praebere.
ausculto, '*to attend*' *in order to catch the sound
and sense.*
audio, '*to hear,*' *also* '*to obey :*' ' dicto audiens
esse.'
excipio : 'avidissimis auribus excepit.'

Inclined . inclinato, propenso, ad credendum animo esse.
proclivus, '*prone,*' *as a characteristic.*

inclinatus, *of inclination at the time* : 'inclina-
tior in Poenos.'

' haud invitus erat ; '   ' *not unwilling.*'

Convinced   mihi persuasum est : 'simulavit se comparatum
et exploratum habere,' *or,* 'se haec affir-
mantibus fidem habere professus est ; '
convinco *means* ' *to confute.*'

Intended .   'id agi credo, ut fiat seditio.'

Ready for   paratus ad agendum.
 action   ' promptissima ad bella gens,' *as a characteristic.*

Dissemble.   simulare, '*to falsely pretend to be,* or, *do
something.*'

dissimulare, ' *to falsely pretend not to be,* or
not to do something.'

praetendere, '*to put a plausible face on anything.*'

Dissembler   ' homo totus ex fraude et mendacio ; ' ' simula-
tor ac dissimulator ; ' ' fictos ejus simula-
tosque vultus recordamini.'

Play . . .   ludere : ' it lusum Maecenas.'

Quoit. . .   discus : ' indoctusve pilae, discive, trochive,
quiescit.'

Disturbed .   ' tanquam importunitate eorum offensus ; ' ' im-
portunitatem eorum moleste ferens, vel
stomachatus.'

Snare . .   laqueus, ' *a noose, gin* : ' 'laqueis captare feras
et fallere visco.'

insidiae, ' *an ambush* : ' 'insidias struere.'

plagae, retia, ' *nets* : ' 'aper incidit in plagas.'

fovea, '*pit-fall* : ' ' quoniam in foveam incidit,
prematur.'

Like to . .   velle : ' quod vult valde vult.'

pervelle : ' aliquid pervelle videre.'

' libentissime id spectarem.'

' nullum hoc potius viserent spectaculum.'

15.

15. *Upon this Ovando . . .*

Praeparatio.

'Upon this.' As '*Anacona*' was the first word in the last sentence, '*Ovandius*' may appropriately begin this: suggesting a kind of contrast between the false Spaniard and his victim. 'With demonstrations of pleasure;' here we feel the want of some particle like the Greek δή, or ὡς δή with a participle. The danger is lest we give an undue prominence to the idea of hypocritical pleasure. '*Simulato gaudio*' would express the meaning, but would be too much for the place. We must have an eye to proportion. Perhaps '*reginae voluntati scilicet obsequens*,' or '*libenter obsecutus*,' would do, or, '*ut doli, sceleris secreti conscius.*'

'Badge of knighthood.' '*Bulla*' is sufficiently analogous to be used here.

'Hanged,' that is till she was dead. '*Suspendo*' alone is not enough.

Constructio.

The prefect, obeying most cheerfully the queen's wish, requests her to be present at the general's quarters with all the nobility; that he wanted to talk with them; signifying, as I think, that he would explain the method of the mock fight. Meanwhile he surrounds the building with cavalry, places the infantry in spots most opportune, gives orders to the officers, that, as soon as they should see himself, during the colloquy, put his right hand to the equestrian bulla, which hung (subjunctive, being a part of his instructions) *from his*

*neck, they were all to rush in and bind the queen and nobles.
All things therefore are done according to his intention. The
whole band of Indians caught by treachery with the queen
herself were seized. Anacona alone was led out from the
general's quarters: the rest shut up there, the buildings
having been set on fire, were burnt. And not (nor) long
after the queen was killed by hanging; the province was
laid waste.*

Materia.

Demonstra- **tion**	species: 'paucis ad speciem tabernaculis relictis;' 'falsa specie deceptus;' 'vultu in speciem gaudii conficto.'
To come .	adesse, *better than* venire, advenire, *or* per-venire.
Quarters .	hospitium, '*temporary lodging*;' 'hospitio excepit advenas.' deversorium, '*inn.*' praetorium, '*general's quarters,*' *as here.*
Signify . .	significare: 'hoc mihi significasse et annuisse visus est;' 'nutu significat se intelligere.' indicare: 'supercilia maxime indicant factum.'
Explain .	explano: 'rem obscuram vobis explanabo;' 'volo et docere et explanare.' expono: 'exponam vobis totam hujus rei rationem modumque.' explico: 'hoc definitione explicabo.' expedio, *poetical*: 'altius omnem expediam prima repetens ab origine famam.'
Show . .	spectaculum: 'apparatissimum id spectaculum.' res ludicra, certamen ludicrum. Olympiorum sollenne ludicrum. 'rationem hujus ludi tibi exponam.'

Conjecture conjicio : 'quantum ego conjiciam.'
opinor : 'ut opinor ; ' 'ut veri simile videtur.'

Surround . circumdare : 'circumdedit urbem muro ; ' 'circumdare oppido equitatum.'

Place . . dispono : 'custodias disposuit locis opportunis ;'
'opportunissimo quoque loco constituit
milites.'

In talking . inter loquendum : 'colloquium est, quum in
unum locum loquendi causa convenimus.'

Badge of bulla : 'mox ubi bulla rudi demissa est aurea
knighthood collo.'
annulus equestris : 'annulum invenit—eques
factus est.'

Rush in . . irrumpere, *implies 'breaking through an ob-
stacle.'*
invadere, '*attack* : ' 'invadit regem ferro.'
irruere : 'irruimus, densis et circumfundimur
armis.'

Bind . . . vincire : 'gravibus vincite catenis ; ' 'arrep-
tamque coma, flexis post terga lacertis,
vincla pati cogit.'

Fall out . accido : 'forte accidit ut—'
evenio : 'res omnis ex sententia evenit.'
fieri : 'ut saepe fit.'

Secure . . comprehendo : 'comprehensi sunt sontes.'

Set fire . . incendere : 'incensae aedes.'

Burnt . . 'vivi combusti sunt.'

Hang . . suspendere : 'ab infelici arbore reste sus-
pendito.'

Desolated . vasto : 'provincia fuit ferro et igne vastata.'
populo : 'feris populandas tradere terras.'
desolo : 'et desolavimus agros.'

16.

22. *Then replied that valiant knight . . .*

PRAEPARATIO.

In dealing with the proper names in this piece, it will be a gain to substitute '*Horatius*' for 'Sir Marmaduke;' as the name is suggestive of a similar incident recorded by Livy. Instead of the knight of chivalry our hero will be a proud Ramnian or Titian, and following out the analcgy we may call 'the esquire' '*a client of Horatius.*' Thus the surroundings will all be tinged with a Roman colour, and if we give ourselves for the time to this illusion, we may catch some of the spirit of Livy, and find ourselves using the same syntax as he is accustomed to use.

The words 'my friends,' suggest that his friends had been advising him to take to the river; and so the translation suggested below will be adequate even if we do not bring in '*my friends*' in the vocative case. It is not desirable to render the English into Latin word for word, but to regard the piece as a whole, and to render idea for idea, so that the entire piece of Latin shall be equivalent to the entire piece of English. We may omit a word where it is inconvenient in the Latin, taking care however to compensate by placing it somewhere else where it will be more appropriate, never losing sight of the main object, which is to be intelligible.

Notice in such expressions as '*he was drowned,*' '*he was hanged,*' '*he swam ashore,*' the Latin is more precise than the English: say, '*aqua submersus periit,*' '*suspendio interemptus est,*' '*nando ad litus pervenit.*'

CONSTRUCTIO.

To his friends advising (trying to persuade) these things, Horatius, most brave soldier as he was, thus replied: 'Far be it from me that I should be said to have met a vain death having been drowned: you too, beware lest you do so! Why not rather follow me? I will open a way for you through the enemies right up to the bridge.' Thereupon, spurs having been set to his horse, while he redoubles blows right and left, —a man of both a tall and robust body—he escaped unhurt himself, and opened a passage to (those) following behind. Whom thus valiantly fighting his nephew, who, his horse having been killed, was lying wounded, with a loud voice implored, 'that he would not desert him.' Then Horatius, 'Mount behind me,' (he) says, 'upon my horse.' But he answered, that his strength had failed him. By chance then up came a certain young man, a client of Horatius, who, the youth having been placed on his horse after he himself had descended, says, 'Praetor, whither thou shalt go we will follow.' Thus having followed him to the bridge both reached a place of safety. The rest to (the number of) about a hundred knights, and five thousand footmen, except those who, few in number, had crossed the river by swimming, were utterly cut to pieces.

MATERIA.

Never . . nunquam, *generally.*
non—unquam, *emphatic.*
'*Never!*' 'absit!' 'absit omen!' 'Dii prohibeant!' 'ne sirit hoc Jupiter!'
Drown . . aqua submersus pereo.
For nothing *Adjective*, incassus: 'incassi labores.'
irritus: 'irritum inceptum.'

Adverb, frustra, *refers to the person disappointed.* '

nequicquam, *to the failure of result.*

incassum *implies a want of consideration, by which failure might have been foreseen.*

Do not . . *Prohibitory*, ne facite, '*don't.*'

ne ita faciatis, '*see that you don't.*'

ne feceritis, '*you must not do it :*' 'tu ne cede malis, sed contra audentior ito?'

warning, 'cave hoc facias,' 'cave ne facias:' 'tu cave defendas, quamvis mordebere dictis;' 'vade, vale: cave ne titubes, mandataque frangas;' 'occursare capro, cornu ferit ille, caveto.'

dissuasive, nolite ita facere: 'vendere quum possis captivum, occidere noli.'

entreating : 'parce pias scelerare manus!'

the disjunctive, '*neither,*'—'*nor,*' *in such sentences is* ' ne,'—'neve,'—'neu,' *not* 'ne-que:' 'ne taxum propius sine, neve rubentes ure foco cancros.'

Follow . . sequor : 'sequor, et qua ducitis adsum.'

Clear . . aperio : 'ventus incendio viam aperuit.'

Passage. . via : *in most general sense,* '*way* :' 'qui sibi semitam non sapiunt, alteri monstrant viam;' 'fit via vi.'

iter, '*a going,*' '*walk* :' 'dicam in itinere,' '*as we go along.*' '*Way,*' '*road* :' 'patefecit illis iter in Galliam.'

transitus : 'flumine impeditus erat transitus exerc⬛s.'

semita, '*path* :' 'quae fuerat quondam semita facta via est.'

Bridge . . pons : 'saxeus ingenti quem pons amplectitur arcu.'

Spur . . . calcar: 'nil nocet admisso subdere calcar equo.'

Plunge . .	immergo : 'inter mucrones se hostium immersit.'
Blow. . .	plaga ; *inflicted as a punishment* : 'gaudet plagarum strepitu.'
	ictus, '*strokes that wound* :' 'nunc dextra ingeminans ictus, nunc ille sinistra.'
Unhurt . .	illaesus, integer, incolumis, sospes.
Pass . . .	evado, *with notion of escaping*.
Tall . . .	procerus : 'celsior ille gradu procera in membra.'
Stout . .	robustus : 'quantas ostendat robusto pectore vires.'
Nephew .	nepos : 'non cecidit patruus dum stat in urbe nepos.'
Save . . .	servo : 'Di patrii servate patrem, servate nepotem !'
	eripio : 'eripe me his malis.'
Behind . .	pone : 'pone subit conjux, ferimur per opaca locorum.'
Strength .	vires : 'non te destituit animus, sed vires meae.'
Presently .	mox : 'mox ubi finis adest.'
	brevi : 'Titius Romana brevi venturus in ora.'
Same, the .	idem, eadem, ĭdem, ejusdem.
Place on .	impono, *suggests the 'putting on from above,'* as sellam, jugum : *but also in wider sense.*
	subicio, '*lifting up*' *of an object*: 'ipsa man subicit gladios ac tela ministrat ;' 'corpora saltu subjiciunt in equos;' 'pavidum regem in equum subjecit.'
	the dative after subicio, *would mean* '*put under*,' 'subjecit ova gallinae.'
Will . . .	volo : 'quocumque vis.'
	libet, '*you like* :' 'ut libet.'
	more emphatic : 'quocumque fert animus.'
Remained .	'*all who remained*,' *adjective*, reliquus, '*re-*

>   *maining after the subtraction of a certain*
>   *quantity* : ' 'reliqui fugae se mandarunt.'
>   ceteri (*no nom. sing. masc.*), '*the rest*'
>   *viewed as a whole* : 'erant perpauci
>   reliqui : ceteri dimissi.'

Swim   . . nando trajicere.

17.

25. *The next year the Portuguese mariners . . .*

PRAEPARATIO.

If we persist in trying to translate word for word we
shall hardly find an equivalent Latin verb to the verb
'discover' here.   Let us neglect single words, and translate the thing signified.   Say, '*came to Madeira an island
unknown before,*' which is equivalent in sense, although
the word '*discover*' nowhere appears in it.

The order of words may be made subservient to clearness.   Contrasted words should be brought together.
In this piece, 'Madeira' and the 'timber' from which it
derives its name should be placed in juxtaposition.

'Its rarest commodity.' We must not adhere too closely
to the English words, and forms ; the superlative here may
be more adequately expressed in Latin, by, '*became in-no-
other-commodity more unfruitful,*' '*fit,* or *facta est, nullo
alio proventu infecundior.*' 'Of discovery.'   The Latin
idiom prefers concrete words, and personal agents, to
abstract terms ; say '*people exploring.*' 'It is clear,' etc.
Shall we put this into the oratio obliqua, or retain the
oratio recta?   The safest way for beginners is to retain

the oratio recta wherever it occurs in the English: they are less likely to get into difficulties. The choice of the one, or the other, is not indeed a matter of indifference, but still a matter for individual taste and judgment. Try to think which Livy or Caesar would have used in each case.

CONSTRUCTIO.

The following year the Lusitani were carried to Madeira, an island unknown before : undertaking the culture of which land a most adverse thing befell them. For, while they give their attention to the clearing of woody places, by chance they made a fire, which widely straying ragèd for seven years, so that at last Madeira, which drew its name from 'Materia,' the trees having been consumed, became of no other produce more unproductive. But the promontory Boiadorium, which runs out from the African shore, had been for a long time the limit of their journey to people exploring the Austral region. Which, of itself formidable, (to such a degree, ending in a rocky ridge, it rages with tide sweeping past, and with eddies), wonders, feigned in the fables of mariners concerning the terrestrial and marine things, which lay (subjunctive, as resting on the testimony of the sailors) *beyond, had rendered much more terrible. 'It is a certain fact,' such was their talk, 'that beyond this promontory there are absolutely no inhabitants. A land more naked than Libya, it hath no water, no trees, no grass. Nay more, the sea there is so shallow that at a distance of three miles from the mainland it hardly exceeds a depth of one ell ; but if any ship shall have sailed beyond that cape, in so great violence of contrary billows there will be no return for it.'*

Mariners . navita; *archaic and poetical form*: 'navita de ventis, de tauris narrat arator.'
usual prose form, nauta.

Attempt . . conor: 'vides Demosthenem multa perficere: nos multa conari.'
suscipio: ' aut ne suscipias aut perfice.'
Substantive: 'incepto desistere coacti sunt.'

Cultivate . colere: 'arva et vineta et oleas et arbustum colimus;' *also figurative*: 'amicitiam, artes liberales.'

Accident . . casus: 'nullum hujusmodi casum respectabant ;' 'res improvisa mihi accidit.'

Clear . . . purgo, *of trees*: 'cum falcibus purgarunt loca.'

Kindle . . accendo, *' to kindle with a view to use:'* 'unctas accendite taedas ;' 'ignem subjiciunt lignis.'
incendo, *' to set fire to with a view to destruction.'*

Fire . . . ignis, *' the element :'* incendium, *' the fire when made,' as a bonfire*: 'dispersa immittit silvis incendia pastor.'

Spread . . pervagor: 'usque ad ultimas terras pervagatus est rumor.'
extendo: 'ignis extenditur per campos.'
Adverb: 'furit late flamma.'

Burn . . ardeo: 'fertilis accensis messibus ardet ager.'

End, in the eo exitu ut, ita ut: ' unde factum est ut ea terra arboribus omnino careret.'

Timber . . materies, *only in nom. and accus. sing.* ; materia, *usual form*, *' timber with a view to use :'* 'jacet omnis ad undam navibus faciundis apta materies.'
lignum, *' wood :'* 'lignum in silva quaeris.'

Commodity fructus: ' fertilis ager vario fructu.'

proventus : 'uberi vinearum proventu.'

Rare . . . rarus : 'vitio parentum rara juventus ;' 'infelix frugibus terra ;' 'infecunda quidem, sed laeta et fortia.'

Africa . . *the name received by the Romans from the Carthaginians as designating their own country; Greek,* Libya. *Thence the whole quarter of the globe south of the Mediterranean Sea.*

Libya : 'aestu torretur Libya.'

Limit . . limes, *masc.; 'a cross-path between fields,' 'a boundary:'* 'limes agro positus ;' '*limit* :' 'aestuat infelix angusti limite mundi.'

finis, '*bound* :' 'est modus in rebus, sunt certi denique fines.'

modus, '*measure not to be exceeded* :' 'modum aliquem et finem orationi facere.'

terminus : 'oratoris facultatem non illius artis terminis, sed ingenii sui finibus describere.'

Southern . meridianus : 'pars orbis meridiana,' *contemplated from north of the equator.*

australis : 'regio australis.'

Cape . . . promontorium, superavit, vel, flexit, '*weathered the cape.*'

Formidable formidolosus : 'bellum terribile ac formidolosum.'

Terminate . *Active* : 'circulus finiens qui a Graecis ὁρίζων nominatur.'

Neuter, desino : 'desinit in piscem mulier formosa superne.'

Ridge . . dorsum : 'dorsum immane mari summo.'

jugum : 'immensis tumet Ida jugis.'

Rock . . . saxum : 'ecce petunt rupes praeruptaque saxa capellae.'

scopuli : 'terra tribus scopulis vastum pro-currit in aequor.'

Currents . fretum, '*a race* :' 'rapido in freto deprehensi.'

aestus, '*tide* :' 'quid de fretis et marinis aesti-bus dicam ?'

vortex, '*eddy* :' 'citatior solito amnis trans-verso vortice dolia impulit ad ripam.'

gurges, '*whirlpool* :' 'deficientibus animis hauriebantur gurgitibus.'

Fancy . . somnium : 'velut agri somnia.'

commentum : 'opinionum commenta delet dies.'

fabula : ' ficta et commenticia fabula.'

ficta res : 'veris falsa et mente ficta miscet.'

Beyond . . *Preposition*, ultra : *Adjective*, ulterior.

It is clear . liquet, '*has been made clear* :' 'si liquebit mundum providentia regi.'

constat, '*it is undisputed* :' 'quid porro quae-rendum est ? Factumne sit ? At constat. A quo ? At patet ;' 'constat inter omnes eum virum probum esse.'

haud *or* non dubium est : 'haud dubium est quin uxorem nolit filius ducere ;' 'periisse me una haud dubium est.'

Whatever . omnino : 'ita fit ut omnino nemo possit esse beatus.'

prorsus : 'verbum prorsus nullum intelligo.'

Bare . . . nudus : 'ut vidua in nudo vitis quae nascitur arvo.'

Grass ' . . gramen : 'gramina carpit equus.'

herba : 'cespitis herba viret.'

Shallow. . brevis, 'fossa brevis ;' 'brevia vadosa dicit, per quae vadi pedibus potest.'

Fathom. . ulna : 'tres pateat coeli spatium, non amplius, ulnas.'

H

Violent . .   *Adjective*, violentus : ' non illo in mare pur-
                    pureum violentior influit amnis.'
                  turbidus, saevus, atrox.
                  Substantive : ' magna vi saevit ibi mare.'

Return . .   redeo, ' *come back again* : ' ' quinque greges
                    illi, et quina redibant armenta.'
                  revertor, *deponent, and*, reverto, *neuter* :
                    ' nescit vox missa reverti.'
                  reversio, *subst. as opposed to* reditus, *implies a
                    return before the objective point of the
                    journey had been reached.*

18.

27. *One of the ringleaders was* . . .

Praeparatio.

The proper names here had better have a Latin termination added, and be made to look as like Roman names
as possible. While doing the piece we might help our
imagination by calling one, Marcus Junius, and the other,
Titus Flaminius, and when the piece was finished, and the
barbarous names could no longer distort our attention, we
might restore Michael and Thomas to their places : or
let them appear modestly under the initials M. and T.

The tone and temper of a piece may be intensified
sometimes by expressing in words what is implied in the
original : e. g. we may fairly assume that T. Flammock
lost no opportunity of airing his importance, although the
historian does not say so in so many words ; ' *Se vendi-
tabat dictitando legem cum illis stare.*'

Often more is gained by translating by analogy than by literal translation : e. g. although '*saga sumere*' does not literally mean 'to put on harness,' yet to a Roman ear it would convey the meaning intended. Neither is '*tumultus*' the literal Latin for 'war,' but a 'Scottish tumult,' on the analogy of the oft-recurring '*Gallici tumultus*,' would call up in the hearer's mind a more precise image of the thing signified than '*bellum*' would. 'Journeys' means 'expeditions,' 'campaigns.'

'Poll and pill,' 'to strip and peel,' or 'rob,' '*spoliare et compilare.*'

CONSTRUCTIO.

One leader of sedition was a certain M. Josephus, a blacksmith, a man forward of tongue and most greedy of fame. The other T. Flammoccius, a lawyer, who commonly, if anything had happened, by repeatedly saying that the laws stood with them, obtained great authority among his fellow townsmen. He, whilst he advertized himself to the plebs by discoursing learnedly, as if he knew how to stir up war, peace being unbroken, denied that in a Scottish tumult it was allowable by law for tax to be demanded of the people, or to be paid ; that, in point of fact, for meeting the expenses of that kind of warfare, it had been provided by law, that money should be collected from another source ; not to say, when all was quiet, and war was only held forth as a pretext for spoiling and pillaging citizens. That by no means then ought they to offer themselves like sheep to be shorn, but as (that which) became men, to assume their war cloaks, and to take arms in their hands.

MATERIA.

Ringleader   caput : 'capita conjurationis ejus securi per-
cussi sunt.'
concitator : 'tumultus ac turbae concitator.'
dux : 'dux seditionis.'

Smith . .   faber : 'fabros ferrarios et tignarios secum
habet.'

Talker . .   lingua procax : 'largus opum, lingua melior ; '
'nimius sermonis ; ' 'famae avidissimus.'

Lawyer . .   juris consultus : *abbreviated*, Ictus.
juris, jure peritus, *so most often used adjec-
tivally.*
leguleius, *contemptuously.*

Neighbour   popularis : 'populares ac sodales sui.'

Commonly   vulgo : 'verum illud verbum est vulgo quod
dici solet.'

Side . . .   stare ab, cum, pro : 'a bonorum causa stetit ; '
'cum di prope ipsi cum Hannibale sta-
rent.'

Sway . . .   auctoritas : 'Dumnorix multum apud eos
auctoritate valebat.'

Learnedly .   sermocinari :   'exquisitius sermocinabatur,
ingenii venditandi aut memoriae osten-
tandae causa.'

Never break   salvus : 'nunc agi cum populo potest, salvis
auspiciis, salvis legibus.'

Subsidy . .   collatio, '*money* :' 'stipis aut decumae collatio.'
subsidium, '*aid.*'

Journey . .   iter, *in military sense*, '*campaign.*'
expeditio : 'expeditionem suscepit contra
Persas.'

Much less .   nedum, *indicating that 'whereas a certain
thing is not, another thing can still less
be* :' 'optimis temporibus nec P. Popilius ·
nec Q. Metellus vim tribuniciam sustinere

　　　　　potuerunt, nedum his temporibus sine
　　　　　vestra sapientia salvi esse possimus.'

Quiet . . *Verb*, paco : ' pacatae tranquillaeque civitates.'

Pretence . *Verb*, obtendo, praetendo.

Shear . . tondeo : ' infirmas tondebat oves ; ' ' hunc
　　　　　tondebo auro usque ad cutem.'

19.

31. *The cruelty wreaked . . .*

PRAEPARATIO.

' Dumb figures.' This must be translated not word for
word, but by analogy. The Roman soldiers and gladiators
used to exercise their skill and strength in sword play,
upon a post or stake ; ' *exercebant se ad palum.* '
' Cradle,' not a child's cradle, but a cage or pen, probably.
Look out ' *cavea* ' and ' *crates.* '

' Siesta : ' the Spanish for ' *sexta hora,* ' ' his mid-day
repose.'

' Alguazil,' a Moorish word, naturalized in Spain :
here ' provost-martial.' ' Martyrdom,' used here in a
derivative sense, not ' death for religion,' but ' execution,' ' cruel and undeserved punishment ; ' ' *supplicium* '
points to the right meaning. ' He intended.' The Latin
idiom would prefer ' *had* intended,' ' *destinaverat animo.* '

CONSTRUCTIO.

*It is monstrous the (how much of) cruelty the Spaniards
exercised towards their captives. L. Cassius is our authority
(author) that on one occasion they hung up thirteen Indians,
'to the honour (if you please) of Christ and his twelve
apostles.' That (on) these, suspended at such a height as to*

touch (imperfect subjunctive) *or, that they touched* (aorist subjunctive) *the ground with their feet, the Spaniards as if they were exercising at the stake, by cutting them proved their blades. At another time also, he says he saw some Indians inclosed in a certain wooden den, being burnt alive. Of whom howling when the noise proved annoying to the Spanish officer taking midday rest in his tent, he ordered the soldier who presided over the execution that he should kill the captives immediately. But he, so that they might not fail to (might not not) exhaust their torments in the manner in which he had destined, gagged the mouths of the wretches: did not kill them.*

MATERIA.

Cruelty. . *Substantive*, crudelitas ; *of wanton cruelty* : 'quae est atrocitas animi in exigendis poenis ; ' 'animi causa crudelitatem exercere.'

Verb, saevio ; *of cruelty under the influence of rage* : 'constat in Trojanos saevitum esse.'

Excessive . immensus : 'laudisque immensa cupido.'

immane : 'immane quantum irae exarserunt.'

Honour. . honoris causa, *or*, in honorem : 'plurimus in Junonis honorem.'

The inverted commas in the English suggest that the historian wishes to show that the Spaniards are answerable for this impiety and that he does not approve of it. This implied thought might be expressed in Latin directly by 'scilicet,' *or*, 'si diis placet.'

Disturb. . molestus : 'abscede hinc, molestus ne sis.'

molestiam exhibere, facere, praebere, '*to cause annoyance.*'

Charge . . praesum : 'ille statuis faciendis praeerat, hic exercitui.'

Despatch . conficio, '*make an end of*:' 'ea sica me paene confecit.'

Gag . . . obturo : 'os tibi obturabo.'

obstruo : 'cujus aures morbus obstruxit.'

20.

33. *The messengers who were sent . . .*

PRAEPARATIO.

The English is easy to understand. Be careful to secure the leading ideas, and key words in the first draft. Thus, '*Missi sunt qui dolo abstraherent incolas.*' '*Hi promittebant se illos ad beatas insulas deducturos esse.*' '*Hoc praetextu deceptos multos ad Hispaniolam asportaverunt.*' '*Abrepti et in metallum dati sunt.*' '*Ibi multi inedia perierunt, nonnulli effugere conati sunt.*' '*Unus, qui olim faber fuerat, per silvas elapsus, ad oram maris pervenit.*' '*Ibi, ut erat arte fabrili peritus caesa arbore ratem qualemcunque fecit.*'

We have now given an idea of what we want to say, in a simple, but intelligible form. We have a secure basis to work upon. We can now modify, fill up, add details, alter the form where necessary, and adapt it more closely to the original, with less chance of distorting the general meaning by dwelling upon and unduly magnifying the less important details.

CONSTRUCTIO.

Those who were sent (imperfect if more than one occasion is meant, pluperfect if one special occasion is referred to) *to draw away the inhabitants into servitude, guile being employed against men too little suspicious, pretended that it had been enjoined on them by the gods, that they should carry away the Lucayans with them to the happy islands, where dwelt* (subjunctive, this being the representaton of the messengers) *their ancestors, and if any one had been dear in life. By which enticements allured very many were taken away thence to Hispaniola, that condemned to the mines, they might complete their remaining age in labouring. So after they learnt the truth many abstaining from food died of starvation : others, hope having been cast away, kept-enduring a miserable life ; others endeavoured to flee away to their native country. One of the latter, who had formerly been a worker in wood, having stolen through the forests, arrived at the northern coast of Hispaniola. There, a tree having been cut down, when, upon beams made out of it he had laid cross beams made of smaller trunks and with the fibres and roots of shrubs that grow in that region had bound them together compactly, at the same time stuffing the cracks with leaves and twigs, he made I know not what ship.*

MATERIA.

Simple . .   '*free from guile,*' simplex : 'vir simplex et apertus.'

          '*easily imposed upon,*' credo : 'non is sum qui credam.'

          credulus, *adject.* : 'vatem me dicunt, sed non ego credulus illis.'

Convey . .   avehere : 'in alias terras avecti.'

Blest . . fortunatae, fortunatorum insulae : 'beata peta-
mus arva, divites et insulas.'

Elysium : 'mittimur Elysium ; ' 'devenere
locos laetos et amoena vireta Fortunatorum nemorum, sedesque beatas.'

Dear . . . carus, *general term* : 'at longe patria est
longe carissima conjux.'

dilectus, *of family love* : 'O luce magis dilecta
sorori.'

Decoy . . allicio, inesco : *of a baited trap.*

pellicio : 'militem donis, populum annona
pellexit.'

decipere, '*take by false pretence.*'

Hunger . . fames, '*desire for food,*' *also* '*famine* :' 'fame
enecare, consumere.'

inedia, '*lack of food,*' *of voluntary starvation* : 'inedia vitam finivit ille philosophus,' *so,* mortem, necem, sibi fame
conscivit.

Despair . . spe abjecta, ad summam desperationem venire.

Patient . . 'toleranter ferre dolorem ; ' 'asellus et pla-
garum et penuriae tolerantissimus.'

Make one's　elabor : 'anguilla est, elabitur ; ' 'mediis
way　　　 . elapsus Achivis.'

evado : 'exsuperat jugum, silvaque evadit
opaca.'

iter facere, *general expression,* '*to journey,*'
'*march.*'

of force : 'fit via vi.'

of obstacles : 'per obstantia nitor.'

of heights : 'juga montis superavit.'

Stem . . truncus : 'cibus per truncos et per ramos
diffunditur omnes.'

'*stalk,*' stirps, *from the botanical point of
view* : 'arborum radices stirpesque.'

Beam . . tignum : 'duo tigna transversa injecerunt.'
trabs, *compacted of several* tigna.

Lash . . . connecto, ' *tie one thing on to another.*'
colligo, ' *bind together.*'
alligo, ' *bind,*' *or,* ' *tie to.*'
deligo, ' *bind so as to hang from,*' *and generally of binding a smaller object to a larger.*

Stringy . . fibratus : 'radix fibrata.'
fibra : 'arbores quae rectam non habent radicem plurimis nituntur fibris.'

Shrub . . frutex, arbustum, *in plur.*

Interstice . rima : 'navis agit rimas, explete.'
commissura.

Leaves . . folia et sarmenta.

Kind of . . ' *any kind soever,*' *with disparagement* : 'carmina lector commendet dulci qualiacunque sono.'
nescio quis : ' causidicum nescio quem.'

21.

34. *He then laid in a store* . . .

Praeparatio.

It is a principle in Latin composition not to begin with details, but to state the larger proposition first, and fill in the details afterwards. Thus in the first sentence it helps to clear the ground if we say first, the 'Indian prepared viaticum,' and then proceed to enumerate the particulars.

This piece being very simple narrative and containing nothing of argument, and little of explanation, ought to be rendered in short sentences, and in language as direct as possible.

Speeches quoted in *oratio recta* are introduced by '*inquit*,' or '*ait*,' the verb being placed always after the first word, or words, of the quotation.

'Caravel.' Use '*navis*,' 'ship:' the general word, first. If you can light upon a closer equivalent afterwards, use it instead of '*navis*.'

CONSTRUCTIO.

Which being done, he prepares food for the journey. He lays up a store of Indian corn, and sets by some pitchers of water. Then, two other mortals, a man and a woman, both related to himself, having been received into the ship, the three together, furnished with oars, loose the vessel. The guide of the way (was) the north star. And so, for many days and nights, they are borne along by oars, tide, wind. And now they had lost sight of Hispaniola, hated prison : and, a run of 200 miles about, having been accomplished, hope had grown that they would see Lucaya again. And the Indian, 'Be of good heart, sister mine,' says (he), 'not many suns more will arise for us, before that we shall revisit our native soil.' Scarcely had he said those (words) when (and) Lo, far off on the extreme sea, a sight seeming (to be) of a black colour, at first affects them with joy, fancying that they saw (infinitive imperfect) their fatherland. Presently despair took-the-place-of joy, when it was known that what they had thought to be land, was a Spanish galley. And without delay (nor delay), the raft having been descried, the enemy are borne in rapid course towards the fugitives. Arrested they carry them away to Hispaniola.

MATERIA.

Store . . . 'condere et reponere.'

Maize . . far Indicum.

Water vessel cadus, '*jar* :' 'vina bonus quae deinde cadis onerarat Acestes.'

dolium, '*cask*,' '*bucket*.'

amphora, '*jar*,' *pitcher*.'

Related . propinquus : *general term, opp. to* alienus.

cognatus, '*by birth* :' is mihi cognatus fuit.'

necessarius : '*connected by a bond*,' *either of relationship or friendship.*

Furnish . instruere : 'instructae atque ornatae omnibus rebus copiae.'

North Star. Arctos, *sing.*: 'versa ab axe suo Arctos erat.'
Pl. : 'Arctos Oceani metuentes aequore tingui.'

Septemtrio : 'gens Hyperboreo septem subjecta Trioni ;' 'stellae, quas nostri septem soliti vocitare triones.'

Guide . . 'dux femina facti.'

Out of view abscondo : 'abscondit in aere telum,' '*he shot it out of sight*;' 'phaeacum abscondimus arces,' '*lose sight of*.'

conspectus : 'fugere e conspectu ejus.'

Cheer . . animus, '*courage*:' 'quare bono animo es ;' 'fac sis bono animo.'

'*hope*:' 'magnus mihi animus est hodiernum diem initium libertatis fore.'

Dawn . . dilucesco : 'omnem crede diem tibi diluxisse supremum.'

'surgit aurora ;' 'sol oritur ;' 'soles occidere et redire possunt.'

Native land patria, natale solum.

Sky line . *technically*, 'orbis finiens,' *or* 'circulus qui aspectum nostrum definit ;' 'margo maris extremi.'

	procul : 'apparet Camarina procul.'
Object . .	macula, '*spot*,' *regarded as a blemish.*
	species : 'nova atque inusitata.'
	'nescio quae visa procul species.'
	res : 'objecta prospicientium oculis.'
Fancy . .	opinor, puto, fingo mente : 'principatum sibi
	opinionis errore finxerat.'
Caravel. .	liburna, '*a galley*.'
	lembus, '*a pinnace* :' 'ducit lembum jam
	directum navis praedatoria.'
	triremis : '*a war ship*.'

22.

37. *They had been informed that* . . .

PRAEPARATIO.

Before putting pen to paper, read over carefully this and the following four pieces. Master the whole story, distinguish the actors in it, and learn the plot and result of the whole adventure, before attempting to tell the story in a foreign language. '*Respice finem*,' find out what the end is, and keep it in view, from the beginning.

'They,' i. e. the royalist soldiers, who wanted to capture Rainsborough, the parliamentary general, and then, by an exchange of prisoners, to ransom Langdale, their own general. Rainsborough had his head quarters at Doncaster. Morrice sallied forth on this adventure from Pomfret castle, then in the hands of the king's men : with intent to bring back Rainsborough prisoner to Pomfret.

The proper names, as usual, present a difficulty, the names of towns of course, if they existed in Roman times, must be ascertained. In this exercise we may be allowed, in our first draft, to substitute ordinary Latin names for

Langdale, Morrice, Rainsborough, while Cromwell may safely be designated the '*dictator.*' We do not find that Roman proper names are derived from places so often as in English, so that we are debarred from translating Langdale for instance according to its meaning; ' De longa valle ' would be a barbarism. Where a proper name happens to be significant, as 'Taylor,' we might render it by ' *Sertorius:*' ' Brown,' by ' *Fuscus ;*' ' Carpenter,' by ' *Fabricius ;*' ' Bacon,' by ' *Porcius,*' and so forth.   Titles such as, ' sir,' and ' my lord,' were not used by the Romans, except as titles of the emperors, and may be omitted.

CONSTRUCTIO.

When it was announced that M. Longinus (him alone at that time the royalist soldiers recognised as military-commander) after the defeat of the Scottish army, having been captured in battle was being detained (passive infinitive imperfect) *in Nottingham castle in strict custody, Marius* (or *Mauritius*), *with twelve horsemen, a chosen band, set out at nightfall, with the (that) design, that he should capture C. Rabirius, by whom as a hostage Longinus might be redeemed.   These then, since all were well acquainted with the locality and the roads, made so great progress, that at dawn they emerged into the high road (public way) which leads from Eboracum.   There the sentinels who were at (that) post, as (being people) by whom there was no enemy to be feared from that direction, with too little curiosity, inquired, 'From whence they were present ?'   But they, when they had answered negligently enough to those (questions), in turn, questioned, ' where the prefect was,' (saying) that they were bringing a letter for him sent from (or by) the dictator.*

MATERIA.

Acknow-ledge	agnosco : '; n me agnoscetis ducem?' nosco, ' *to admit* :' ' illam partem excusationis nec nosco nec probo.'
Strict . .	intentus: 'intentiore custodia eum asservabant.'
Custody .	custodia: (1) '*protection*,' (2) '*guards.*' (3) ' *watchfulness*,' ' *look out place.*' (4) ' *restraint* : ' ' nec cuiquam uni custodiam Philopoeminis credebant.' (5) '*prison* : ' ' Lentulus in custodia necatur.'
Ransom .	redimo : ' tu redimes me, si me hostes inter-ceperint?'
Thereby .	eo obside : ' ut obsides accipere non dare con-sueverint ; ' ' retinere aliquem obsidem.'
Acquainted	peritus, gnarus: ' duces earum regionum peritissimi.'
Went so far	procedo : ' longius processit; ' ' haud multum processit,' *of space*. proficio, *of general progress*. progredior : ' tridui viam progressi.'
Put them-selves	evado : ' per praeruptum saxum in Capitolium evasit.'
Direction .	regio, ' *a straight line* :' ' e regione moveri,' ' *to move in a straight line*,' *opposed to* ' declinare.' ' luna quum est e regione solis,' ' *right over against.*' ' ea regione qua Sergius erat,' ' *in that quarter where.*'
Negligently	incuriose : ' pacis modo incuriose agere ; ' ' parum curiose inquirere.' negligenter, *opp. to* diligenter : ' negligenter audientes ; ' ' satis negligens.'
Letter . .	litterae missae, ' *a letter sent.*' litterae allatae, ' *a letter received.*'

23.

38. *The guards sent one to show . . .*

' The general,' viz. Rainsborough.

' They knew,' viz. Morrice and his party knew. ' They were to pass,' i. e. the adventurers had to pass. The obligation, or necessity may be expressed either by a gerundive, ' *trajiciendum erat illis,*' or by ' *necesse erat,*' or by '*qua sola viâ ad castellum rediri potuit.*'

' Their officer,' viz. Morrice.

' The general,' viz. Rainsborough.

' Some of the horse,' viz. the Cromwellians.

' Who only went in.'   Here instead of the *aorist*, as in the English, the *pluperfect* would be used in Latin. Either, ' *qui profectus esset* (*or*) *discessisset, ad conveniendum ducem*' (subjunctive because part of the statement of the men = *who, as they said, had gone*, etc.), or directly, ' *eum autem profectum esse ducis conveniendi causâ.*'

One of the guards therefore was sent, who might point out to them where the prefect dwelt : to whom nevertheless it was by no means unknown (minime fefellit) *that he lodged in the hospice the most comfortable of as many as there are there. Whither when it was come* (by them), *the door having been opened, three of the conspirators* (implied in the English narrative, expressed in the Latin for the sake of clearness) *enter the house ; the rest hasten by a straight course further on, to that bridge, which, in the extreme part of the town must be crossed by (people) going to Pontefract ('Broken bridge'). There, and not contrary to expectation, the watch meets them, horsemen and footmen : with whom talk having been joined, they pass the time, until their comrades should return, pretending that they were waiting for their officer, who just now had gone away* (subjunctive, as being the statement of the soldiers, not of the historian) *to-have-a-meeting-with the commander. At the same time they request that wine may be brought. But the sentinels not-in-the-least suspecting them to be foes, ordered cups to be brought, 'was there anything of news,' they ask, and answer, chatting whatever (came) into their heads. And now, it being sufficiently clear light, some began to dismount, some to depart to their quarters, as if having performed their morning duties.*

MATERIA.

Guards . . custos, *most general term, 'guardian.'*
custodia, *abstract for concrete* : 'clam transire propter custodias non poterant.'
vigiliae, '*night watch,' ' sentries.'*
excubiae, '*guards,' keeping watch night and day.*

Show . . monstro, demonstro, '*to show' for information* : 'non monstrare viam eadem nisi sacra colenti.'
ostendo, '*to expose to view.'*
indico, '*to show by pointing.'*

Lay at . . 'deversari apud aliquem,' '*to lodge with.'*
'devertere ad cauponem,' '*to put up at a tavern.'*
habito, *of permanent dwelling.*

I

Of them .	*for the sake of greater clearness, say* 'the royalist soldiers,' *or,* 'the conspirators,' *use a phrase devoid of all ambiguity.*
Rode on .	*no need to use a word meaning* 'to ride' *unless for the sake of emphasis to discrim- inate from* 'walking,' 'sailing,' *etc.*
Other end .	pars extrema, *inserted more conveniently and perspicuously in describing the locality of the bridge.*
Were to pass	trajicio, *active and neuter* : 'copias suas Caesar Rhenum trajecit;' 'exercitus propter altitudinem fluminis trajicere non poterat.'
Expected .	spes, opinio, *subst.* : 'quod non praeter spem, praeter opinionem, evenit.'
Entertain .	*of passing the time,* 'tempus terere, loquendo, jocando, sermones conferendo.'
Went to speak to	convenio, adeo, *with accusat.* 'convenire aliquem colloquendi, vel consulendi causa.'
Call for . .	posco : 'pocula poscimus.'
News . . .	novum : 'num quid novi est rogo?' 'si quid novi acciderit' *mostly implying bad news.* res novae, 'revolution,' 'political innovations.'
Talk negli- gently	'quicquid in buccam venerit, scribere, dicere, garrire :' *the* 'venerit' *is sometimes omitted.*
Court of guard	statio, praesidium ; *but consider the purpose of their going, and translate according to the sense : having come off duty, the soldiers went* 'ad sua quisque tecta,' *or* 'ad tectum,' *to their quarters in the barracks.*

24.

39. *They who went into the inn . . .*

PRAEPARATIO.

'Two of them,' viz. of the adventurers.

'The soldier,' viz. one of the Cromwellians.

'To put on his clothes.' Infinitive after 'would.' In the English of to-day we should leave out '*to*,' the sign of the infinitive.

'The fellow;' for the sake of clearness, say the 'servant,' *servus*, which word will naturally suggest '*cetera familia, quae nondum somno experrecta erat.*'

There is no difficulty in this passage arising from argument, or, reasoning, but there is a chance of confusing the persons. Our chief object, as ever, ought to be to make things plain to the reader, and to do this we must know what we wish to say. That knowledge will help us more than minute rules and directions. We can only hope to make clear to others, what is first clear to ourselves.

CONSTRUCTIO.

Meanwhile the horsemen, who we said above went into the inn, interrogate the servant, who, the household being still asleep, had opened the door, where the general is, for so the soldiers called Rabirius. The servant showing them his sleeping-room they ascend two (of them). The third, to whom had been given the care of watching the horses, while he waits outside the door, exchanges talk with the soldier, who had been guide of the way to (them) coming from the guard-station. And now, the two conspirators having entered the bed-room, found Rabirius as yet lying in bed, yet awakened by the noise, although very slight, of (them) approaching. So not (nec) *thereupon delaying, they warn him, ' that he is taken, that it is open to him to choose, whether he would rather off-hand be killed (he perceived them (to be) sufficiently prompt to do that), or without violence, his clothes having been put on, be placed on a horse made ready for this use, and accompany themselves about to go to Broken bridge.*

ı

MATERIA.

Fellow . . puer, servus, *speaking from a Roman point of view.*

Chamber . i. e. '*sleeping chamber,*' cubiculum ; *here the Latin will be more precise than the English.* Camera, *would attract our attention to the architecture.*

Stay below foris maneo : ' qui foris manserat equos cústodiendi causa,' ' qui extra portam ceteros opperiebatur.'

Held . . *not* retineo, *unless the horses showed a desire to run away* ; *here be more general than in the English.*

Talk with . garrire, loqui, serere, caedere sermones.

The little noise *that is, ' the noise although little,' ' however little :*' ' quamvis levissimo strepitu.'
in Latin it is usual to express the logical connexion, which in English is only implied.

In his power integrum : ' non est integrum Pompèio con-
silio tuo jam uti.'

Would be killed or i. e. '*preferred to be :* ' ' utrum mavis abire an occidi ? ' ' malo mori quam foedari.'

Resistance 'sine reluctatione,' *is perhaps too clumsy* ; 'sine vi,' *would do, or,* ' volens.'

Mounted . subjicio, *implying rather acceptance of help.*
impono : *suggesting passive resistance.*

25.

40. *The present danger awakened him* . . .

PRAEPARATIO.

' One of *them*,' the conspirators; a noun, or a proper
name, or some other distinctive word, had better be sub-
stituted in the Latin for an ambiguous pronoun, wherever
perspicuity requires the change.   That ' *he* ' might be
mounted behind ' *him.*'   *Who* behind *whom* ?   Try to
make this impossible to be misunderstood in the Latin.
Would ' *ut victus victori alligaretur,*' help us ?   Or, ' *tum
vero Rabirius exclamare coepit, quum id agi intelligeret ut
ipse equiti averso alligaretur* ? '   Let our first object be to
make the main statements clear and definite.   More than
half the difficulty will be overcome when we have distinguished what is important, what is indispensable to the
right understanding of the story, from what is less important.

CONSTRUCTIO.

*Present danger dispelled stupor from Rabirius.   He
promised that he would be obedient to their word; and
would put on his clothes as quickly as he could.   Then his
sword having been taken away they escort him out of doors.
Meanwhile, he who was guarding the horses, had sent away
the soldier, and had given-him-injunctions that he should re-
seek his own (comrades) and procure drink and if anything
else was ready to hand.   But Rabirius, having come out of*

doors ('*foras egressus*' is better than '*in viam egressus*,' because the '*ex*,' '*in*' are unsymmetrical, and would grate on a Roman ear) *when, contrary to expectation, he saw all things empty of soldiers, nor any one to be present, save one who was holding the horses, presently they lifting him on to the horse that he might be tied to the back of the rider, began to resist and to cry out. Him resisting, since there was no hope of carrying him away, they transfix with swords; and, he being left dead on the ground, flee away to their own (comrades), no chance of pursuing being given to any of those who were within.*

MATERIA.

Awaken .   expergefacio : 'expergefactus e somno.'

            excutio : 'excute corde metum;' 'excusso somno.'

            discutio : 'sole orto est discussa caligo;' 'discussit terrores animi.'

Wait upon   appareo : 'apparere consulibus solebat.' *So* 'apparitor;' *but here go straight to the point and say,* 'se dicto audientem fore.'

Make haste propero, festino, maturo, celero : 'maturare datur, quae mox properanda forent.'

Lead down deduco : 'eum concionari conantem de rostris deducunt;' 'magna multitudo optimorum civium me de domo deduxit.'

            duco, *generic* : 'ducite ab urbe domum.'

Stairs . . scalae : *but there is no need to dwell on this detail of house construction, in this place.*

Go . . . *use a compound verb in preference to a simple, if, as is generally the case, it adds clearness* : 'abeo,' *here, is better than* 'eo.'

Against . . *Preposition* : 'in eorum adventum;' *or, conj.* 'dum:' 'Tityre, dum redeo, brevis est via, pasce capellas.'

Behind . . 'aversus,' *turned away* ; ' 'adversus,' '*front-ing*: ' 'scribit in aversa Picens epigram-mata charta,' i. e. ' *on the back of*: ' 'aver-sas traxit in antra boves,' '*dragged back-wards*.'

a tergo, post tergum : 'manibus post terga revinctis.'

Bind . . . ligo ; ad, '*to* : ' 'adligatus est ad palum ; ' de, '*from* ;' *or*, '*up to* :' 'viros ac feminas ad stipitem deligari jussit ; ' cum, '*together* :' 'i, lictor colliga manus.'

Struggle . luctor : ' in reluctantes dracones.'

repugno, reclamo.

Rode away *not* ' abequito ;' *although this word occurs once in Livy, use a more general term* '*departed quickly*.'

26.

41. *When those at the bridge* . . .

PRAEPARATIO.

'Those at the bridge.' Let us recapitulate the story for the sake of clearness. The royalist party consisted of twelve horsemen, led by Morrice. First, they all rode to the inn, a Cromwellian soldier being told off to show them the way. Three entered the inn. Ten rode on to the bridge leading to Pomfret, where they waited gossiping with the guards. The guards about this time, being off duty, disperse, most of them, to their quarters. The three have by this time killed Rainsborough, and are making with all speed for the bridge.

The remainder of the story, related in the present passage, will now be quite clear.

'Their garrison,' the royalist garrison at Pomfret.

' The town,' Doncaster.

' Their general,' Rainsborough.

' The devil.' This is a conception not known, at least under this name, to the Latin writers of the Augustan age.

What then was their substitute? Not ' *demons,*' for at that time the ' δαίμονες ' had not yet lost their character. *Demon* is Greek; the equivalent Latin word is ' *genius,*' or ' *lar,*' both virtuous and benevolent powers.

Let us try the most general idea first. ' *Putabant id divinitus esse factum* : ' 'they thought it was supernatural.' This would do. But the diabolical element is hardly taken into account. Can we get a step nearer? Would ' *larvae* ' help us? *Larvae* are hobgoblins who frighten people, and play evil pranks, as in Plautus we read: ' *Haec quidem, edepol, larvarum plena est !* ' ' *Why, the woman is possessed !* '

Probably, ' *larvarum id opera fieri vel, factum esse putabant* ' would be intelligible to a contemporary of Cicero, and suggest the state of perplexity in which the townsmen found themselves.

CONSTRUCTIO.

Whom when the rest from the bridge saw approaching, for so they had agreed upon before, being prepared for the deed, and sufficiently aware what had to be done, having turned upon the guards they slew many. The rest fled in distraction; and the way was cleared. And so, not with unaccomplished purpose, albeit they had missed the prey so boldly sought, a band having been formed, using as much speed as was necessary, by a shorter route they returned again to the camp. Meanwhile so great terror invaded the

*townsmen and garrison soldiers, that, since they could find
out nothing from Rabirius himself, whom they found lying-
dead on the ground, nor any one else in sight, they thought
the deed to have been done by the agency of evil spirits
(goblins).   Nor in the so great trepidation of all, could they
sufficiently unravel a method by which a foe, whom they had
not even seen, was to be pursued.*

MATERIA.

Saw . . . video, *most general term.*
  cerno, '*distinguish with the eyes.*'
  aspicio, '*behold,*' '*look at.*'
  conspicio, '*catch sight of,*' '*view.*'
  conspicor, '*catch sight of.*'
  specto, '*to be a spectator,*' '*to look on.*'
  intueor, '*to gaze at.*'

Knowing . satis gnari quid faciendum esset.

**In distrac-
  tion** } amens, inops animi : temere, effuse, fugientes.

Miss . . . 're infecta revertor.'
  'destinatum non ferire : 'a destinato aberarre,'
    literally of shooting at a mark.
  'irritus legationis,' '*having failed in his mis-
    sion* ;' 're infecta.'
  fallo : 'spes praedae eos fefellerat ; ' 'res spem
    fefellit.'
  frustror : 'jam me saepe spes frustravit,' *or*
    'frustrata est,' *deponent.*
  amitto, '*to let slip.*'

Adventure res, facinus, inceptum, alea.

Lusty . . 'plagam luculentam accepit,' '*he received a
    lusty blow.*' *But it is better to construe the
    thought than the word* : 'tam audax in-
    ceptum.'

Joined . . 'agmine facto ;' *or*, 'in unum collecti.'

Garrison . castra, *often* 'aestiva,' *or* 'hiberna,' *as the case may be.*

Consterna- 'pavor, ac consternatio.'

tion . . trepidatio: 'nec opinata res plus trepidationis fecit.'

attonitus, obstupefactus, stupens, '*thunder-struck.*'

Information comperio, *verb* : 'nihil compertum habuit.'

Anybody . *after negative,* 'quisquam.'

Recollect . 'expedire rationem :' 'quemadmodum expediam exitum hujus institutae orationis, non reperio.'

27.

49. *Travelling through a forest* . . .

PRAEPARATIO.

Latin prose has a tendency to be more explicit than English : e. g. 'in a moment :' here it is better to insert '*ita faciam,*' or '*jumenta convertam,*' which is only implied in the English. 'The storm ;' state in full, '*iram domini,*' or '*Caesaris furentis rabiem.*' It is not enough to hint at the meaning as in English. 'He shall turn.' Turn what? The object must be expressed in the Latin.

'Had done so.' Done what? Turned the horses and carriage. This must be stated explicitly in the Latin.

So in such phrases as 'those from the citadel,' the Latin idiom requires an explicit statement, as '*ii qui ab arce venerant.*' 'A letter from the king,' '*epistola ab rege missa.*'

Cicero will be the best model for this piece. Such treatises as that *De Officiis* (*vide De Off.* 3. 61), *De Divinatione, De Natura Deorum,* abound in anecdotes.

Constructio.

By chance, making a journey through a forest bordered on each side by marshes, he suddenly conceived in his mind I know not what whim for returning, and bade the coachman turn the horses.   To him delaying the king repeated the order.   Then the coachman answering that he would do it shortly, that the road was too narrow there, Paullus inflamed with anger leapt down from the carriage, and (to) the equerry being summoned gave orders that he should stop the horses, and chastise the man too little obedient.   But he, wishing to allay the rage of his master, said that the driver would turn the team as soon as it could be done.   To whom Paullus, 'Both thou, scoundrel, and yonder one are good-for-nothing.   May I perish miserably unless he shall have turned the carriage at once.   It must be obeyed, what I order, at whatsoever peril.'   Meanwhile the coachman had fulfilled his orders, yet only in such a way that having been badly mauled he made a pretty good atonement.

Materia.

With . .   cingo : 'via utrimque paludibus cincta;' 'quae media inter paludes per silvam ducebat.'

Recollected   subeo : 'subiit animo aliquid;' 'venit in mentem nescio quid;' 'subiit nescio quae lubido revertendi.'

Driver . .   redarius, *'coachman ;'* auriga, *'charioteer.'*

Turn . . .   *insert the object turned* : currum, equos, jumenta.

Do . . .   cesso, *'to be slow about a thing:'* 'imus in adversos.   Quid cessas ?'

Repeated .   itero : haec resonis iterabat vocibus, 'Heu ! Heu !' 'bis terque clamavit;' 'id repetens iterum monebat.'

Leapt out .   desilio, *with the object of punishing the driver* :
                  'curru fremebundus ab alto desiluit.'

                  exsilio, *regards rather the point from which
                  the impulse originated* : 'impetu pertur-
                  batus exsiluisti.'

Carriage .   vehiculum, currus, 'currum agere,' 'curru
                  vehi.'

                  bigae, '*carriage and pair.*'

                  rheda, *four wheeled* : 'rhedarum transitus
                  arcto vicorum inflexu.'

                  carpentum, *two wheeled, for ladies.*

                  pilentum, *easy carriage, for ladies.*

                  carruca, *travelling carriage.*

                  cisium, '*cab.*'

Equerry .   equiso, '*groom.*'

                  stipator, '*personal attendant.*'

                  satelles, '*king's guard.*'

                  pedisequus, '*lacquey.*'

Chastise .   castigo, '*to punish,*' *for the good of the person
                  punished* : 'Cicero dicit pueros non verbis
                  solum, sed etiam verberibus castigandos
                  esse.'

                  punire, *by way of retribution.*

Him . . .   parum obedientem, *implied in the context.*

Allay . .   sedo : 'sedavit animos, iram, militum.'

                  mitigo, animum, dolorem, ferocitatem.

                  mulceo, aliquem dictis.

Turn . . .   conversurum. *The object must be expressed* :
                  'jumenta eum conversurum esse dixit.'

As soon as   quum primum id fieri posset.

                  quam primum : 'ut quam primum possis,
                  redeas ;' 'huic mandat, ut ad se quam
                  primum revertatur.'

You   furcifer, qui furcam fert, *an instrument of
scoundrel   punishment in the form of a fork placed
                  on the neck* : 'servus per circum quum

virgis caederetur, furcam ferens ductus
est.'   *A term of reproach, 'jail-bird.'*

nequam, *from* ne-aequus, '*worthless,*' '*good
for nothing*;' *opposed to* frugi, '*respect-
able* :' ' malus et nequam es.'

Break my   *literally,* 'vel si cervicem mihi fregerit,' *but say,*
neck   'male peream ni . . .' *a common form of
imprecation. So,* 'di te perdant, di de-
. aeque omnes te perduint nisi . . .'   *This
is the spirit of the Czar's exclamation.*

All hazards 'quocumque periculo meo.'

The mo-   e vestigio : 'e vestigio loci et temporis;'
ment   ' repente e vestigio ex homine tamquam
aliquo Circaeo poculo factus est Verres.'

statim : ' statim dimisit nuntios.'

confestim : ' confestim aut ex intervallo aliquid
consequi.'

Too late to ita tamen ut, *a favourite idiom in Latin* : '*yet
with this modification, that he got a
beating.'*

To save him- male mulcatus, *literally* '*badly mauled.'*
self a sound '*sound,*' luculentus: 'ipse plagam luculentam
beating.   accepit ;' '*he got a shrewd knock,*' '*a
pretty hard knock.'*

poenas luculentas dederit, i. e. '*great, serious
atonement.'*

28.

50. *An order against wearing boots . . .*

PRAEPARATIO.

The title of 'Czar' must of course be rendered by
Caesar.

'Boots.' It will be advisable at this point to consult

the Dictionary of Antiquities, to find out what the Romans wore on their feet, whether they habitually wore shoes, or sandals? When and on what occasions they wore boots? Till that is done we shall be at a loss how to deal with the 'purple tops.' Meanwhile, will these expressions help us? '*Mutavit calceos.*' '*Veniam caligatus in agros.*' '*Appositam nigrae lunam subtexit alutae.*'

'Nobleman.' '*Senator*' would do here, not because 'senator' is equivalent in all senses to 'nobleman,' but with reference to Caesar: because it was so often a senator that was the victim of Nero's or Caligula's capricious cruelty. We want every key word to be not only appropriate in itself, but suggestive of cognate images. '*Nobilis*' would rather fix the attention too exclusively on his rank. '*Optimates,*' this word is suggestive of oligarchs and factions, with which we have nothing to do here.

'Pelisse.' Consult some book on Roman antiquities, to find out how the Romans were clothed.

'Work.' We must be careful in choosing our word. '*Laboro*' is too suggestive of toil and distress. '*Opera*' with appropriate verb might help. But look out '*vaco,*' and trace it through all its meanings and usages, and then decide. Compare σχολάζειν μουσικῇ in Greek. Consider whether there is not a closer relation really between the first sentence and the second sentence than is expressed in the English. This will decide the form of the two sentences.

'Order against.' The language of legal forms and prohibitions must be consulted, and we must adopt some word or formula that may be suggestive. Such are '*Lege XII Tabularum cautum est, ne quis civem in servitutem vindicaret.*' '*Intra muros urbis mortuum ne sepelito,*

*neve urito.'　'Parricidii reum infelici arbore reste sus-
pendito.'　'Consulem edicere, ut senatus senatusconsulto
ne optemperet.'　'Edicere est ausus ut senatus ad vestitum
rediret.'*

CONSTRUCTIO.

*When it had been provided by edict, that no one should
wear boots bordered with a purple edging, very strict notice
was taken of offenders. The tyrant therefore (so) bidding,
a certain one thus booted, while he is borne in a carriage
along the street, was compelled to halt by a policeman. But
he (began) to protest, to imprecate evils on himself, if these
were not the only boots he had at hand, to deny that he
would cut the border off them. Then indeed two officers,
each, a leg of him sitting in the droschsky having been seized,
pull off his boots, dismiss him with bare feet.*

*By chance walking in the city he saw a senator, who
stood gazing at some workmen of his own occupied in
planting trees, to whom Caesar, 'Ho there you, what are
you doing?' and he, 'I am giving my leisure to the labour
of (those) planting.' But Caesar, 'Oh indeed!' Then,
being turned to the lictor, 'Draw off from this man his
pelisse,' he says, 'Give him a spade.' And to the Senator,
"Lo, the implement! Do you yourself give your labour
to the planting.'*

MATERIA.

Order . . edictum, '*a manifesto,' issued by ediles, tribunes,
dictator, consuls, emperor, praetor.*

Wearing . induo, *but more explicitly*: 'ne quis calceos
... indutus in publico incederet.'

Enforced . animadverto, '*to notice for punishment,' 'take
notice of*:' 'illud facinus animadverten-

dum est ; ' ' in Marcianum, ut in libertum, palam animadversum est.'

Police . . vigiles, lictores, milites : ' rarus venit in cenacula miles.'

' viator,' *an officer who summons people before a magistrate.*

Stop . . . *intrans.* consisto, sto : ' stat contra starique jubet.'

Remonstrate reclamo : ' ab universo senatu reclamatum est.'

Droschsky cisium : 'inde cisio ad urbem celeriter advectus domum venit.'

Let go . . dimitto : ' hostem ex manibus dimittet.'

Street . . via : ' ibam forte viâ sacrâ sicut meus est mos.'

vicus, *'row of houses, quarter of a town*:' 'dictus sceleratus ab illa vicus;' ' *village*,' ' *canton*:' si quis Cobiamacho, qui vicus inter Tolosam et Narbonem est, deverteretur.'

platea, *street, square*: ' purae sunt plateae.'

Stopped to look at . specto, *a continuous tense of a verb meaning ' to look at,' will be enough here.*

Workman. opera, *used generally in the plural* : ' plures operas conduxit.'

Plant . . sero : ' serit arbores quarum aspiciet baccam ipse nunquam.'

Do . . . ago : ' quid agis?' *' what are you about ?'* also, *' how are you ?'* ' *how do you do ?*'

facio : ' quid facis?' *' what are you doing ?'* ' quid faceret miser ? ' *' what could he do, poor man ?*'

Merely . . ' nihil nisi ;' ' nihil aliud facio quam ;' ' id ago ut operae serentium vacem.'

Spade . . pala : ' palas sibi emendas ait, ut hortum fodiat.'

ligo, ' *hoe*:' ' purgare ligonibus arva.'

There now eccam, i. e. ' ecce illam palam.'

29.

51. *One pathetic yet ludicrous occurrence* . . .

PRAEPARATIO.

'Pathetic,' 'ludicrous,' we must not expect the Latin equivalent in the form of an adjective; we must determine the exact sense of 'pathetic' and 'ludicrous,' and express it by any parts of speech we can.

'Number of them,' beware of attempting word for word translation. '*Numerus eorum, manus eorum, copia eorum pertinentium,*' would be ambiguous, meaningless, or ungrammatical

'Suicide,' neither shall we find this in the form of a single equivalent noun-substantive in Latin. '*Conscisco*' is the key word: which look out in the dictionary.

CONSTRUCTIO.

Concerning voluntary death among the Indians this circumstance is narrated; fitted to excite both pity and laughter. Some of those, not a small band, who were slaves of one master, had determined to bring death upon themselves by hanging, if perchance they might be able to escape the miseries and labours of life. But the master, having been made acquainted with their design, came among them just then about to kill themselves, and ' Prythee, a rope,' he says, 'for me ; for by me too it has been resolved to die with you.' At the same time he informs them, that he cannot live without them, for that to be deprived of their usefulness was intolerable, that, whither they were about to go, thither it must be gone by himself also. Therefore the slaves, believing that they would not escape out of his hands even after death,

K

determined to remain in life ; and the halters having been regretfully laid down proceeded to return (imperfect) *to their several (own) tasks.*

MATERIA.

Suicide .	voluntaria mors : 'aut capiendus exsilio locus aut consciscenda mors voluntaria.'
Came upon	supervenio: 'addit se sociam timidisque supervenit Aegle.'
	intervenio : ' sponsae pater intervenit.'
	deprehendo : 'in aliquo scelere deprehendi.'
	intercedo, *generally for the purpose of interference.*
Go seek .	' cedo restim,' '*here, give me a rope.*' ' Cedo' *is an old imperative form. It implies haste, authority, familiarity, and so differs from* ' da,' ' praebe,' ' effer.' ' *Quick ! I say !*'
Must . . .	*the obligation depends on the resolve of the speaker* : *say,* ' certum est.'
Gave to understand	doceo : ' docui per literas id nec opus esse nec fieri posse.'
Future state	'ne post mortem quidem carere malis homines puto.'
Agreed . .	convenit: 'inter omnes conveniebat ut abirent.'
	statuo : 'statuerunt nihil de illo dicere.'
Lay aside .	depono : 'deposuit fasces.'
With sorrow	aegre : 'discessit aegre ferens:' ' invitus haec scribo.'
Labour . .	pensum, '*task-work of slaves* :' 'pensum meum confeci.'

30.

62. *With the theft of the palladium* . . .

What do we know about the Palladium? Why the theft? Who were the thieves, that—

> '*Fatale aggressi sacrato avellere templo*
> *Palladium, caesis summae custodibus arcis,*
> *Corripuere sacram effigiem?*'

We must learn the circumstances of the theft of the image of Minerva, by the impious Tydides, '*scelerumque inventor Ulixes*,' before we can see the fitness of the comparison.

We should then refer to Livy for a standard of description, and a pattern to copy. The exploit of M. Scaevola in Livy ii. 12, or that of Horatius Cocles ii. 10, will be found useful reading before beginning to put Fernando's exploit into Latin. Another night adventure of desperate hardihood is that of Nisus and Euryalus recorded in the ninth Aeneid.

The first difficulty is how to deal with the proper names: and this will depend on the method we adopt in regard to the whole piece. The best way will be in our first draught to look at everything from the point of view of our master, Livy. Let the hero be Horatius, Mucius, or Fabius. Let Veii stand for Granada. Let the mosque be represented by a Veientine temple. The other accessories will easily accommodate themselves. Our Fabius may be represented as nailing up a tablet on altar, wall, or statue, and so vindicating that temple to the service of the gods of Rome. There would be no impropriety in his rededicating the temple to the 'mother of the Gods.'

By passing through this process the composition can hardly fail to imbibe a classical colouring. This is our immediate object.

CONSTRUCTIO.

Not unworthy to be compared with the theft of the Palladium seems the exploit of F. P. Pulcherius. Who, when the Spaniards were besieging Granata city, having meditated a design of almost reckless audacity, is related to have said to his comrades standing round, 'Which of you, O youths, will be present as sharer with me about to dare a matter-of almost desperate hazard?' And they say that not one of those who heard, although the disposition of the man, bold even to rashness, was known to all, hesitated to (quin) give in his name. Accordingly, fifteen having been chosen out of more, the ablest both of body and spirit, in the dead of night he led out from the camp. Then having proceeded cautiously to the city, they reached a postern gate of the wall looking towards the river Darro, and guarded by foot-soldiers There, most of those who kept watch being buried in sleep, since that incursion was unexpected, they burst through the gates. There followed a confused struggle.

MATERIA.

Siege . . . oppugnatio, *subs.* oppugno *verb*; *of active attack, and, generally, hostile proceedings for the purpose of capturing a town*: 'oppugnari coeptum est Saguntum.'
obsidio, obsideo; *siege by investment, block-ade*: 'ab obsidione liberavit urbem.'
expugnatio, expugnare; *capture by storming.*

Peril . . . alea : 'periculosae plenum opus aleae.'

Rash . . perdita audacia; temeraria virtus.

Hardihood   'etsi nota erat viri usque ad temeritatem audax indoles.'

Hesitate .   dubito, '*to hesitate from ignorance or misgiving*:' 'nolite dubitare quin credatis.'

haesito, *through embarrassment.*

cunctor, *from lack of resolution* : 'utrisque cunctantibus periculum summae rei facere.'

cesso, '*to hang back*,' *generally from slothfulness* : 'ad arma cessantes concitet;' 'ne quis in eo quod me viderit facientem · cesset.'

Step forward nomen do, profiteor, *of volunteers.*

Dead of .   media nocte, concubia nocte.

Until . .   quoad ; *but another form of logical connection would be preferred in Latin* : '*having marched forward they reached.*'

Postern . .   posticus, *adj.* '*at the back* :' ostium.

posticum, '*the back door* :' 'atria servantem postico falle clientem.'

Opened . .   specto : 'ad meridiem spectat.'

Attack . .   incursio : 'subitas hostium incursiones sustinere.'

Chance . .   confusum certamen: 'caeco Marte pugnatum est.'

Adv. forte : 'quae forte fortuna fieri putamus.'

Medley. .   temere : 'pepulerunt ut forte temere in adversos montes agmen erigeret.'

31.

63. *Fernando stopped not to take* . . .

Praeparatio.

When the classical names such as Mucius, Veii, Vesta, or whichever we may have chosen to represent Pulgar, Granada, and the rest, have served their turn, we may

restore the originals.   But even here it will be as well to
retain as much of the classical form as possible.   Let
each name have a Latin termination.   Fernandus, Petreius,
Pulgaris, or Pulcherius, would sound like Latin.   We
might even venture to translate Pulgar, by Pulex; for
that surname was once borne by a M. Geminus Servilius
Pulex.

We might also restore Granata.   But there is no need
to displace 'the mother of the gods:' and no absolute
necessity for bringing in '*Christiani*,' where '*nostri*' would
do.   Moslems might be rendered '*Mauri*,' or even '*barbari*,' and so we shall not have travelled beyond the words
sanctioned by the best classical authors.

'Christian warrior' may be sufficiently expressed by
'*hostis*,' such was Fernando's aspect at the moment.   His
most striking characteristic in the eyes of the astounded
Granadinos was that he was an armed enemy.

CONSTRUCTIO.

*The rest then fighting chance-medley, Pulcherius himself,
the contest being omitted, his horse being put to full speed,
while fires sparkle struck out at every step, speeding through
the streets, arrived at the temple which stands out the most
celebrated in that city.   Then he leapt down from his horse,
and bending on his knee at the porch, dedicates to the mother
of the gods that fane, as if vindicated into the rightful
possession of his country's gods.   In witness of which dedi-
cation, when, a tablet, which he had brought with him,
inscribed with the name of the goddess, he had affixed to the
temple with his dagger, his horse having been mounted, he
hastened back again to the gate.   Meanwhile a clamour
having been raised by the sentinels, an alarmed bustle spread*

(impersonal, '*coeptum est trepidari*') *all over the city: soldiers flocked together from all sides: all were stupefied at the miracle of an armed enemy hastening from the inner part of the city. But he, some, who stood in his way, being thrust off, others slain, reached his own (men), who, by strenuously fighting, still held the gate. Thence all betook themselves in safety to their camp.*

MATERIA.

Stopped not omitto, praetermitto : 'certamen praetermisit ;'
           'a certamine se abstinuit.'

Spur . . . calcar : 'subdo calcaria ;' 'addit equo calcar.'

Gallop . . citato equo feror.

Strike . . excudo : 'scintillam excudit Achates.'

Bound . . gressus : 'gressus glomerare superbos.'
           gradus : 'tertio quoque gradu substitit.'
           saltus : 'saltu super ardua venit Pergama Durateus equus.'

Portal . . tecti limen.
           janua, porta : 'vestibulum ante ipsum.'

Kneel . . in genua procumbo.
           genibus nitor ; genua submitto.

Possession vindico : 'videor id meo jure quodam modo vindicare.'

Dedicate . dedico, dico, consecro.

Ceremony. caerimonia, *not explicit enough here.*
           say 'dedicatio,' *which is the ceremony meant.*

Took and }
  nailed   } *Aorist tense.*

Inscribe . inscribere: 'in statua incripsit, "Parenti optime merito ;"' 'ut, si quae essent incisae aut inscripta literae, tollerentur ;' 'aram condidit dedicavitque ingenti rerum a se gestarum titulo ;' 'signa cum titulo laminae aeneae inscripto.'

Nailed . . affigo : 'signa Punicis affixa delubris ;' 'leges ad parietem fixae clavis ferreis.'

Dagger . . pugio, *from* pungo : ' *dirk.*'

          sica, ' *a curved dagger.*'

Alarm . . 'clamor "ad arma" cives concitantium.'

Uproar . . tumultus : 'omnia belli trepido concussa tumultu.'

          Verb, trepidare coepit : 'trepidari coeptum est.'

Astonished stupeo : 'vigiles attoniti et stupentibus similes.'

Overturn . subverto : 'subvertit mensam.'

          sterno : 'manu tum sternit Aphidnum.'

          caedo : 'protinus innumerae caedunt pineta secures ;' caede sterno.

          dejicio, *of objects shot at from a distance.*

          detrudo, ' *push,*' ' *thrust down.*'

          affligo, ' *dash down.*'

          proturbo : 'hostes hinc cominus proturbamus.'

Retreat . . 'tuto se in castra recepit equitatus.'

          Subs., 'Caesar receptui cani jussit.'

32.

78. *We went down stairs directly . . .*

CONSTRUCTIO.

We went down into the street forthwith, well satisfied to have found some one who was willing to afford us protection. Many there (were) the bodies of dead (people), many of the dying (that) we saw. At the same time it was (possible) to hear many piteous voices, such as would touch any nature however savage. To us stepping over the bodies, when it was come to Catharine's (church) a horseman comes in the way, a man of the highest dignity. He, as he caught sight

of us, and saw me indeed covered with blood, having turned
towards our guide, says, ' Fellow-soldier, beware that you do
no evil to those (istis) *persons.' Next addressing my wife,*
he asks, ' whether the house he saw (subjunctive) *was ours?'*
But she says, yes. Then the knight, ' But thou,' he says,
' do not depart from my side : lead us to yonder house ; I
promise you (plural, i.e. *both of you*) *faith and protection.'*
Then looking at me, whilst he stretches his right hand
towards the soldiers, he says to me, ' Citizens of Magde-
burgh, with you lies the blame of this destruction, in whose
power it was to do otherwise.'

MATERIA.

Stairs . . scalae : ' scalis habito tribus et altis ;' *but say*
here ' in plateam descendimus,' *which is*
the main point.

Protector . tutor : ' *guardian of minors, women.*'
patronus : *in relation to* ' cliens.'
defensor : ' patronus, defensor, custos coloniae.'
better say ' aliquem qui nobis tutelam prae-
stare vellet.'

Barbarian . barbarus : ' neque civitas ulla tam immanis
ac barbara est.'
barbaria : *the quality*, ' ista vero quae et
quanta barbaria est ;' ' immane facinus
quod nulla barbaria posset agnoscere.'
say ' voces miserabiles quae nullam non bar-
bariam tangere possent.'

Walk . . incedo : ' incedis per ignes suppositos cineri
doloso.'

Fellow-sol-
dier } commilito : ' " commilito," quis jussit?'

Yonder . . iste, *when the second person is used* : ' istaene
sunt tuae aedes ?'

ille, *with the other persons* : 'rogavit, nos-
traene essent illae quas cerneret aedes?'

Say yes . . aio; *opposed to* ' nego:' 'hodie uxorem ducis?
Aiunt;' *'they say, yes.'*

Make a sign *say* 'dum intendit dextram ad milites.'

Occasion . culpa : 'penes vos est culpa hujus cladis, o
cives!'

33.

79. *The soldier who had used me ill . . .*

CONSTRUCTIO.

*Then the soldier who had used me ill, an occasion being
offered, secretly withdrew himself.   We enter into the house :
we find it crowded with robbers ; whom our knight, who
was of tribunician rank, commanded to go away.   Then he
said he had it in his mind to lodge with us, and, two
soldiers having been left for a guard, departed, having
promised that he would soon return.   We therefore give a
very good breakfast, and that most gladly, to our guardians.
They on the other hand (begin) to congratulate us, because
we (who) had fallen into the hands of the tribune.   Before
long (they begin) to ask for wages, for (they represented)
that they, whilst they bestow their attention on protecting us,
were gaining nothing, that the others were acquiring not a
little booty : therefore that it was fair, that (men) who un-
willingly continued inactive should be compensated by a
payment.*

MATERIA.

Treat . . . habeo : 'accurate ac liberaliter te habebant.'

Steal away surripio : 'surripuisti te mihi.'

subduco : 'de circulo se subduxit;' 'clam te
subduxisti mihi.'

Crowded . refercio : 'domus erat aleatoribus referta, plena ebriorum ; ' 'refertum mare prae-donum.'

Lodging . deverto : 'mihi in animo est devertere ad cauponem.'

deversor, deverso : 'cum Athenis apud Lysiam deversarem.'

Breakfast . prandium, *'a late breakfast,' 'lunch :'* 'adduxit Titium ad se ad prandium.'

jentaculum, *'early breakfast,' taken by children and invalids :* 'epulas interdum quadri-fariam dispertiebat, in jentacula et prandia et cenas commissationesque.'

Compliment gratulor : 'tibi gratulor quod te summa laus persecuta est.'

beatum, felicem dico : 'omnes me felicem di-cebant qui talem filium haberem.'

Fall into . incido : 'incidit in Scyllam qui vult vitare Charybdim.'

Booty . . praeda, 'praeda ante parta.'

Safeguard . custodia : 'dum regis custodiae operam dant.'

Inactive . *Subs.,* desidia, inertia, otium : 'cessantium inertiam castigant.'

Adj., 'sedemus desides domi spectatores otiosi calamitatis.'

Verb, 'cessamus et nihil agimus.'

Equivalent *Verb,* compenso : 'summi labores nostri magna compensati gloria.'

34.

80. *Upon this I gave them* . . .

CONSTRUCTIO.

To them making these demands I gave four gold (coins); *with which wages content, of such* (Lat. *qua* = for of such) *humanity were they, of their own accord they offered their*

services (operam) *for the collecting of our friends, if (there
was) any one we wanted to be placed in safety at our house.
I answered that there was one most familiar, who, as far as
I could conjecture, had fled to the temple of Concord; if by
their means he should have escaped safe and sound, that I
undertook to say that he would pay back a good recompense.
And so one of the two, my maidservant being his companion,
hastened to the temple, summons my friend by name twice and
three times; no answer was made to him calling: nor was
any mention of him brought to us after that.*

Materia.

Demand .   'postulantibus quatuor aureos dedi.'
Rose-nobles aureus : 'si contigit aureus unus.'
Search for   'ad conquirendos amicos nostros.'
Place   colloco : 'ibi exercitum hiemandi causa collo-
          cavit.'
Conjecture   quantum conjicerem, *subjunctive, because given
         as part of the speaker's representation to
         the guards. 'As far (I told them) as I
         could guess.' If the speaker appealed
         directly to the general reader he would
         use the indicative. 'As far as I (the
         historian) guessed; for between you and
         me, I had come to the conclusion that he
         had taken refuge in the cathedral.'*
Escaped to effugio, *regards the locus ex quo*; confugio,
         the locus ad quem.
         many verbs compounded with cum *imply
         motion, or intention to a certain point*:
         jacio, *'I throw';* conjicio, *'I aim at';*
         tendo, *'I stretch';* contendo, *'I hasten
         towards.'*
Saved . . 'si eorum ope salvus evasisset,' *pluperfect,
         because the escape must have preceded the*

payment, both events however being in the future.

Called . . cico, clamo, voco : 'nomine amicum meum vocabam ;' 'quis vocat ?' 'quis nominat me ?' 'Creusam iterumque iterumque vocavi.'

Mention . 'mentio nobis perlata est ;' 'qua de re tecum mentionem feceram.'

35.

85. *Such irreverent jests . . .*

CONSTRUCTIO.

That indeed (was said) not reverently enough, (or, too little reverently) : it does not however imply scoffing : for to jest thus is the part of one dreading and fearing the gods as much as of one despising. Nor is it to be supposed that the general's jokes were displeasing to the soldiers : nay rather (it is to be supposed) that they produced a belief in the hearers (participle), *that the consul, in saying these things, had a conviction that the gods would be propitious to him ; not otherwise than if any one, over his cups, should wish to indulge a pert slave. To this was added that Papirius performed very well the part of a general. For he is said to have practised a trick, celebrated in our, (i.e. modern), warfare also, with good issue, namely that, the panniers having been taken off, camp followers mounted on mules, in the midst of the contest, should show themselves to the Samnites, both on flank and on rear. Immediately, through both armies the rumour runs that Sp. Carvilius is present for the assistance of his colleague. Then indeed the Romans with all their cavalry and infantry, a charge having been made, break through the ranks of the Samnites, and turn them to flight. The greatest part of the infantry betook themselves into the camp, or inside the walls of Aquilonia. The cavalry, the nobility of the whole race, when they had disentangled themselves from the mass of fugitives* (participle) *fled to Bovianum.*

MATERIA.

Irreverent. 'id quidem parum verecunde: non tamen irrisionem necessario arguit: namque ita cavillari paventis et extimescentis deos perinde ac contemnentis est.'

Jests . . . jocus, *plural* joca: 'joca tua plena facetiarum;' 'ludo et joco ubi licet quum gravibus seriisque rebus satisfecerimus.'

ludus: 'ludus discendi non lusionis.'

cavillatio; frivola est; dicacitas salsa.

lepor, '*a pretty conceit,' or, 'a pleasant manner of conversing.'*

sales, '*jests,' 'sallies of ingenious raillery;'* 'sale et facetiis Caesar vicit omnes.'

facetiae: 'alias in verbo, alias in re inesse dicuntur facetiae.'

Servant. . servus, verna, minister: *which aspect of 'service' is presented to us? If servitude, use 'servus,' opposed to 'dominus.' If attendance, or waiting on, then 'minister,' opposed to 'magister.' If familiarity, with condescension on one side and pertness on the other,* 'verna,' *opposed to* 'herus:' 'vernasque procaces pasco libatis dapibus;' 'erat, tamquam verna, joco mordente facetus.'

Trick . . dolus: 'dolus an virtus, quis in hoste requirat.'

ars: 'nota jam callidus arte.'

Camp servants	lixae, '*sutlers*:' 'lixae permixti cum militibus.' calones : 'insidentes mulis calones.'
Baggage mules	jumenta sarcinaria : 'speculum civilis sarcina belli ;' 'detractis mularum clitellis impo-nendos calones curavit.'
Flank and rear	'a latere et a tergo Samnitibus impetum faci-unt.'
Clear	expedio : 'vix illigatum se triformi Pegasus expediet chimaerae.'

36.

113. *There is nothing in history* . . .

. CONSTRUCTIO.

To (men) reading the memorials of things, nothing else more useful is offered, than those records concerning the departure from life of illustrious men, which declare to us how they bore themselves in that supreme necessity. It is permitted also to add this (remark), that no events are re-corded which can more either move, or delight the mind of a reader. The reason of which thing (I imagine), consists in this, that out of all the things which are narrated about any man whatsoever, no other case, except death, can possibly befall each one of the readers (participle). *For how few, hope that they will ever take part in a battle or a triumph. But as often as we contemplate the lot of one about to die, we cannot help* (facere), *but (that we) consider everything he may say or do, with attentive mind: seeing that we are sure that we shall some day be in like fortune. Certainly to act the rôle of a general or a philosopher, or to guide the repub-lic does not fall to every man ; to act the part of a dying (man) sooner or later there is no one to whom it will not fall.*

MATERIA.

Sensible .	*Verb*, 'quae tantopere commoveant mentes ;' 'cetera quae vacuas tenuissent carmine mentes.'
Any . . .	quivis, '*any you please*,' '*every one* :' 'non cuivis homini contingit adire Corinthum.'
	quisquam, *always after negative* : haud quisquam, '*not any one.*'
Every one .	unusquisque, '*each individual.*'
	universi, '*all together.*'
	singuli, '*each severally.*'
One man in a million	*translate the thought, not the words* : 'quotus enim quisque.'
	rarus : 'rari quippe boni.' .
	pauci : 'pauci e multis.'
Cannot forbear	'non possumus facerē quin attente contemplemur ;' 'non possumus quin attendamus animum ad ea ;' 'non possumus non teneri.'
History . .	historia : 'erat enim initio historia nihil aliud nisi annalium confectio ;' 'nihil est in historia pura et illustri brevitate dulcius ;' 'quicquid Graecia mendax audet in historia.'
	memoria : 'liber quo iste omnium rerum memoriam breviter complexus est.'
	monumenta : 'commendare aliquid monumentis ;' 'monumenta rerum gestarum.'
Add . . .	'adde super dictis quod non levius valeat ;' 'addit etiam illud, equites non optimos fuisse.' *Notice that* 'illud,' *like the Greek* ἐκεῖνο, *is used to introduce a statement,* = '*this,*' '*this which I will now mention.*'
No parts in history which	'nulla res memorantur quae magis animum lectoris commoveant.'
Characters	*the metaphor here is taken from the stage* :

personam : 'quam magnum est, personam in republica tueri principis.'

also, gerere, agere.

May never act '*may*,' *it is possible that* : 'fieri potest ut partes ducis agamus.' *Notice however that* '*potest*,' *by itself, never means, 'it is possible;' it invariably means, 'he,' 'she,' or 'it is able.'*

est ut : 'est ut viro vir latius occupet campum.'

'non cuivis homini contingit regnare : cuique homini mori contingat necesse est.'

37.

114. *An infant comes into the world . . .*

· CONSTRUCTIO.

An infant produced into the light appears at first helpless and devoid of reason. Presently, it acquires strength, and, (its) body growing, the faculties of the mind are nourished. And, at first indeed, comes on the wanton age of childhood; to this succeeds the ardour of youth; next he is ranked among men, and becomes possessed of manly prudence.
' *Having reached this age for a little while he remains in a stand, flourishing with vigorous and unimpaired reason. Thence he feels-beforehand that he is becoming weak and inactive; diseases diminish his vigour, his eyes grow dim, his ears grow deaf. Not now do the joys of life, the conversation of friends, the society of children delight him. To the earth out of which he was made doth man bend himself; nor can his feet any longer support the burden of his tottering body: having sunk down on his bed he breathes out*

his spirit. At length buried in the earth he is resolved into his original dust. What then? Shall this body live again? Nature denies that man can live again. But a voice sent down from heaven thus exhorts us, 'Lo! I am the resur- rection and the life! who believes in me, he shall live, although he be dead.'

MATERIA.

Comes into editus in lucem, prodit.
               'nudus humi jacet infans indigus omni vitai auxilio.'

World . . orbis terrarum; homines; natura rerum.
          as a rule avoid 'mundus.' *There are in- numerable ways of expressing 'world' in Latin, according to the aspect presented for the occasion by this Protean 'world;' '*mundus,*' the Briton's favourite word, is rarely the right one.*
          lux *is appropriate here, of birth.*
          for the general sentiment of the passage compare Horace Ars Poet. 158:
          'Reddere qui voces jam scit puer et pede certo
          Signat humum, gestit paribus colludere, et iram
          Colligit ac ponit temere et mutatur in horas.
          Imberbus juvenis, etc. .   .   .   .
          Conversis studiis, aetas animusque virilis
          Quaerit opes   .   .   .   .   .
          Multa senem circumveniunt incommoda.'

Reason . . ratio, '*the intellectual faculty*:' 'omnia quae rationem habent praestant iis quae sunt rationis expertia.'
          mens, '*mind,*' *thinking faculty*: 'mens cui regnum totius animi a natura tributum est.'
          intelligentia, *the faculty by which the soul perceives existing objects.*

Childhood.   infantia, *sometimes extended over the first seven years of life.*

pueritia, puerilis aetas, anni, tempus.

Youth . .   adolescentia, *from fifteen to thirty*: 'citius adolescentiae senectus quam pueritiae adulescentia obrepit?'

also, people are called 'juvenes' *from twenty to forty.*

Manhood .   aetas virilis : 'nonnunquam illa aetas dicitur composita, Graece καθεστηκυῖα ἡλικία.'

Stationary.   quae in vestigio stat.

quae consistere videtur : *so, of disease*: 'videndum morbus an increscat, an consistat, an minuatur.'

in statione, *rare*: 'navis quae manet in statione,' '*without moving.*'

Society . .   consuetudo : 'is cum hominibus nostris consuetudinem, familiaritatem, amicitiam jungere volebat.'

'hominum cetus et celebrationes obire,' '*to go much into society.*'

Ground. .   humus : 'dejécto in humum vultu ;' 'reptat humi puer.'

Totter . .   labo, '*to be on the point of falling*:' 'paries labat, labuntur saxa, caementae cadunt.'

nuto, '*to nod to its fall.*'

titubo, '*to stagger*:' 'titubans annisque meroque.'

Resolved .   *loosed again*: 'gleba in pulverem resolvitur;' 'homo dicitur ab humo unde factus est, qua humabitur.'

Live again   'reviviscat Curius aut eorum aliquis.'

Resurrection   *this being a quotation, the words of the Vulgate ought to be used.*

38.

115. *We pass the first years . . .*

CONSTRUCTIO.

*We pass the first years of this life of ours in the darkness
of ignorance, those which follow in pain and labour, the last
part in grief and remorse, and the whole span-of-life in
error. Nor do we suffer ourselves to enjoy fully even a
single serene and cloudless day. For why? If we examine
this matter with sincerity, we shall certainly confess that our
troubles spring from ourselves. Virtue alone can render us
superior to Fortune. We desert the former leader, and it is
necessary that we contend with odds against us. Fortune
mocks us; she rolls us bound to her wheel: at her own
pleasure she either raises or depresses. Yet her power rests
upon our weakness. This is an inveterate evil indeed, but
(one) which may be cured* (impersonal), *for (there is)
nothing (which) a constant and sublime mind cannot effect.
The best remedies, as far as I have found out, are the dis-
courses of wise men, and the study of good letters. But to
these must be added the consent of the soul, for unless this*
(qui nisi) *be present the counsels even of the best advisers*
(participle and adverb) *become vain.*

MATERIA.

Pass . . . vitam, aetatem, tempus terere; *rather with a
notion of wasting*: 'diem sermone terere
segnities mera est.'
    dego: 'omne tempus aetatis sine molestia
degere.'

Life . . . vita, *generic term*: 'vita animantium.'

aetas, *considered as a period of time*: 'vix hominis aetas esset suffectura,' *a man's life-time would hardly be enough.*

Pain . . . dolor, *bodily or mental suffering*; also, *indignation from an insult* : 'dolor excitat iras;' 'nec solos tangit Atridas iste dolor.'

Grief . . aegritudo, *uneasiness of mind* : 'aegritudine mori.'

maeror, *mourning, sorrow* : 'maeror est aegritudo flebilis.'

luctus : 'est aegritudo ex ejus qui carus fuit interitu acerbo.'

Remorse . *no single word*; *suggestive words are* sollicitudo, dolor, cura quae remordet ; 'desiderium libertatis remordet animos.'

Standard . vexillum, '*military flag*:' 'ut vexillum tolleres.'

signum : 'signa relinquere,' '*to desert.*'

Wheel . . rota : 'versatur celeri fors levis orbe rotae.'

'multos, alterna revisens, Lusit et in solido rursus Fortuna locavit.'

Weakness . infirmitas corporis, animi ; *opposed to* firmitudo, robur.

debilitas, *from defects* : *opposed to* integritas, sanitas.

imbecillitas, '*helplessness.*'

Power . . vis, vires.

potestas.

potentia : 'nate meae vires, mea magna potentia solus.'

Mind . . . mens : 'mens sana in corpore sano.'

animus : 'quam elato quam excelso est animo.'

Discourse . sermo, *conversation* : 'sermones sapientium consuetudo bonorum.'

39.

116. *What gratitude do we not owe . . .*

CONSTRUCTIO.

Of how grateful a mind then ought we to be, towards those excellent men, who, although they departed from life many ages before us, yet by their writings still live, and converse with us, who are our guides and masters, and, in this navigation of life, in which our bark is continually agitated by storms of angers and of desires, perform as it were the duty of pilots.   For so philosophy directs us by a sure and not (nec) *difficult journey into a safe port.   I am not however aiming at this, O my friend, namely to exhort you,* (non id ago ut te adhorter) *to those studies of letters which I value most.   Nature, indeed, has given you a mind capacious of all knowledge, but Fortune has denied you leisure.   Still you, if at any time it has been allowed you to withdraw yourself a little from public business, have straightway betaken yourself to the conversations of philosophers.   Nor does it escape my notice that your memory not seldom performs for you the duty of a book.*

MATERIA.

Gratitude . *Subs.*, gratia : 'meritam alicui gratiam persolvere, referre,' '*to show gratitude.*'
gratiam habere alicui, '*to feel.*'
grates agere, '*to thank.*'
Adj., gratus : 'gratissimo animo bonos prosequimur ;' 'bene de se meritis gratum se praebet;' 'ut quam gratissimus erga te esse cognoscerer.'

Age . . . aetas, '*time of life* :' 'aetate puer.'
aurea aetas ; '*period* :' 'vixi annos bis centum, nunc tertia vivitur aetas.'

aevum, *poet.* : 'nunc aequali tecum floresceret
    aevo.'

seculum :. 'aliquot seculis post Scipio Car-
    thaginem cepit.'

tempora : 'antiquis temporibus.'

anni : 'multis ante annis.'

Works . . opus : 'habeo magnum opus in manibus.'

scriptum : 'cum eorum inventis scriptisque se
    oblectent.'

Pilot . . . gubernator, '*helmsman*:' 'qui sedet ad guber-
    nacla rei publicae.'

rector : 'rectorem navis compellat voce Me-
    noetes.'

Navigation , navigatio : 'in portum ex longa navigatione
    venimus.'

Verb, 'in hoc tam procelloso mari navigantibus
    nullus portus nisi mortis est.'

Storm . . '*tempest*:' 'subito coorta est atrox tem-
    pestas.'

procella, '*squall*:' 'tempestates et procellae
    rerum.'

hiems, '*winter*:' 'ab illa die pessima mutati
    coepit amoris hiems;' 'noctem hiememque
    ferens.'

Passions . 'perturbationes et motus animi quae Graeci
    πάθη vocant;' 'irae, odia, cupiditates, luc-
    tus, libidines.'

Taste . . *Subs.,* judicium, '*critical*:' 'sentitur latente
    judicio velut palato;' 'judicium subtile
    videndis artibus.'

elegantia, '*refinement*:' 'patris elegantia tincta
    filia.'

gustatus, '*appreciation*:' 'verae laudis gusta-
    tum non habere.'

studium : 'studio philosophandi imbutus;' 'a
    juris studio non abhorrens.'

Adj., 'animum habet sapientiae avidissimum;'
'mens omnis doctrinae capax.'

Leisure . .   otium : 'otio qui nescit uti plus negotii habet;'
'in otio de negotio cogitare oportet.'

Affairs . .   res : 'a rebus gerendis senectus abstrahit.'

Memory   .   memoria : 'memoriam bonam, firmam, immo
tenacissimam habet;' 'hoc in memoria mea
penitus insedit.'

Adj., 'mendacem memorem esse oportet.'

Instead . .   *Prep.,* pro : 'pro verbo proprio subjicitur aliud.'
Subs., loco, *when one thing counts for another*:
'te in germani fratris dilexi loco.'
vice : 'fungar vice cotis acutae.'

40.

117. *The prospect of* . . .

CONSTRUCTIO.

*The hope of a life about to be after death secretly refreshes
and consoles me. This beautifies with a certain glad
appearance all things that are about* (me). *This for me re-
joicing doubles pleasures, alleviates the burden of evils to me
afflicted. So long I can bear with equal mind annoyances
and misfortunes, diseases and pains, death itself, and, what
is worse than death, the loss of those whom I have loved, as
long as I have in view the everlasting joys of the life to
follow* (participle), *where neither fear nor apprehension is
present, nor pain, nor sorrow, no bitterness of disease, no
separation of friends. Why therefore should any one be so
odious as to tell me that these things are vain and fictitious?
Does he deserve well who announces evils? But if it is a
dream, allow me thus to dream pleasant things such as to*
(relative) *make me both happier and better.*

MATERIA.

Prospect . spes : ' spes est expectatio boni ; ' ' spes diutur-
nitatis et imperii.'
prospectus, *mostly of things within sight*:
' praebere prospectum navium.'
Verb, futura prospicere.

Future life vita futura, *better*, vita post mortem futura :
' expone igitur, si potes, remanere animos
post mortem.'

Comfort . solatium : ' vacare culpa magnum est solatium;'
' solatia luctus exigua ingentis.'
consolatio : ' stultam senectutem praeterita
aetas nulla consolatione permulcere
potest.'
Verb, ' in hoc communi malo consoletur se
conscientia optimae mentis.'

Nature . . *consider what the word ' nature ' means here.*
natura rerum, *' the cosmogony.'*
natura habitusque locorum, *' the physical
features.'*
natura deorum, *' the nature of gods.'*
better say here, ' omnia quae circa sunt,' *or*
' in prospectu sunt.'

Eternity . *Adjective*, aeternus, *of time without beginning
or end.*
sempiternus, *' everlasting*:' ' negant quidquam
esse sempiternum.'
Substantive, aeternitas : ' aeternitate fruuntur
animi.'
immortalitas : ' ea quae Socrates supremo
vitae die de immortalitate animorum
disseruit.'

Officious . molestus : ' abscede hinc, molestus ne sis.'
odiosus : ' odiosa et ingrata dona ; ' ' odiosa et
inepta sedulitas.'

Delusion .	*Verb*, 'fallor, an hoc verum est? verum est, non fallimur.'
	Subs., 'an me ludit amabilis insania?' 'certe est mentis gratissimus error.'
	Adj., 'falsum est id totum neque solum fictum, sed absurde et imperite fictum.'
Dream . .	somnium: 'quae sopitos deludunt somnia sensus;' 'eho! quae tu somnias; hic homo non sanus est.'
	'sine me hac ficta felicitate laetari.'
	'his rebus pascor, his delector, his perfruor.'
Happier .	'in te retinendo fuit Asia felicior quam nos in deducendo.'
	'nec enim melior vir fuit Africano quisquam, nec clarior.'

41.

130. *The generality of mankind . . .*

Taking Cicero, who deals with similar themes in the Tusculan Questions, for our model, we may adopt a somewhat argumentative style in this passage.

CONSTRUCTIO.

What?   Do not the greater part of men so live that they do not receive the least (bit) of pleasure from this so various and multiplied beauty of things which the vicissitudes of Nature display?   The sun's rising and setting, the diverse appearance of the waning and waxing moon, the fourfold mutations of seasons, and revolutions of stars, which are not effected without the greatest charm and variety of shapes and colours—all these things with many people are held in the number of things commonplace and habitual.   So true it is that they neither delight by their beauty, nor move by their grandeur the minds of those who, made blunter by daily habit, have no other regard for natural things, unless in so far as they subserve the comforts of human life.

There is no one, I fancy, who cannot remember a time when this fair show of the universe affected him gazing with no admiration; but to many will come to mind the remembrance that it first occurred to him to feel more rightly about the works of nature, then, when, in early youth, he was busied with the studies of Greek and Latin letters.

MATERIA.

World . . *Adv.*, hic: 'ubi ego sum? hicine an apud mortuos? Neque apud mortuos neque hic es.'

Subs., 'haec etiam in terris pulcritudo excitavit cupiditatem ea caelestia visendi.'

Scenery. . *no single equivalent, use some combination of such words as* forma, species, pulcritudo, amoenitas: 'amoenitates orarum et litorum.'

Ordinary . quotidianus: 'quotidianae vitae consuetudo.'
vulgaris: 'rarum hoc et haud vulgare.'
usitatus: 'usitatus honos pervulgatusque.'

Magni-   majestas: 'majestas templorum.'
ficence   splendor: 'harum rerum splendor omnis et amplitudo.'

Useful . . commodus: 'nec pecori opportuna nec commoda Baccho.'
utilis: 'utile lignum navigiis.'
Subs., utilitas: 'hominis utilitati agri omnes et maria parent.'
commodum: 'ex incommodis alterius sua comparant commoda.'
commoditas: 'plurimas et maximas commoditates amicitia continet.'

Remember   recordor, memini : 'sed parum est me hoc
                meminisse, spero etiam te, qui oblivisci
                nihil soles, nisi injurias, reminiscentem re-
                cordare ;' 'recordari pueritiae memoriam.'
                venit in mentem : 'tibi tuarum virtutum veniat
                in mentem ;' 'venit hoc mihi in mentem
                te tum aegrotasse.'

Study . . 'Literarum studia alit honos.'

42.

17. *There was then an illustrious . . .*

On account of his great age : propter provectam aetatem.

That the Senate was going to vote for the peace : patres in ea
sententia esse ut pax cum Pyrrho fieret.

Received him and led him : excipiunt et in curiam deducunt.

A respectful silence : tum ob reverentiam viri silentio omnium facto.

I wish I had been : utinam, ut sum caecus oculis, sic etiam auribus
surdus essem.

Voted for the war : bellum contra regem decreverunt.

43.

18. *After the battle of Panormus . . .*

Weary of the war : quos jam belli pertaesum erat.

Not so entirely but that : non tam penitus—ut non acciperent ;
or, ut nollent accipere.

According to the well known story : *say*, satis nota est fabula.

Under promise to return : jurejurando astrictus se rediturum si.

Arrival : '*I arrive at a place*' *is not* 'advenio,' *but* 'pervenio.'

As being no longer. '*To be a citizen*' *is* inter cives censeri.

Of their own body : *say*, ex eo ordine.

In the presence : coram legatis ; *or*, praesentibus legatis.

44.

20. *Sedition was spreading . . .*

The defence had been entrusted, etc. *It is better in Latin to
make Camillus the subject (a personal subject is generally
preferred in Latin) and to say, ' He had been left as pro-consul
with one legion and a small band,' etc.*

Proconsul : 'Proconsul,' *or,* 'proconsule:' *both are found.*

Small: 'exiguus,' *and* 'modicus,' *are often good substitutes for* 'parvus.'

From his late masters. *It would make the story clearer to say,* quas artes in castris Romanis stipendia merens edoctus erat.

Claimed the honours of conqueror. *Speaking from the Roman point of view, we might say,* insignia triumphalia ob victoriam ut debita sibi dari poposcit.

Was not aware: 'nescivit,' *or,* 'eum fefellit' *would do in a general way, but as being more suitable to the man, and the position, say,* neqne tum praesensit quam non diuturna ea fortuna foret.

45.

24. *We are told that Valerian . . .*

We are told: memoriae traditur Valerianum, *with infinitive to follow.*

Spectacle: majestatis afflictae spectaculum.

Foot: 'vestigium' *may be used for* 'pedem.'

To remember: *say,* nullis amicorum vocibus flexum fuisse ferunt, saepe monentium memor esset, etc. (*with or without* ut).

Pledge: pignus.

Insult: contumelia.

Sunk: occumbo.

Skin: *we cannot be too explicit in Latin, say,* cutem corpore detractam et faeno in speciem hominis fartam, in celeberrimo Persarum templo per multos annos servatam fuisse.

Real monument: *for the sentiment compare,* 'Exegi monumentum aere perennius.'

So often: *say,* '*which very many, the Romans erected, with vain arrogance.*'

Moral and pathetic: *we must not always expect to find the same ideas expressed in the same parts of speech in the two languages ; therefore we shall frequently have to explain the English. Say then,* Haec fabula mentibus et ad misericordiam et ad virtutem promovendis apta, num fide digna sit ambigi potest. *Notice that* 'potest ambigi' *is used impersonally.*

46

26. *When Dolabella was proconsul . . .*

Dolabella. *It is usual on the first mention of a person to give both praenomen and nomen* : say, Cn. Dolabella.

Taken the lives : vita privaverat, *not* vitis.

Confessed. *Imperfect, i.e. whenever she was asked.*

The said husband: ille idem maritus, et filius alterum filium mulieris exceptum insidiis occidisset.

' Pygmalion Sychaeum clam ferro incautum superat, factumque diu celavit.'

Put the case : referre ad concilium.

On the one hand, on the other : ' et—et.'

The crime of poisoning, etc. *Be as explicit as possible* : veneficium quo maritus et filius necati essent.

Crimen, '*the charge* :' scelus, '*the wickedness* :' facinus, '*the bad deed*.'

A well deserved punishment had been, etc. : digna tamen paena in homines sceleratos vindicatum esset.

47

132. *A dervise travelling through Tartary . . .*

A dervise travelling : forte Anacharsis dum per Scythiam iter facit. *For Anacharsis, see* Herodotus iv. 46. 75. *There is no term in Latin co-extensive with ' dervise.' If the anecdote turned upon ' dancing' as a form of religion,* ' Gallus,' *a priest of Cybele, might do. But the aspect presented to us here is that of the intelligent traveller. As a general expression* ' philosophus quidam' *would do. But '* Anacharsis' *suggests the most prominent qualities of the dervise in this story. Similarly,* 'Solon' *might serve our turn, with reference to his visit to Sardis, and his interview with Croesus. See* Herod. i. 29.

By mistake, thinking it to be a public inn : fertur in regias aedes intravisse perperam id hospitium publicum esse credens.

Laid down his wallet and spread his carpet : peram deposuit, tegetem substravit, more patrio in ea discubiturus ; ' cum baculo peraque senex' *is used of a Cynic philosopher* : ' ausa Palatino tegetem praeferre cubili.'

Before he had been there long: nec diu ibi requieverat et unus ex stipatoribus regiis eum conspicatus rogavit.

Intended to pass the night there: cogitare se in illo hospitio noctem commorari.

Not an inn but: miles increpitare et dicere illam domum regiam non deversorium esse.

48.

133. *During this debate the king . . .*

During this debate: dum haec agitantur.

How he could be so dull: qui posset ita hebes esse ut internoscere nequiret. ' Qui ' *is the ablative of* ' quis.'

O king, give me leave to ask you: 'Tua, rex,' inquit, 'bona venia liceat mihi pauca interrogare?' ' liceat,' *subj.*: ' *might I be allowed.'*

Who lodged in this house: quis primus in his aedibus, postquam aedificatae sunt, commoratus est?

The king replied: rex majores suos ait.

The king told him that he himself did: 'Egomet ipse,' inquit rex, 'hic habito.'

A house that changes: quae domus tam saepe inquilinos mutat; inquilinus, ' *a lodger,'* dominus, ' *an owner,'* incola, ' *an inhabitant,'* hospes, ' *a guest.'*

You will rightly call: eam recte dixeris non regiam sed hospitium; hospitium: 'ex vita ita discedo tamquam ex hospitio non tamquam ex domo;' deversorium: 'commorandi enim natura deversorium nobis, non habitandi locum dedit;' insula: ' *a building inhabited in flats,'* ' *a block.'*

49.

135. *While engaged in hunting . . .*

They shake off the indolence peculiar to their nature: excussa desidia quod proprium gentis vitium est; inertia, ' *lack of energy:'* ' segnities atque inertia;' desidia, ' *sloth:'* ' vitanda est improba Siren desidia.'

Their sagacity, and address, are equal: par illis in praeda indaganda sagacitas, et in conficienda dexteritas.

If they attack openly: si palam cum feris congredi opus sit.

It is almost impossible to escape their toils: si dolo circum-venire, ratio effugiendi prorsus nulla apparet.

Sharpened by emulation, *in parenthesis*: adeo mentes humanas acuit aemulatio, impellit necessitas.

Has struck out many inventions: multa et nova excogitavit quae venantibus prosint: 'extundo,' *poet.* '*to hammer out*:' 'pater ipse colendi haud facilem esse viam voluit, primusque per artem movit agros, curis acuens mortalia corda, nec torpore gravi passus sua regna veterno—ut varias usus meditando extunderet artes.'

The most singular of these: inter quae, singulari laude digna, est veneni cujusdam inventio.

The blood fixes and congeals: cogitur extemplo sanguis et concrescit, et quantumvis valida bestia exanimis concedit.

50.

143. *Gulliver thus relates . . .*

Gulliver: *instead of* 'Gulliverus,' *say* 'Ulysses,' *or* 'aretalogus quidam,' *and see* Juvenal xvi. 15.

Blefuscudians: 'Hippogerani,' *better than* 'Blefuscudiani.'

Lilliput; Pygmaei: 'Pygmaeus parvis currit bellator in armis.'

Half moon: lunato agmine.

Up to my neck: quum capite solo eminerem; 'graditurque per aequor jam medium, necdum fluctus latera ardua tinxit.'

Fears: metu exemptus est.

Within hearing: quum jam prope ab litore abessem ita ut vox mea audiri posset.

Long live: 'Ave rex Pygmaeorum, imperator invictissime!'

THE END.

July, 1888.

𝕿𝖍𝖊 𝕮𝖑𝖆𝖗𝖊𝖓𝖉𝖔𝖓 𝕻𝖗𝖊𝖘𝖘, 𝕺𝖗𝖋𝖔𝖗𝖉,

LIST OF SCHOOL BOOKS,

PUBLISHED FOR THE UNIVERSITY BY

HENRY FROWDE,

AT THE OXFORD UNIVERSITY PRESS WAREHOUSE,
AMEN CORNER, LONDON.

** All Books are bound in Cloth, unless otherwise described.

LATIN.

Allen. *An Elementary Latin Grammar.* By J. BARROW ALLEN, M.A.
Fifty-seventh Thousand . . . . Extra fcap. 8vo. 2s. 6d.

Allen. *Rudimenta Latina.* By the same Author. Extra fcap. 8vo. 2s.

Allen. *A First Latin Exercise Book.* By the same Author. *Fourth Edition.* . . . . Extra fcap. 8vo. 2s. 6d.

Allen. *A Second Latin Exercise Book.* By the same Author.
Extra fcap. 8vo. 3s. 6d.

[*A Key to First and Second Latin Exercise Books : for Teachers only.*]

Jerram. *Anglice Reddenda ; or Extracts, Latin and Greek, for Unseen Translation.* By C. S. JERRAM, M.A. *Fourth Edition.*
Extra fcap. 8vo. 2s. 6d.

Jerram. *Anglice Reddenda.* SECOND SERIES. By C. S. JERRAM, M.A.
Extra fcap. 8vo. 3s.

Jerram. *Reddenda Minora ; or, Easy Passages, Latin and Greek, for Unseen Translation.* For the use of Lower Forms. Composed and selected by C. S. JERRAM, M.A. . . . . . . Extra fcap. 8vo. 1s. 6d.

Lee-Warner. *Hints and Helps for Latin Elegiacs.*
Extra fcap. 8vo. 3s. 6d.

[*A Key is provided : for Teachers only.*]

Lewis and Short. *A Latin Dictionary,* founded on Andrews' Edition of Freund's Latin Dictionary. By CHARLTON T. LEWIS, Ph.D., and CHARLES SHORT, LL.D. . . . . 4to. 25s.

Nunns. *First Latin Reader.* By T. J. NUNNS, M.A. *Third Edition.*
Extra fcap. 8vo. 2s.

Papillon. *A Manual of Comparative Philology* as applied to the Illustration of Greek and Latin Inflections. By T. L. PAPILLON, M.A. *Third Edition.*
Crown 8vo. 6s.

Ramsay. *Exercises in Latin Prose Composition.* With Introduction, Notes, and Passages of graduated difficulty for Translation into Latin. By G. G. RAMSAY, M.A., Professor of Humanity, Glasgow. . *Second Edition.*
Extra fcap. 8vo. 4s. 6d.

Sargent. *Passages for Translation into Latin.* By J. Y. SARGENT, M.A. *Seventh Edition.* . . . . . . Extra fcap. 8vo. 2s. 6d.

[*A Key to this Edition is provided : for Teachers only.*]

Caesar. *The Commentaries* (for Schools). With Notes and Maps.
By CHARLES E. MOBERLY, M.A.
     The Gallic War. Second Edition . . . . . Extra fcap. 8vo. 4s. 6d.
     The Gallic War. Books I, II. *Just ready.*
     The Civil War . . . . Extra fcap. 8vo. 3s. 6d.
     The Civil War. Book I. *Second Edition.* . . Extra fcap. 8vo. 2s.

Catulli Veronensis *Carmina Selecta,* secundum recognitionem
ROBINSON ELLIS, A.M. . . . . . . Extra fcap. 8vo. 3s. 6d.

Cicero. *Selection of interesting and descriptive passages.* With Notes.
By HENRY WALFORD, M.A. In three Parts. *Third Edition.*
                                          Extra fcap. 8vo. 4s. 6d.
     Part I. *Anecdotes from Grecian and Roman History.* . limp, 1s. 6d.
     Part II. *Omens and Dreams; Beauties of Nature.* . . limp, 1s. 6d.
     Part III. *Rome's Rule of her Provinces.* . . . . limp, 1s. 6d.

Cicero. *De Senectute.* With Introduction and Notes. By LEONARD
HUXLEY, B.A. *In one or two Parts* . . . . Extra fcap. 8vo. 2s.

Cicero. *Pro Cluentio.* With Introduction and Notes. By W. RAMSAY,
M.A. Edited by G. G. RAMSAY, M.A. *Second Edition.* Extra fcap. 8vo. 3s. 6d.

Cicero. *Selected Letters* (for Schools). With Notes. By the late
C. E. PRICHARD, M.A., and E. R. BERNARD, M.A. *Second Edition.*
                                          Extra fcap. 8vo. 3s.

Cicero. *Select Orations* (for Schools). *First Action against Verres;
Oration concerning the command of Gnaeus Pompeius; Oration on behalf of
Archias; Ninth Philippic Oration.* With Introduction and Notes. By J. R.
KING, M.A. *Second Edition.* . . . . . Extra fcap. 8vo. 2s. 6d.

Cicero. *In Q. Caecilium Divinatio* and *In C. Verrem Actio Prima.*
With Introduction and Notes. By J. R. KING, M.A.
                                       Extra fcap. 8vo. *limp,* 1s. 6d.

Cicero. *Speeches against Catilina.* With Introduction and Notes. By
E. A. UPCOTT, M.A. *In one or two Parts.* . . Extra fcap. 8vo. 2s. 6d.

Cicero. *Philippic Orations.* With Notes, &c. by J. R. KING, M.A.
Second Edition. . . . . 8vo. 10s. 6d.

Cicero. *Select Letters.* With English Introductions, Notes, and Appendices. By ALBERT WATSON, M.A. *Third Edition.* . . . 8vo. 18s.

Cicero. *Select Letters.* Text. By the same Editor. *Second Edition.*
                                       Extra fcap. 8vo. 4s.

Cornelius Nepos. With Notes. By OSCAR BROWNING, M.A.
Third Edition. Revised by W. R. INGE, M.A. . . Extra fcap. 8vo. 3s.

Horace. With a Commentary. Volume I. *The Odes, Carmen
Seculare,* and *Epodes.* By EDWARD C. WICKHAM, M.A., Head Master of
Wellington College. *New Edition. In one or two Parts.* Extra fcap. 8vo. 6s.

Horace. *Selected Odes.* With Notes for the use of a Fifth Form. By
E. C. WICKHAM, M.A. *In one or two Parts.* . . Extra fcap. 8vo. 2s.

Juvenal. *XIII Satires.* Edited, with Introduction, Notes, etc., by
C. H. PEARSON, M.A., and H. A. STRONG, M.A. . . . Crown 8vo. 6s.
           Or separately, Text and Introduction, 3s.; *Notes,* 3s. 6d.

Livy. *Selections* (for Schools). With Notes and Maps. By H. LEE-
WARNER, M.A. . . . . Extra fcap. 8vo
     Part I. *The Caudine Disaster.* . . . . . limp, 1s. 6d.
     Part II. *Hannibal's Campaign in Italy.* . . . limp, 1s. 6d.
     Part III. *The Macedonian War.* . . . . . limp, 1s. 6d.

Livy. *Book I.* With Introduction, Historical Examination, and Notes. By J. R. SEELEY M.A. *Second Edition.* . . . . . 8vo. 6s.

Livy. *Books V—VII.* With Introduction and Notes. By A. R. CLUER, B.A. *Second Edition.* Revised by P. E. MATHESON, M.A. *In one or two parts.* . . . . Extra fcap. 8vo. 5s.

Livy. *Books XXI—XXIII.* With Introduction and Notes. By M. T. TATHAM, M.A. . . . . . Extra fcap. 8vo. 4s. 6d.

Livy. *Book XXII.* With Introduction and Notes. By the same Editor. *Just ready.*

Ovid. *Selections* (for the use of Schools). With Introductions and Notes, and an Appendix on the Roman Calendar. By W. RAMSAY, M.A. Edited by G. G. RAMSAY, M.A. *Third Edition.* . Extra fcap. 8vo. 5s. 6d.

Ovid. *Tristia*, Book I. Edited by S. G. OWEN, B.A. Extra fcap. 8vo. 3s. 6d.

Persius. *The Satires.* With Translation and Commentary by J. CONINGTON, M.A., edited by H. NETTLESHIP, M.A. *Second Edition.* 8vo. 7s. 6d.

Plautus. *Captivi.* With Introduction and Notes. By W. M. LINDSAY, M.A. *In one or two Parts.* . . . . Extra fcap. 8vo. 2s. 6d.

Plautus. *Trinummus.* With Notes and Introductions. By C. E. FREEMAN, M.A. and A. SLOMAN, M.A. . . . . Extra fcap. 8vo. 3s.

Pliny. *Selected Letters* (for Schools). With Notes. By the late C. E. PRICHARD, M.A., and E. R. BERNARD, M.A. *New Edition. In one or two Parts.* . . . . Extra fcap. 8vo. 3s.

Sallust. *Bellum Catilinarium* and *Jugurthinum.* With Introduction and Notes, by W. W. CAPES, M.A. . . . Extra fcap. 8vo. 4s. 6d.

Tacitus. *The Annals.* Books I—IV. Edited, with Introduction and Notes for the use of Schools and Junior Students, by H. FURNEAUX, M.A. Extra fcap. 8vo. 5s.

Tacitus. *The Annals.* Book I. By the same Editor. Extra fcap. 8vo. *limp*, 2s.

Terence. *Adelphi.* With Notes and Introductions. By A. SLOMAN, M.A. . . . . Extra fcap. 8vo. 3s.

Terence. *Andria.* With Notes and Introductions. By C. E. FREEMAN, M.A., and A. SLOMAN, M.A. . . . . . . Extra fcap. 8vo. 3s.

Terence. *Phormio.* With Notes and Introductions. By A. SLOMAN, M.A. . . . . Extra fcap. 8vo. 3s.

Tibullus and **Propertius.** Edited, with Introduction and Notes, by G. G. RAMSAY, M.A. *In one or two Parts.* . . . Extra fcap. 8vo. 6s.

Virgil. With Introduction and Notes, by T. L. PAPILLON, M.A. In Two Volumes. . . . Crown 8vo. 10s. 6d.; Text separately, 4s. 6d.

Virgil. *Bucolics.* With Introduction and Notes, by C. S. JERRAM, M.A. *In one or two Parts.* Extra fcap. 8vo. 2s. 6d.

Virgil. *Aeneid I.* With Introduction and Notes, by C. S. JERRAM, M.A. Extra fcap. 8vo. *limp*, 1s. 6d.

Virgil. *Aeneid IX.* Edited with Introduction and Notes, by A. E. HAIGH, M.A. . . . Extra fcap 8vo. *limp* 1s. 6d. *In two Parts.* 2s.

GREEK.

Chandler. *The Elements of Greek Accentuation* (for Schools). By H. W. CHANDLER, M.A. *Second Edition.*   Extra fcap. 8vo. 2s. 6d.

Liddell and Scott. *A Greek-English Lexicon*, by HENRY GEORGE LIDDELL, D.D., and ROBERT SCOTT, D.D. *Seventh Edition.*   4to. 36s.

Liddell and Scott. *A Greek-English Lexicon*, abridged from LIDDELL and SCOTT's 4to. edition, chiefly for the use of Schools. *Twenty-first Edition.* Square 12mo. 7s. 6d.

Veitch. *Greek Verbs, Irregular and Defective :* their forms, meaning, and quantity ; embracing all the Tenses used by Greek writers, with references to the passages in which they are found. By W. VEITCH, LL.D. *Fourth Edition.* Crown 8vo. 10s. 6d.

Wordsworth. *Graecae Grammaticae Rudimenta in usum Scholarum.* Auctore CAROLO WORDSWORTH, D.C.L. *Nineteenth Edition.*   12mo. 4s.

Wordsworth. *A Greek Primer, for the use of beginners in that Language.* By the Right Rev. CHARLES WORDSWORTH, D.C.L., Bishop of St. Andrew's. *Seventh Edition.*   Extra fcap. 8vo. 1s. 6d.

Wright. *The Golden Treasury of Ancient Greek Poetry ;* being a Collection of the finest passages in the Greek Classic Poets, with Introductory Notices and Notes. By R. S. WRIGHT, M.A.   *New edition in the Press.*

Wright and Shadwell. *A Golden Treasury of Greek Prose ;* being a Collection of the finest passages in the principal Greek Prose Writers, with Introductory Notices and Notes. By R. S. WRIGHT, M.A., and J. E. L. SHADWELL, M.A. . . . . . . Extra fcap. 8vo. 4s. 6d.

A SERIES OF GRADUATED READERS.—

Easy Greek Reader. By EVELYN ABBOTT, M.A. *In one or two Parts.* . . . . Extra fcap. 8vo. 3s.

First Greek Reader. By W. G. RUSHBROOKE, M.L., Second Classical Master at the City of London School. *Second Edition.* Extra fcap. 8vo. 2s. 6d.

Second Greek Reader. By A. M. BELL, M.A. Extra fcap. 8vo. 3s. 6d.

Fourth Greek Reader ; being Specimens of Greek Dialects. With Introductions and Notes. By W. W. MERRY, D.D., Rector of Lincoln College. . . . . . . Extra fcap. 8vo. 4s. 6d.

Fifth Greek Reader. Selections from Greek Epic and Dramatic Poetry, with Introductions and Notes. By EVELYN ABBOTT, M.A. Extra fcap. 8vo. 4s. 6d.

THE GREEK TESTAMENT.—

Evangelia Sacra Graece. . . . Fcap. 8vo. *limp*, 1s. 6d.

The Greek Testament, with the Readings adopted by the Revisers of the Authorised Version. Fcap. 8vo. 4s. 6d. ; or on writing paper, with wide margin, 15s.

Novum Testamentum Graece juxta Exemplar Millianum. 18mo. 2s. 6d. ; or on writing paper, with large margin, 9s.

Novum Testamentum Graece. Accedunt parallela S. Scripturae loca, necnon vetus capitulorum notatio et canones Eusebii. Edidit CAROLUS LLOYD, S.T.P.R., necnon Episcopus Oxoniensis.

18mo. 3*s.* ; or on writing paper, with large margin, 10*s. 6d.*

A Greek Testament Primer. An Easy Grammar and Reading Book for the use of Students beginning Greek. By REV. E. MILLER, M.A.

Extra fcap. 8vo. 3*s. 6d.*

Outlines of Textual Criticism applied to the New Testament. By C. E. HAMMOND, M.A. *Fourth Edition.*   .   Extra fcap. 8vo. 3*s. 6d.*

Aeschylus. *Agamemnon.* With Introduction and Notes, by ARTHUR SIDGWICK, M.A. *Third Edition. In one or two Parts* . Extra fcap. 8vo. 3*s.*

Aeschylus. *Choephoroi.* With Introduction and Notes, by the same Editor. . . . . . . Extra fcap. 8vo. 3*s.*

Aeschylus. *Eumenides.* With Introduction and Notes, by the same Editor. *In one or two Parts.* . . . . . Extra fcap. 8vo. 3*s.*

Aeschylus. *Prometheus Bound.* With Introduction and Notes, by A. O. PRICKARD, M.A. *Second Edition.* . . . Extra fcap. 8vo. 2*s.*

Aristophanes. *The Clouds.* With Introduction and Notes, by W. W. MERRY, D.D. *Second Edition.* . . . . . Extra fcap. 8vo. 2*s.*

Aristophanes. *The Acharnians.* By the same Editor. *Third Edition. In one or two Parts.* . . . . . Extra fcap. 8vo. 3*s.*

Aristophanes. *The Frogs.* By the same Editor. *New Edition. In one or two Parts.* . . . . Extra fcap. 8vo. 3*s.*

Aristophanes. *The Knights.* By the same Editor. *In one or two Parts.* . . . . Extra fcap. 8vo. 3*s.*

Cebes. *Tabula.* With Introduction and Notes, by C. S. JERRAM, M.A.

Extra fcap. 8vo. 2*s. 6d.*

Demosthenes. *Orations against Philip.* With Introduction and Notes. By EVELYN ABBOTT, M.A., and P. E. MATHESON, M.A., Vol. I. *Philippic I and Olynthiacs I—III. In one or two Parts.* . . . Extra fcap. 8vo. 3*s.*

Euripides. *Alcestis.* By C. S. JERRAM, M.A. Extra fcap. 8vo. 2*s. 6d.*

Euripides. *Helena.* By the same Editor. . Extra fcap. 8vo. 3*s.*

Euripides. *Heracleidae.* By the same Editor. Extra fcap. 8vo. 3*s.*

Euripides. *Iphigenia in Tauris.* With Introduction and Notes. By the same Editor. . . . . Extra fcap. 8vo. 3*s.*

Euripides. *Medea.* With Introduction, Notes and Appendices. By C. B. HEBERDEN, M.A. *In one or two Parts.* . . Extra fcap. 8vo. 2*s.*

Herodotus. Book IX. Edited with Notes, by EVELYN ABBOTT, M.A. *In one or two Parts.* . . . . . . Extra fcap. 8vo. 3*s.*

Herodotus. *Selections.* Edited, with Introduction, Notes, and a Map, by W. W. MERRY, D.D. . . . . . . Extra fcap. 8vo. 2*s. 6d.*

Homer. *Iliad,* Books I–XII. With an Introduction, a brief Homeric Grammar, and Notes. By D. B. MONRO, M.A. Extra fcap. 8vo. 6*s.*

Homer. *Iliad,* Book I. By the same Editor. *Third Edition.*

Extra fcap. 8vo. 2*s.*

Homer. *Iliad,* Books VI and XXI. With Notes, &c. By HERBERT HAILSTONE, M.A. . . . . . . Extra fcap. 8vo. 1*s. 6d.* each.

Homer. *Odyssey*, Books I–XII. By W. W. MERRY, D.D. *New Edition. In one or two Parts.* . . . . Extra fcap. 8vo. 5s.

Homer. *Odyssey*, Books XIII–XXIV. By the same Editor. *Second Edition.* . . . . Extra fcap. 8vo. 5s.

Homer. *Odyssey*, Books I and II. By the same Editor.
Extra fcap. 8vo. each 1s. 6d.

Lucian. *Vera Historia*. By C. S. JERRAM, M.A. *Second Edition.*
Extra fcap. 8vo. 1s. 6d.

Plato. *The Apology*. With Introduction and Notes. By ST. GEORGE STOCK, M.A. *In one or two Parts.* . . . Extra fcap. 8vo. 2s. 6d.

Plato. *Meno*. With Introduction and Notes. By ST. GEORGE STOCK, M.A. *In one or two Parts.* . . . . Extra fcap. 8vo. 2s. 6d.

Sophocles. (For the use of Schools.) Edited with Introductions and English Notes by LEWIS CAMPBELL, M.A., and EVELYN ABBOTT, M.A. New and Revised Edition. 2 Vols. . . . . Extra fcap. 8vo. 10s. 6d.
Sold separately, Vol. I. Text, 4s. 6d. Vol. II. Notes, 6s.

☞ *Also in single Plays. Extra fcap. 8vo. limp,*
Oedipus Tyrannus, Philoctetes. New and Revised Edition, 2s. each.
Oedipus Coloneus, *Antigone.* 1s. 9d. each.
Ajax, *Electra,* *Trachiniae.* 2s. each.

Sophocles. *Oedipus Rex:* Dindorf's Text, with Notes by W. BASIL JONES, D.D., Lord Bishop of S. David's. . Extra fcap. 8vo. *limp*, 1s. 6d.

Theocritus. Edited, with Notes, by H. KYNASTON, D.D. (late SNOW). *Fourth Edition.* . . . . Extra fcap. 8vo. 4s. 6d.

Xenophon. *Easy Selections* (for Junior Classes). With a Vocabulary, Notes, and Map. By J. S. PHILLPOTTS, B.C.L., Head Master of Bedford School, and C. S. JERRAM, M.A. *Third Edition.* . Extra fcap. 8vo. 3s. 6d.

Xenophon. *Selections* (for Schools). With Notes and Maps. By J. S. PHILLPOTTS, B.C.L. *Fourth Edition.* . . Extra fcap. 8vo. 3s. 6d.

Xenophon. *Anabasis*, Book I. With Notes and Map. By J. MARSHALL, M.A., Rector of the High School, Edinburgh. . . Extra fcap. 8vo. 2s. 6d.

Xenophon. *Anabasis*, Book II. With Notes and Map. By C. S. JERRAM, M.A. . . . . Extra fcap. 8vo. 2s.

Xenophon. *Anabasis*, Book III. By J. MARSHALL, M.A.
Extra fcap. 8vo. 2s. 6d.

Xenophon. *Cyropaedia*, Book I. With Introduction and Notes. By C. BIGG, D.D. . . . . Extra fcap. 8vo. 2s.

Xenophon. *Cyropaedia*, Books IV, V. With Introduction and Notes, by C. BIGG, D.D. . . . . . Extra fcap. 8vo. 2s. 6d.

Xenophon. *Hellenica*, Books I, II. With Introduction and Notes. By G. E. UNDERHILL, M.A. . . . . . Extra fcap. 8vo. 3s.

EARLY AND MIDDLE ENGLISH, &c.

Mayhew and Skeat. *A Concise Dictionary of Middle English.* By A. L. MAYHEW, M.A., and W. W. SKEAT, Litt. D. . . Crown 8vo. 7*s. 6d*

Skeat. *A Concise Etymological Dictionary of the English Language.* By W. W. SKEAT, Litt. D. *Third Edition.* . . . Crown 8vo. 5*s. 6d.*

Tancock. *An Elementary English Grammar and Exercise Book.* By O. W. TANCOCK, M.A., Head Master of King Edward VI's School, Norwich. *Second Edition.* . . . . . . Extra fcap. 8vo. 1*s. 6d.*

Tancock. *An English Grammar and Reading Book,* for Lower Forms in Classical Schools. By O. W. TANCOCK, M.A. *Fourth Edition.* Extra fcap. 8vo. 3*s. 6d.*

Skeat. *The Principles of English Etymology. First Series.* By W. W. SKEAT, Litt. D. . . . . Crown 8vo. 9*s.*

Earle. *The Philology of the English Tongue.* By J. EARLE, M.A., Professor of Anglo-Saxon. *Fourth Edition.* . . Extra fcap. 8vo. 7*s. 6d.*

Earle. *A Book for the Beginner in Anglo-Saxon.* By the same Author. *Third Edition.* . . . . Extra fcap. 8vo. 2*s. 6d.*

Sweet. *An Anglo-Saxon Primer, with Grammar, Notes, and Glossary.* By HENRY SWEET, M.A. *Third Edition.* . . Extra fcap. 8vo. 2*s. 6d.*

Sweet. *An Anglo-Saxon Reader.* In Prose and Verse. With Grammatical Introduction, Notes, and Glossary. By the same Author. *Fourth Edition, Revised and Enlarged.* . . . . Extra fcap. 8vo. 8*s. 6d.*

Sweet. *A Second Anglo-Saxon Reader.* By the same Author. Extra fcap. 8vo. 4*s. 6d.*

Sweet. *Anglo-Saxon Reading Primers.*

    I. *Selected Homilies of Ælfric.* Extra fcap. 8vo. *stiff covers,* 1*s. 6d.*
    II. *Extracts from Alfred's Orosius.* Extra fcap. 8vo. *stiff covers,* 1*s. 6d.*

Sweet. *First Middle English Primer, with Grammar and Glossary.* By the same Author. . . . . Extra fcap. 8vo. 2*s.*

Sweet. *Second Middle English Primer.* Extracts from Chaucer, with Grammar and Glossary. By the same Author. . . Extra fcap. 8vo. 2*s.*

Morris and Skeat. *Specimens of Early English.* A New and Revised Edition. With Introduction, Notes, and Glossarial Index.

    Part I. From Old English Homilies to King Horn (A.D. 1150 to A.D. 1300). By R. MORRIS, LL.D. *Second Edition* . . Extra fcap. 8vo. 9*s.*
    Part II. From Robert of Gloucester to Gower (A.D. 1298 to A.D. 1393). By R. MORRIS, LL.D., and W. W. SKEAT, Litt. D. *Third Edition.* Extra fcap. 8vo. 7*s. 6d.*

Skeat. *Specimens of English Literature,* from the 'Ploughmans Crede' to the 'Shepheardes Calender' (A.D. 1394 to A.D. 1579). With Introduction, Notes, and Glossarial Index. By W. W. SKEAT, Litt. D. *Fourth Edition.* Extra fcap. 8vo. 7*s. 6d.*

Typical Selections from the best English Writers, with Introductory Notices. *Second Edition.* In Two Volumes. Vol. I. Latimer to Berkeley. Vol. II. Pope to Macaulay. . . Extra fcap. 8vo. 3*s. 6d.* each

A SERIES OF ENGLISH CLASSICS.

Langland. *The Vision of William concerning Piers the Plowman,* by WILLIAM LANGLAND. Edited by W. W. SKEAT, Litt. D. *Fourth Edition.* Extra fcap. 8vo. 4*s.* 6*d.*

Chaucer. I. *The Prologue to the Canterbury Tales ; The Knightes Tale ; The Nonne Prestes Tale.* Edited by R. MORRIS, LL.D. *Fifty-first Thousand.* . . . . Extra fcap. 8vo. 2*s.* 6*d.*

Chaucer. II. *The Prioresses Tale ; Sir Thopas ; The Monkes Tale ; The Clerkes Tale ; The Squieres Tale, &c.* Edited by W. W. SKEAT, Litt. D. *Third Edition.* . . . . Extra fcap. 8vo. 4*s.* 6*d.*

Chaucer. III. *The Tale of the Man of Lawe ; The Pardoneres Tale ; The Second Nonnes Tale ; The Chanouns Yemannes Tale.* By the same Editor. *New Edition, Revised.* . . . Extra fcap. 8vo. 4*s.* 6*d.*

Gamelyn, The Tale of. Edited by W. W. SKEAT, Litt. D. Extra fcap. 8vo. *stiff covers,* 1*s.* 6*d.*

Minot. *The Poems of Laurence Minot.* Edited, with Introduction and Notes, by JOSEPH HALL, M.A. . . . Extra fcap. 8vo. 4*s.* 6*d.*

Wycliffe. *The New Testament in English,* according to the Version by JOHN WYCLIFFE, about A.D. 1380, and Revised by JOHN PURVEY, about A.D. 1388. With Introduction and Glossary by W. W. SKEAT, Litt. D. Extra fcap. 8vo. 6*s.*

Wycliffe. *The Books of Job, Psalms, Proverbs, Ecclesiastes, and the Song of Solomon*: according to the Wycliffite Version made by NICHOLAS DE HEREFORD, about A.D. 1381, and Revised by JOHN PURVEY, about A.D. 1388. With Introduction and Glossary by W. W. SKEAT, Litt. D. Extra fcap. 8vo. 3*s.* 6*d.*

Spenser. *The Faery Queene.* Books I and II. Edited by G. W. KITCHIN, D.D.

    Book I. *Tenth Edition.* . . . . Extra fcap. 8vo. 2*s.* 6*d.*
    Book II. *Sixth Edition.* . . . . . Extra fcap. 8vo. 2*s.* 6*d.*

Hooker. *Ecclesiastical Polity,* Book I. Edited by R. W. CHURCH, M.A., Dean of St. Paul's. *Second Edition.* . . . Extra fcap. 8vo. 2*s.*

Marlowe and Greene.—MARLOWE'S *Tragical History of Dr. Faustus,* and GREENE'S *Honourable History of Friar Bacon and Friar Bungay.* Edited by A. W. WARD, M.A. *New Edition.* . . Extra fcap. 8vo. 6*s.* 6*d.*

Marlowe. *Edward II.* Edited by O. W. TANCOCK, M.A. *Second Edition.* . . . . . Extra fcap. 8vo. *Paper covers,* 2*s.* *cloth,* 3*s.*

Shakespeare. Select Plays. Edited by W. G. CLARK, M.A., and W. ALDIS WRIGHT, M.A. . . . . Extra fcap. 8vo. *stiff covers.*

    The Merchant of Venice. 1*s.*   *Macbeth.* 1*s.* 6*d.*
    Richard the Second. 1*s.* 6*d.*   *Hamlet.* 2*s.*

Edited by W. ALDIS WRIGHT, M.A.

The Tempest. 1*s.* 6*d.*	*Coriolanus.* 2*s.* 6*d.*
As You Like It. 1*s.* 6*d.*	*Richard the Third.* 2*s.* 6*d.*
A Midsummer Night's Dream. 1*s.* 6*d.*	*Henry the Fifth.* 2*s.*
Twelfth Night. 1*s.* 6*d.*	*King John.* 1*s.* 6*d.*
Julius Cæsar. 2*s.*	*King Lear.* 1*s.* 6*d.*

Shakespeare as a Dramatic Artist; *a popular Illustration of the Principles of Scientific Criticism.* By R. G. MOULTON, M.A. Crown 8vo. 5s.

Bacon. *Advancement of Learning.* Edited by W. ALDIS WRIGHT, M.A. *Third Edition.* . . . . . . Extra fcap. 8vo. 4s. 6d.

Milton. I. *Areopagitica.* With Introduction and Notes. By JOHN W. HALES, M.A. *Third Edition.* . . . . Extra fcap. 8vo. 3s.

Milton. II. *Poems.* Edited by R. C. BROWNE, M.A. 2 vols. *Fifth Edition.* . Extra fcap. 8vo. 6s. 6d. Sold separately, Vol. I. 4s., Vol. II. 3s.

In paper covers :—

Lycidas, 3d.   *L'Allegro*, 3d.   *Il Penseroso*, 4d.   *Comus*, 6d.

Milton. III. *Paradise Lost.* Book I. Edited with Notes, by H. C. BEECHING, M.A. . Extra fcap. 8vo. 1s. 6d. *In white Parchment*, 3s. 6d.

Milton. IV. *Samson Agonistes.* Edited with Introduction and Notes by JOHN CHURTON COLLINS. . . . Extra fcap. 8vo. *stiff covers*, 1s.

Clarendon. *History of the Rebellion.* Book VI. Edited with Introduction and Notes by T. ARNOLD, M.A. . . Extra fcap. 8vo. 4s. 6d.

Bunyan. *The Pilgrim's Progress, Grace Abounding, Relation of the Imprisonment of Mr. John Bunyan.* Edited by E. VENABLES, M.A. Extra fcap. 8vo. 5s. *In white Parchment*, 6s.

Dryden. *Stanzas on the Death of Oliver Cromwell; Astræa Redux; Annus Mirabilis; Absalom and Achitophel; Religio Laici; The Hind and the Panther.* Edited by W. D. CHRISTIE, M.A. . Extra fcap. 8vo. 3s. 6d.

Locke's *Conduct of the Understanding.* Edited, with Introduction, Notes, &c. by T. FOWLER, D.D. *Second Edition.* . . Extra fcap. 8vo. 2s.

Addison. *Selections from Papers in the 'Spectator.'* With Notes. By T. ARNOLD, M.A. . Extra fcap. 8vo. 4s. 6d. *In white Parchment*, 6s.

Steele. *Selected Essays from the Tatler, Spectator, and Guardian.* By AUSTIN DOBSON. . . Extra fcap. 8vo. 5s. *In white Parchment*, 7s. 6d.

Berkeley. *Select Works of Bishop Berkeley*, with an Introduction and Notes, by A. C. FRASER, LL.D. *Third Edition.* . . Crown 8vo. 7s. 6d.

Pope. I. *Essay on Man.* Edited by MARK PATTISON, B.D. *Sixth Edition.* . . . . Extra fcap. 8vo. 1s. 6d.

Pope. II. *Satires and Epistles.* By the same Editor. *Second Edition.* Extra fcap. 8vo. 2s.

Parnell. *The Hermit.* . . . . . *Paper covers*, 2d.

Johnson. I. *Rasselas.* Edited, with Introduction and Notes, by G. BIRKBECK HILL, D.C.L. Extra fcap. 8vo. *limp*, 2s. *In white Parchment*, 3s. 6d.

Johnson. II. *Rasselas; Lives of Dryden and Pope.* Edited by ALFRED MILNES, M.A. . . . . . . Extra fcap. 8vo. 4s. 6d.

Lives of Pope and Dryden. . . . . *Stiff covers*, 2s. 6d.

Johnson. III. *Life of Milton.* Edited, with Notes, etc., by C. H. FIRTH, M.A. . . . Extra fcap. 8vo. *stiff covers*, 1s 6d.; *cloth*, 2s. 6d.

Johnson. IV. *Vanity of Human Wishes.* With Notes, by E. J. PAYNE, M.A. . . . . *Paper covers*, 4d.

Gray. *Selected Poems.* Edited by EDMUND GOSSE.
Extra fcap. 8vo. *Stiff covers*, 1s. 6d. *In white Parchment*, 3s.

Gray. *Elegy, and Ode on Eton College.* . . *Paper covers*, 2d.

Goldsmith. *Selected Poems.* Edited, with Introduction and Notes, by
AUSTIN DOBSON. . . . . Extra fcap. 8vo. 3s. 6d.
In white Parchment, 4s. 6d.

Goldsmith. *The Traveller.* Edited by G. BIRKBECK HILL, D.C.L.
Extra fcap. 8vo. *stiff covers*, 1s.

The Deserted Village. . . . . *Paper covers*, 2d.

Cowper. I. *The Didactic Poems of* 1782, with Selections from the
Minor Pieces, A.D. 1779-1783. Edited by H. T. GRIFFITH, B.A.
Extra fcap. 8vo. 3s.

Cowper. II. *The Task, with Tirocinium*, and Selections from the
Minor Poems, A.D. 1784-1799. By the same Editor. *Second Edition.*
Extra fcap. 8vo. 3s.

Burke. I. *Thoughts on the Present Discontents; the two Speeches
on America.* Edited by E. J. PAYNE, M.A. *Second Edition.*
Extra fcap. 8vo. 4s. 6d.

Burke. II. *Reflections on the French Revolution.* By the same
Editor. *Second Edition.* . . . . . Extra fcap. 8vo. 5s.

Burke. III. *Four Letters on the Proposals for Peace with the
Regicide Directory of France.* By the same Editor. *Second Edition.*
Extra fcap. 8vo. 5s.

Keats. *Hyperion*, Book I. With Notes, by W. T. ARNOLD, B.A.
Paper covers, 4d.

Byron. *Childe Harold.* With Introduction and Notes, by H. F. TOZER,
M.A. . . . Extra fcap. 8vo. 3s. 6d. *In white Parchment*, 5s.

Scott. *Lay of the Last Minstrel.* Edited with Preface and Notes by
W. MINTO, M.A. With Map.
Extra fcap. 8vo. *stiff covers*, 2s. *In Ornamental Parchment*, 3s. 6d.

Scott. *Lay of the Last Minstrel.* Introduction and Canto I, with
Preface and Notes by W. MINTO, M.A. . . . *Paper covers*, 6d.

FRENCH AND ITALIAN.

Brachet. *Etymological Dictionary of the French Language*, with
a Preface on the Principles of French Etymology. Translated into English by
G. W. KITCHIN, D.D., Dean of Winchester. *Third Edition.*
Crown 8vo. 7s. 6d.

Brachet. *Historical Grammar of the French Language.* Translated
into English by G. W. KITCHIN, D.D. *Fourth Edition.*
Extra fcap. 8vo. 3s. 6d.

Saintsbury. *Primer of French Literature.* By GEORGE SAINTS-
BURY, M.A. *Second Edition.* . . . . Extra fcap. 8vo. 2s.

Saintsbury. *Short History of French Literature.* By the same
Author. . . . . Crown 8vo. 10s. 6d.

Saintsbury. *Specimens of French Literature.* . . Crown 8vo. 9s.

Beaumarchais. *Le Barbier de Séville.* With Introduction and Notes by Austin Dobson. . . . . . . Extra fcap. 8vo. 2s. 6d.

Blouët. *L'Éloquence de la Chaire et de la Tribune Françaises.* Edited by Paul Blouët, B.A. (Univ. Gallic.) Vol. I. *French Sacred Oratory.* Extra fcap. 8vo. 2s. 6d.

Corneille. *Horace.* With Introduction and Notes by George Saintsbury, M.A. . . . . . . Extra fcap. 8vo. 2s. 6d.

Corneille. *Cinna.* With Notes, Glossary, etc. By Gustave Masson, B.A. . . . . Extra fcap. 8vo. *stiff covers,* 1s. 6d. *cloth,* 2s.

Gautier (Théophile). *Scenes of Travel.* Selected and Edited by G. Saintsbury, M.A. . . . . Extra fcap. 8vo. 2s.

Masson. *Louis XIV and his Contemporaries;* as described in Extracts from the best Memoirs of the Seventeenth Century. With English Notes, Genealogical Tables, &c. By Gustave Masson, B.A. Extra fcap. 8vo. 2s. 6d.

Molière. *Les Précieuses Ridicules.* With Introduction and Notes by Andrew Lang, M.A. . . . . . . Extra fcap. 8vo. 1s. 6d.

Molière. *Les Femmes Savantes.* With Notes, Glossary, etc. By Gustave Masson, B.A. . Extra fcap. 8vo. *stiff covers,* 1s. 6d. *cloth,* 2s.

Molière. *Les Fourberies de Scapin.* } With Voltaire's Life of Molière. By
Racine. *Athalie.* } Gustave Masson, B.A. Extra fcap. 8vo. 2s. 6d.

Molière. *Les Fourberies de Scapin.* With Voltaire's Life of Molière. By Gustave Masson, B.A. . Extra fcap. 8vo. *stiff covers,* 1s. 6d.

Musset. *On ne badine pas avec l'Amour,* and *Fantasio.* With Introduction, Notes, etc., by Walter Herries Pollock. Extra fcap. 8vo. 2s.

NOVELETTES :—

Xavier de Maistre. *Voyage autour de ma Chambre.* }
Madame de Duras. *Ourika.* } By Gustave
Erckmann-Chatrian. *Le Vieux Tailleur.* } Masson, B.A.,
Alfred de Vigny. *La Veillée de Vincennes.* } 3rd Edition
Edmond About. *Les Jumeaux de l'Hôtel Corneille.* } Ext. fcap. 8vo.
Rodolphe Töpffer. *Mésaventures d'un Écolier.* } 2s. 6d.

Voyage autour de ma Chambre, separately, limp, 1s. 6d.

Perrault. *Popular Tales.* Edited, with an Introduction on Fairy Tales, etc, by Andrew Lang, M.A. . . . . Extra fcap. 8vo. 5s. 6d.

Quinet. *Lettres à sa Mère.* Edited by G. Saintsbury, M.A. Extra fcap. 8vo. 2s.

Racine. *Esther.* Edited by G. Saintsbury, M.A. Extra fcap. 8vo. 2s.

Racine. *Andromaque.* } With Louis Racine's Life of his Father. By
Corneille. *Le Menteur.* } Gustave Masson, B.A. Extra fcap. 8vo. 2s. 6d.

Regnard. . . . *Le Joueur.* } By Gustave Masson, B.A.
Brueys and Palaprat. *Le Grondeur.* } Extra fcap. 8vo. 2s. 6d.

Sainte-Beuve. *Selections from the Causeries du Lundi.* Edited by G. SAINTSBURY, M.A. . . . . Extra fcap. 8vo. 2s.

Sévigné. *Selections from the Correspondence of* **Madame de Sévigné** and her chief Contemporaries. Intended more especially for Girls' Schools. By GUSTAVE MASSON, B.A. . . . . . Extra fcap. 8vo. 3s.

Voltaire. *Mérope.* Edited by G. SAINTSBURY, M.A. Extra fcap. 8vo. 2s.

Dante. *Selections from the ' Inferno.'* With Introduction and Notes, by H. B. COTTERILL, B.A. . . . . . Extra fcap. 8vo. 4s. 6d.

Tasso. *La Gerusalemme Liberata.* Cantos i, ii. With Introduction and Notes, by the same Editor. . . . . Extra fcap. 8vo. 2s. 6d.

GERMAN, GOTHIC, ICELANDIC, &c.

Buchheim. *Modern German Reader.* A Graduated Collection of Extracts in Prose and Poetry from Modern German writers. Edited by C. A. BUCHHEIM, Phil. Doc.

Part I. With English Notes, a Grammatical Appendix, and a complete Vocabulary. *Fourth Edition.* . . . Extra fcap. 8vo. 2s. 6d.

Part II. With English Notes and an Index. Extra fcap. 8vo. 2s. 6d.

Part III. In preparation.

Lange. *The Germans at Home*; a Practical Introduction to German Conversation, with an Appendix containing the Essentials of German Grammar. By HERMANN LANGE. *Third Edition.* . . . . . 8vo. 2s. 6d.

Lange. *The German Manual*; a German Grammar, a Reading Book, and a Handbook of German Conversation. By the same Author. 8vo. 7s. 6d.

Lange. *A Grammar of the German Language,* being a reprint of the Grammar contained in *The German Manual.* By the same Author. 8vo. 3s. 6d.

Lange. *German Composition*; a Theoretical and Practical Guide to the Art of Translating English Prose into German. By the same Author. *Second Edition* . . . . 8vo. 4s. 6d.

[A Key in Preparation.]

Lange. *German Spelling*: A Synopsis of the Changes which it has undergone through the Government Regulations of 1880 . *Paper cover, 6d.*

Becker's Friedrich der Grosse. With an Historical Sketch of the Rise of Prussia and of the Times of Frederick the Great. With Map. Edited by C. A. BUCHHEIM, Phil. Doc. . . . Extra fcap. 8vo. 3s. 6d.

Goethe. *Egmont.* With a Life of Goethe, etc. Edited by C. A. BUCHHEIM, Phil. Doc. *Third Edition.* . . . Extra fcap. 8vo. 3s.

Goethe. *Iphigenie auf Tauris.* A Drama. With a Critical Introduction and Notes. Edited by C. A. BUCHHEIM, Phil. Doc. *Second Edition.* Extra fcap. 8vo. 3s.

Heine's *Harzreise.* With a Life of Heine, etc. Edited by C. A. BUCHHEIM, Phil. Doc. Extra fcap. 8vo. *stiff covers,* 1s. 6d. *cloth,* 2s. 6d.

Heine's *Prosa,* being Selections from his Prose Works. Edited with English Notes, etc., by C. A. BUCHHEIM, Phil. Doc. Extra fcap. 8vo. 4*s.* 6*d.*

Lessing. *Laokoon.* With Introduction, Notes, etc. By A. HAMANN, Phil. Doc., M.A. . . . . Extra fcap. 8vo. 4*s.* 6*d.*

Lessing. *Minna von Barnhelm.* A Comedy. With a Life of Lessing, Critical Analysis, Complete Commentary, etc. Edited by C. A. BUCHHEIM, Phil. Doc. *Fifth Edition.* . . . Extra fcap. 8vo. 3*s.* 6*d.*

Lessing. *Nathan der Weise.* With English Notes, etc. Edited by C. A. BUCHHEIM, Phil. Doc. *Second Edition.* . Extra fcap. 8vo. 4*s.* 6*d.*

Niebuhr's *Griechische Heroen-Geschichten.* Tales of Greek Heroes. Edited with English Notes and a Vocabulary, by EMMA S. BUCHHEIM. Extra fcap. 8vo. *cloth,* 2*s.*

Schiller's *Historische Skizzen:—Egmonts Leben und Tod,* and *Belagerung von Antwerpen.* Edited by C. A. BUCHHEIM, Phil. Doc. *Third Edition, Revised and Enlarged, with a Map.* . Extra fcap. 8vo. 2*s.* 6*d.*

Schiller. *Wilhelm Tell.* With a Life of Schiller; an Historical and Critical Introduction, Arguments, a Complete Commentary, and Map. Edited by C. A. BUCHHEIM, Phil. Doc. *Sixth Edition.* . Extra fcap. 8vo. 3*s.* 6*d.*

Schiller. *Wilhelm Tell.* Edited by C. A. BUCHHEIM, Phil. Doc. *School Edition.* With Map. . . . . . Extra fcap. 8vo. 2*s.*

Schiller. *Wilhelm Tell.* Translated into English Verse by E. MASSIE, M.A. . . . . Extra fcap. 8vo. 5*s.*

Schiller. *Die Jungfrau von Orleans.* Edited by C. A. BUCHHEIM, Phil. Doc. [*In preparation.*]

Scherer. *A History of German Literature.* By W. SCHERER. Translated from the Third German Edition by Mrs. F. CONYBEARE. Edited by F. MAX MÜLLER. 2 vols. . . . . . . 8vo. 21*s.*

Max Müller. *The German Classics from the Fourth to the Nineteenth Century.* With Biographical Notices, Translations into Modern German, and Notes, by F. MAX MÜLLER, M.A. A New edition, revised, enlarged, and adapted to WILHELM SCHERER'S *History of German Literature,* by F. LICHTENSTEIN. 2 vols. . . . . Crown 8vo. 21*s.*

Wright. *An Old High German Primer.* With Grammar, Notes, and Glossary. By JOSEPH WRIGHT, Ph.D. . . Extra fcap. 8vo. 3*s.* 6*d.*

Wright. *A Middle High German Primer.* With Grammar, Notes, and Glossary. By JOSEPH WRIGHT, Ph. D. . . Extra fcap. 8vo. 3*s.* 6*d.*

Skeat. *The Gospel of St. Mark in Gothic.* Edited by W. W. SKEAT, Litt. D. . . . . Extra fcap. 8vo. 4*s.*

Sweet. An Icelandic Primer, with Grammar, Notes, and Glossary. By HENRY SWEET, M.A. . . . . . Extra fcap. 8vo. 3*s.* 6*d.*

Vigfusson and Powell. *An Icelandic Prose Reader,* with Notes, Grammar, and Glossary. By GUDBRAND VIGFUSSON, M.A., and F. YORK POWELL, M.A. . . . . Extra fcap. 8vo. 10*s.* 6*d.*

MATHEMATICS AND PHYSICAL SCIENCE.

Aldis. *A Text Book of Algebra (with Answers to the Examples).* By W. STEADMAN ALDIS, M.A. . . . . . . Crown 8vo. 7s. 6d.

Hamilton and Ball. *Book-keeping.* By Sir R. G. C. HAMILTON, K.C.B., and JOHN BALL (of the firm of Quilter, Ball, & Co.). *New and Enlarged Edition* . . . . Extra fcap. 8vo. 2s.

   *** *Ruled Exercise Books adapted to the above.* (Fcap. folio, 2s.)

Hensley. *Figures made Easy: a first Arithmetic Book.* By LEWIS HENSLEY, M.A. . . . . Crown 8vo. 6d.

Hensley. *Answers to the Examples in Figures made Easy,* together with 2000 additional Examples formed from the Tables in the same, with Answers. By the same Author. . . . . . Crown 8vo. 1s.

Hensley. *The Scholar's Arithmetic.* By the same Author.
                                       Crown 8vo. 2s. 6d.

Hensley. *Answers to the Examples in the Scholar's Arithmetic.* By the same Author. . . . . Crown 8vo. 1s. 6d.

Hensley. *The Scholar's Algebra.* An Introductory work on Algebra. By the same Author. . . . . . . Crown 8vo. 2s. 6d.

Baynes. *Lessons on Thermodynamics.* By R. E. BAYNES, M.A., Lee's Reader in Physics. . . . . Crown 8vo. 7s. 6d.

Donkin. *Acoustics.* By W. F. DONKIN, M.A., F.R.S. *Second Edition.* Crown 8vo. 7s. 6d.

Euclid Revised. Containing the essentials of the Elements of Plane Geometry as given by Euclid in his First Six Books. Edited by R. C. J. NIXON, M.A. . . . . Crown 8vo.

      May likewise be had in parts as follows :—

Book I, 1s.   Books I, II, 1s. 6d.   Books I-IV, 3s.   Books V-IV, 3s.

Euclid. *Geometry in Space.* Containing parts of Euclid's Eleventh and Twelfth Books. By the same Editor. . . . Crown 8vo. 3s. 6d.

Harcourt and Madan. *Exercises in Practical Chemistry.* Vol. I. *Elementary Exercises.* By A. G. VERNON HARCOURT, M.A.; and H. G. MADAN, M.A. *Fourth Edition.* Revised by H. G. Madan, M.A.
                                       Crown 8vo. 10s. 6d.

Madan. *Tables of Qualitative Analysis.* Arranged by H. G. MADAN, M.A. . . . . Large 4to. 4s. 6d.

Maxwell. *An Elementary Treatise on Electricity.* By J. CLERK MAXWELL, M.A., F.R.S. Edited by W. GARNETT, M.A. Demy 8vo. 7s. 6d.

Stewart. *A Treatise on Heat,* with numerous Woodcuts and Diagrams. By BALFOUR STEWART, LL.D., F.R.S., Professor of Natural Philosophy in Owens College, Manchester. *Fifth Edition.* . Extra fcap. 8vo. 7s. 6d.

Williamson. *Chemistry for Students.* By A. W. WILLIAMSON, Phil. Doc., F.R.S., Professor of Chemistry, University College London. *A new Edition with Solutions.* . . . . . . Extra fcap. 8vo. 8s. 6d.

Combination Chemical Labels. In two Parts, gummed ready for use. Part I, Basic Radicles and Names of Elements. Part II, Acid Radicles. Price 3s. 6d.

HISTORY, POLITICAL ECONOMY, GEOGRAPHY, &c.

Danson. The Wealth of Households. By J. T. DANSON. Cr. 8vo. 5s.

Freeman. *A Short History of the Norman Conquest of England.* By E. A. FREEMAN, M.A. *Second Edition.* . Extra fcap. 8vo. 2s. 6d.

George. *Genealogical Tables illustrative of Modern History.* By H. B. GEORGE, M.A. *Third Edition, Revised and Enlarged.* Small 4to. 12s.

Hughes (Alfred). *Geography for Schools.* Part I, *Practical Geography.* With Diagrams. . . . . Extra fcap. 8vo. 2s. 6d.

Kitchin. *A History of France.* With Numerous Maps, Plans, and Tables. By G. W. KITCHIN, D.D., Dean of Winchester. *Second Edition.* Vol. I. To 1453. Vol. II. 1453-1624. Vol. III. 1624-1793. each 10s. 6d.

Lucas. *Introduction to a Historical Geography of the British Colonies.* By C. P. LUCAS, B.A. . . . . Crown 8vo., with 8 maps, 4s. 6d.

Rawlinson. *A Manual of Ancient History.* By G. RAWLINSON, M.A., Camden Professor of Ancient History. *Second Edition.* Demy 8vo. 14s.

Rogers. *A Manual of Political Economy,* for the use of Schools. By J. E. THOROLD ROGERS, M.A. *Third Edition.* Extra fcap. 8vo. 4s. 6d.

Stubbs. *The Constitutional History of England, in its Origin and Development.* By WILLIAM STUBBS, D.D., Lord Bishop of Chester. Three vols. . . . . Crown 8vo. each 12s.

Stubbs. *Select Charters and other Illustrations of English Constitutional History,* from the Earliest Times to the Reign of Edward I. Arranged and edited by W. STUBBS, D.D. *Fourth Edition.* Crown 8vo. 8s. 6d.

Stubbs. *Magna Carta:* a careful reprint. . . . . 4to. *stitched,* 1s.

ART.

Hullah. *The Cultivation of the Speaking Voice.* By JOHN HULLAH. Extra fcap. 8vo. 2s. 6d.

Maclaren. *A System of Physical Education: Theoretical and Practical.* With 346 Illustrations drawn by A. MACDONALD, of the Oxford School of Art. By ARCHIBALD MACLAREN, the Gymnasium, Oxford. *Second Edition.* Extra fcap. 8vo. 7s. 6d.

Troutbeck and Dale. *A Music Primer for Schools.* By J. TROUT-BECK, D.D., formerly Music Master in Westminster School, and R. F. DALE, M.A., B. Mus., late Assistant Master in Westminster School. Crown 8vo. 1s. 6d.

Tyrwhitt. *A Handbook of Pictorial Art.* By R. St. J. TYRWHITT, M.A. With coloured Illustrations, Photographs, and a chapter on Perspective, by A. MACDONALD. *Second Edition.* . . . 8vo. *half morocco*, 18s.

Upcott. *An Introduction to Greek Sculpture.* By L. E. UPCOTT, M.A. . . . . Crown 8vo. 4s. 6d.

Student's Handbook to the University and Colleges of Oxford. *Ninth Edition.* . . . . Crown 8vo. 2s. 6d.

Helps to the Study of the Bible, taken from the *Oxford Bible for Teachers,* comprising Summaries of the several Books, with copious Explanatory Notes and Tables illustrative of Scripture History and the Characteristics of Bible Lands; with a complete Index of Subjects, a Concordance, a Dictionary of Proper Names, and a series of Maps. . . . . Crown 8vo. 3s. 6d.

*** A READING ROOM *has been opened at the* CLARENDON PRESS WAREHOUSE, AMEN CORNER, *where visitors will find every facility for examining old and new works issued from the Press, and for consulting all official publications.*

☞ *All communications relating to Books included in this List, and offers of new Books and new Editions, should be addressed to*

THE SECRETARY TO THE DELEGATES,
CLARENDON PRESS,
OXFORD.

London : HENRY FROWDE,
OXFORD UNIVERSITY PRESS WAREHOUSE, AMEN CORNER.
Edinburgh : 6 QUEEN STREET.
Oxford : CLARENDON PRESS DEPOSITORY,
116 HIGH STREET.